MIRACLES ALONG COUNTY Q

MIKE McCABE

LITTLE CREEK PRESS

MINERAL POINT, WISCONSIN

Little Creek Press
5341 Sunny Ridge Road
Mineral Point, WI 53565

ORDERING INFORMATION
Quantity sales. Special discounts are available on quantity purchases
by corporations, associations, and others. For details, contact
info@littlecreekpress.com

Orders by US trade bookstores and wholesalers.
Please contact Little Creek Press or Ingram for details.

Printed in the United States of America

Cataloging-in-Publication Data
Name: Mike McCabe, author
Title: Miracles Along County Q
Description: Mineral Point, WI Little Creek Press, 2024
Identifiers: LCCN: 2024918731 | ISBN: 978-1-955656-84-9
Classification: FICTION / Mystery & Detective / Cozy / General
FICTION / Friendship
FICTION / Coming of Age

Book design by Little Creek Press

ACKNOWLEDGMENTS

This book is dedicated to my late brother Dan, one of the brightest stars in the universe ever to go largely unrecognized. Had Dan not been in my life for just over forty years, I would not have this story to tell. It is a tribute to him.

I will be forever grateful for the love, patience and support of my wife and son—Marilyn Feil and Casey McCabe—without whom this book never would have been written.

A huge debt of gratitude is owed to Kristin Mitchell for believing in this story and trusting in an author who waited nearly until retirement age to take his first stab at writing fiction. Thanks also go to Jan Kardys, who did me the considerable favor of reading my first draft and offering extensive recommendations for improvement. Gretchen Eick then went over my revised manuscript with a fine-toothed comb, which led to further refinements. Her contributions to the finished product cannot go unacknowledged. And thank you to my editor, Kevin Campbell, for his tender care and attention to detail.

Lastly, this is a true story. And it's fiction. The people and places in *Miracles Along County Q* are very real but fictionalized. While it took several months to write this story, it's been in the making for six decades. The book got its soul from those who brought me up and many others whose paths crossed mine at one time or another. I owe them most of all.

CHAPTER 1

WHAT CAN'T BE EXPLAINED IS MAGIC. Old Man Morger was fond of saying that, more times than anyone who knew him cared to count. If there's a stitch of truth to it, magic must be in abundant supply in these parts. A lot's unexplained in Faith, surprising since there's not much to the town, just one of those blink-and-you-miss-it places.

Gin Glennon, on the other hand, now she's hard to overlook. A fetching woman, in her 60s by calendar, quite a bit younger by looks. Drives a car with no signs of rust. That alone gets her noticed here. Lives on what locals call the Hill, the good part of town. With every item on her to-do list crossed off, she heads for home. When Gin pulls into the driveway, there is her husband's unnecessarily large truck parked in the garage, a rare sight at four o'clock.

She doesn't go in the house. Doesn't get out of the car. Puts it in reverse, backs out onto the street, drives off. Gin crosses nearly the entire length of Faith in a matter of a minute or two, down the main drag until buckled curbs turn to gravel shoulders of a county trunk highway stretching out into the countryside.

Four hundred yards past the last cluster of houses, she turns off on a path with a pair of foot-wide strips worn bare, a body length apart, a scraggly carpet of crabgrass and white man's foot between them. She comes to a stop, puts the car in park, kills the engine, gets out, crosses a balding lawn, climbs the stairs, enters without knocking. What used to be the Morger place isn't hers, never has been, but Gin knows every square inch.

No one's home. She lingers for a moment, first in the dining room, running her fingers over the tired Formica table before moving on to the adjoining kitchen. The walls are close, visibly patched here and there, one unspackled hairline fracture snaking from ceiling to floor. Cracked linoleum bulges in places, its adhesion long ago lost, crunching under Gin's weight. Her eyes are drawn to a sheet of paper on the discolored countertop next to the sink. Folded at one time, but no longer. On it, three short sentences. Eleven words in all, written with great care, not scribbled. She picks up the page, studies it, puts it down again.

Her gaze darts, as though looking for something, or someone, thoughts drifting. Morger, an acquired taste, that one. Came to love his every eccentricity. Sweet Colette, dear friend, second mother. Those words, that penmanship, the school notebook paper.

Gin proceeds to the cramped sitting room, stopping alongside the shabby armchair she'd been offered a hundred times before. On the bookshelf, the photo album containing a lifetime's worth of memories, of the farm, of travels, of family, in plastic sleeves, fading nonetheless. Two crinkled envelopes tucked inside the album cover. In one, proof of valor. In the other, evidence of immodesty.

She stares absent-mindedly out the clouded front window, seeing nothing that wasn't there 20 minutes earlier, or 20 days, or 20 years ago. The one object in her field of vision that most certainly wasn't there two decades earlier—a glass-covered black contrivance about the size and shape of a candy bar—starts flashing and vibrating, snapping her back to attention. She glances down, takes it up, taps the bar's outer wrapping, speaks to it.

A familiar voice answers. "Where are you?"

"Your place," Gin replies.

"Are Chris and Ana there?"

"Not yet."

"I'll prolly beat them. Will be there in five."

"You got another message."

"Yeah."

"What's it mean?"

"Means I can be who I am, do what I do, be open about it. What's happening is no accident."

"You got all that from it?"

Her question is answered with a clipped laugh.

"I mean, who could possibly decipher that?" Gin says. "It's like secret code."

"Took it to mean it's time to show what I been hiding. Face what I been avoiding. It's okay to be different, okay to do … you know. I s'pose I already knew all that. The message just sorta confirmed it for me."

Gin pivots. "It's amazing what you've done for that kid you took in, what's his name again?"

"Slobodnik. Humphrey Slobodnik. You know what he was called at school?"

Gin makes no guesses out loud, though slob comes immediately to mind.

"Dump. Been kicked his whole life. Ain't a bad kid. Was just living down to what everyone thinks of him."

"Word is the kid's a methhead," Gin protests. "Pulled a knife on a teacher when he was still in school. Got himself expelled. I hear feds are looking for him. Searched the old theater and hotel. Found guns, ammo, stuff for making bombs. They're thinking …"

"He's got nothing to do with it. He's not on meth, he's not cooking, I can tell you that much for certain. And he's not one of them who thinks he's gotta start a civil war."

"They're looking for him, and that's going to lead them to you."

"I've got nothing to hide. Neither does he."

"Why's he called Dump?"

"Why'd I get called Hen? Kids do what they do, started calling him Hump, then later Dump. Maybe it was a play on Humpty Dumpty, how the hell am I supposed to know?"

"His parents sure didn't do him any favors, naming him Humphrey," Gin sympathizes. "I do have to say, from the sounds of it you've done him a world of good."

"Didn't do much."

"Didn't lay a hand on him?"

"What's that got to do with anything?"

"You know what it has to do with."

The line fell silent once more, stayed that way until Gin could bear it no longer. "Maybe you should get out of here. You're free to go, you know that, right? We'll be fine. You don't have to stay ... you don't have to put up with how you're treated here. There's nothing for you here."

"You're here ... Everything I have is here, everything I really care about."

"This place doesn't deserve you."

"It belongs to me as much as it belongs to them."

Gin wanted to protest, but chose not to. She had more to say, but kept it to herself. The call ended. That was that.

CHAPTER 2

NEITHER FAITH'S BUCOLIC CHARM NOR THE TELLTALE signs of economic distress and social discord make the town noteworthy. To this day, what makes Faith remarkable is hiding in plain sight, as is often the case with undiscovered treasure.

Once big enough to merit a dot on the state map of Wisconsin, Faith has been steadily shrinking for years. Now but a tiny speck in the vast expanse that is the middle of nowhere, impossible to locate on any up-to-date map. Faith is in Clark County, the heart of America's Dairyland, halfway between Loyal and Unity. Loyal is home to 1,200 give or take, Unity 300-some.

The tallest structure in town is the water tower, situated not far from a shuttered paper mill and adjacent mill pond. In the winter, the pond is used for snowmobile racing, about all it's good for. Swimming's not advisable, owing to years of discharge from the mill. The fishing's not good either, unless you don't mind bottom feeders like carp, suckers and bullheads. A few locals swear they're decent eating early in the spring as soon as the ice goes out, but most consider them trash fish with a muddy taste.

There used to be an elementary school in town, but that closed down on account of shriveling enrollment. From kindergarten through high school, kids living to the south and west of Faith now ride the bus to Loyal to go to school. Those living in town or to the north and east attend school in Colby, where the cheese bearing the same name originated, no surprise, as there are twice as many cows in Clark County as people.

Most of those who call Faith home today are have-littles, but there are a few have-lots too. West of the mill pond is the high ground, known to everyone in Faith as the Hill. Immaculately kept Colonials and Victorians are surrounded by more modern split levels and ranch styles. Doctor Szymanski's family lives on the Hill. So does Pastor Cash. The Glennons too. One of their neighbors is Jim Slater, who had a brief professional baseball career before returning to Faith after his premature retirement.

The low parts of town east of the water tower and mill pond are where most of Faith lives. Quite a few are of Polish, German, Irish or Norwegian descent and were born here, as were their parents and grandparents. Their ranks are thinning, however, as roughly half of Faith's population today is Latino, mostly first-generation immigrants from Mexico or Central America.

Some dwell in rough-looking mobile homes parked at the end of Third Street beyond where the elementary school was. Faith is so small there is no Fourth Street. Rows of boxy two-story houses and cracker box prefabs, some tidy but aging, others worn and torn, are situated within a few blocks of Main Street, which cuts through the village's heart. What's left of it.

Buildings where there was once a five-and-dime, a bowling alley and a bank stand empty, as does a once-stately brick structure that housed the movie theater and hotel. The local newspaper still operates out of a sparse office on Main Street, and the tavern, liquor store and real estate office are a few doors down. Not far off the main drag is the sole grocery store in town and what used to be the car dealership. A cluster of newer and larger homes dot the periphery of the northwest side where a combination bookstore and coffee shop as well as a natural food cooperative and Mexican cantina have sprung up. That's what lifers in town call New Faith.

Walking from one end of Faith to the other is a brief and leisurely stroll. Surrounding the village are farm fields and scattered wooded patches in every direction. In the summer, vast swaths of green stretch to the horizon. Come autumn, all that green turns shades of brown, yellow, tan, orange and red—with the exception of half or more of the trees that don't turn color. When winter arrives, Faith could just as well be the North Pole, an unassuming encampment surrounded by a sea of white.

As far as the eye can see is not all that far despite the fact that the landscape is fairly flat. Sightlines are intermittently broken by gentle knolls and stands of pines, birches, maples, popples and oaks reaching for the heavens. Also sprinkled across the terrain are lonely homesteads, each with a rectangular barn painted either red or white and, typically, a shingled roof. Jutting from the ground next to the barn is one or sometimes several silos, circular cement towers—or a blue steel one here and there—used for storing feed for cattle. A stone's throw from the barn is the farmhouse, sometimes well kept, sometimes run down. Most of the houses and barns have power lines running to them bringing electricity. A few don't. Those are owned by Amish families.

Curious thing about small towns, there are few places where it's harder to hide but not many where it's easier to keep secrets. Everybody thinks everybody knows everybody. Everybody's wrong.

The townsfolk here in Faith are no exception. Never saw it coming.

The Glennons are a regular topic of discussion in Faith. No surprise, considering they own half the town. Listen in on the locals talking and, at some point, the Moose will come up. Richard Glennon was born and raised up here, the son of an auctioneer known to everyone as Old Dean. Old Dean and his wife Margaret had three sons. First Paul, then Young Dean and finally Richard. Gin calls the youngest son—her husband—Richie, but no one else calls him that. Or Richard or Rich or Dick or Rick. It's been Moose since anyone can remember.

He was an early bloomer, reaching his full height of six-foot one-inch by the middle of ninth grade. He was barrel chested with broad shoulders and a thick neck, still is. He had a strikingly handsome face with straight dishwater blond hair that he kept cropped short, still does. Moose graduated from high school the same year as his lifelong buddy, local baseball legend Jim Slater.

Moose's sport was football. He played fullback on offense, linebacker on defense, a one-man wrecking crew at both positions. He threw vicious blocks to open gaping holes for teammates to run through and was next to impossible to wrestle to the ground when he carried the ball. When opponents took possession, Moose roamed sideline to sideline shedding blockers and demolishing ball carriers.

He was a three-time all-conference selection on both offense and defense, making honorable mention all-state for defense his junior year and second team all-state on both sides of the ball his senior year. Earned an athletic scholarship to play football at the state university in River Falls, hoped to use that opportunity as a springboard to transfer to a Big Ten school, but blew out his knee his first year. Never was the same player after that.

By the time he finished his college degree, Moose was married to his high school sweetheart—Virginia to her parents, Gin to everyone else. Gin Barber was once the most popular girl in school, a cheerleader, homecoming queen and class salutatorian. Every girl hoped to be included in her circle of friends. Every boy dreamed of getting her in the back seat.

With her academic decorations, Gin set her sights on becoming a doctor. A high school guidance counselor saw that as no fit path for a girl and threw cold water on those plans, cautioning her against pursuing a degree from a four-year college. He advised her to consider what he deemed a more practical plan, a two-year vocational school where she could acquire clerical or bookkeeping skills or maybe nursing certification.

Her parents also were sour on the idea of medical school due to the daunting cost, threatening to withhold any financial support if she went through with the idea. Moose wasn't encouraging either, as he was not fond of the idea of Gin going off to some top university somewhere without him. He was well aware that pre-med coursework and then med school, followed by a residency who knows where, probably meant at least 10 years apart. A separation that might very well foil his plans to make her his bride.

Gin relented to the pressures, became Gin Glennon, and lived to regret it. While happy enough by all appearances, it didn't take long for her to become bored out of her skull with the whole arrangement.

Moose, on the other hand, saw endless possibilities when he returned home after college. The people of Faith are hardworking salt-of-the-earth sorts, thankful for their blessings but also prone to misfortune. The Glennons are exceptional, every bit as industrious as their neighbors if not doubly so, more charmed than cursed.

Young Dean and Paul followed in their father's footsteps, taking their place in the auctioneering business. Like their father and brother, they are hulking men well over six feet tall, though less chiseled than Moose. In addition to spelling their father at auctions and learning the ins and outs of an auction house, they joined Moose in taking over the real estate business that Old Dean started. But it was clear in no time that Moose was the one with the enterprising spirit and competitive ruthlessness to thrive in business.

Within a few short years, Moose was calling most of the shots at Glennon Realty, using his share of the proceeds to finance other ventures. He bought the old grocery store, renaming it Glennon's. Then he opened Moose's Bar and Grill and Glennon's Liquor. Not long after that, he entered into a partnership with the owner of the local car dealership, becoming sole owner of Faith Motors several years later. His final acquisition was *The Lantern*, the local newspaper. He made himself publisher and hired an old high school chum as editor.

If you live in Faith, you get your groceries from Moose. You wet your whistle at Moose's. If you're on the younger side, chances are you bought your house from Moose. Moose sold you wheels. Moose's paper tells you what's going on around town. He's not fawned over the way he was in his younger years, but for the most part folks in the community are outwardly respectful and appreciative toward Moose and his family. When there is bellyaching about the Glennons, the family name is rarely invoked. Folks just refer to the Moose. The Moose wants this. The Moose did that.

They don't know the half of it.

To make sense of Faith, some steps need retracing. Forty years ago. That's when the odyssey began, that's when Faith was upended.

Those were brutal times for farmers in the area. Many took on a great deal of debt to upgrade their operations, expanding their herds when milk prices were high. When prices plummeted, they started defaulting on their loans. The banks felt no sympathy. Foreclosures were commonplace, sending ripples throughout the local economy. While devastating for feed mills and farm implement dealers, it was undeniably good for the auction business. Barely 10 years out of high school, Moose was the middleman in dozens of farm sales, taking his commission. When his own liquidity permitted, he bought up some of the land for himself at bargain prices.

Moose and Gin had wasted no time starting a family after marrying during his senior year at college. Their first son, Steve, was born just before Christmas. Mark arrived shortly after New Year's Day two years later. There was a lull in the baby-making for a few years, but by the time Steve turned six and Mark four, Gin was pregnant again.

Privately, Moose marveled at his wife's fertility, as she was spending considerable time away from home helping out her younger sister in the Cities, where Sis worked as a music teacher before having to go on maternity leave near the end of the school year. To his friends at the tavern and even at a few family gatherings, Moose bragged about his potency. One shot's all it took.

Gin's pregnancies had always gone smoothly before, but not this time. Morning sickness wasn't confined to mornings. The nausea and vomiting stopped after a few weeks with her first two pregnancies. Persisted into the third trimester with this one. On top of that, she felt perpetually tired and faint. Doctor Szymanski, a youthful-looking second-generation family physician who took over the local practice from his father, figured she was suffering from anemia. Gave her some iron supplements that helped some with the fatigue but seemed to bring on the vomiting, not to mention diarrhea.

Gin was miserable; the physical ordeal wore her down emotionally. She started feeling depressed, losing her appetite for days at a time. A couple of weeks before the baby was due, Doc Szymanski noticed a sharp jump in her blood pressure. He wanted her checked into the hospital in Marshfield at once so her blood pressure could be carefully monitored and managed. Moose pooh-poohed the idea when Gin told him, but came around when the doctor followed up by telephone to tell him this was nothing to mess around with.

Moose drove Gin the 15 miles to Marshfield, getting her settled into a hospital room before returning to Faith to look after the two boys, help his brothers with an upcoming auction and do a couple of house showings. Gin was in the hospital for a week before going into labor. Moose dropped everything to be there once he got word that the moment had arrived, leaving Steve and Mark with a neighbor.

By the time Moose tied up the loose ends at home and made his way to the hospital, Gin was experiencing rapid-fire contractions. Turns out the doctors induced labor because of her condition. A nurse and attending physician were coaching her to breathe, imploring her to push. The whole idea of childbirth had always made Moose queasy. He stayed in a waiting room for the first two to be born. This time was going to be different, he told himself. He was going to be at his wife's side for the arrival of their third.

Was it ever different.

Her eyes shut tight, beads of sweat formed into streams down her forehead and cheeks. After a particularly intense contraction, her face screwed up in agony, strands of sopping blonde hair pasted to her temples, Gin let out a sob that morphed into a deep, rumbling groan.

"Get it out! Get it out!" she pleaded. She begged the doctor and nurse for pain medication but was told it was too late for that.

Moose fixed his eyes on the doctor. First a look of alarm flashed across his face, then one of panic.

"Oh come on, God dammit, give her something!"

"She's past the point where we can," the doctor said calmly but firmly. His gaze shifted from Moose back to the business at hand. Moose staggered back a step, collected himself, looking over the doctor's shoulder and between his wife's outstretched legs held wide apart by stirrups cupping her feet. His eyes got big. Something emerged from the widening slit, then receded.

The doctor leaned in close. "Now take a really deep breath, Virginia," he said, barely above a whisper.

"Push! Come on now, Mrs. Glennon, one more. Push!"

Something resembling a frankfurter bulged from the opening. Moments later, the sausage started taking the form of a head. Ears, eyes, nose, mouth. Then shoulders, arms, fingers. One more involuntary spasm, another anguished push from Gin, and the rest of the body oozed out into the doctor's cupped hands and then the towel another of the nurses held below.

Moose looked stunned. His eyes darted from the doctor to the nurse to Gin's still-closed eyes to the cord extending from his wife to the towel and back to the doctor. A look of confusion turned to one of disbelief, then to rage.

"*What the hell!*"

Gin's eyes sprung open, meeting her husband's. Panic splashed over her face.

"What's wrong?" she whimpered. "Is it okay?"

"Everything's fine," the doctor replied reassuringly, clearly flustered.

Moose turned his back on them all, then wheeled around again an instant later.

"*What the hell is that?*" he screamed in the general direction of the doctor, then turning his attention toward Gin, veins bulging in his temples. "*Who were you with? Whose is it?*"

"Richie, what are you talking about? Are you all right?" Gin said with a terrified look. "What's happening?"

"Mr. Glennon, please calm down and lower your voice," the obviously shaken nurse at Gin's side interjected sternly while her counterpart patted and rubbed the newborn with the towel as the doctor gently tapped the bottom of its feet, the umbilical cord still attached. The baby cried out, seizing its first breath. Enveloped in the white towel, barely visible, was skin of a smoky ash brown hue, wisps of coal-black hair atop a misshapen head, longer than it was wide, somewhat flat at the back.

"*Stay out of this!*" Moose shouted back at her, quickly shifting his glare to his wife and gesturing toward the baby. "*This isn't mine. ... You God damned whore!*"

"Richie, there's no one else," Gin sputtered as she began to sob, choking on her words. "Only ... you ... I swear."

"*Don't lie to me, you filthy slut!*"

The doctor tried in vain to redirect attention to the baby. The cord needed to be cut, the placenta still needed to be expelled. Gin spoke over him, frantic.

"It's yours," she pleaded, sobbing. "It's yours ... I swear!"

"How can it be mine?" Moose said in a spiteful but somewhat more collected tone. "It's not even the same species."

The doctor, clearly unnerved but determined to restore order, interrupted. "Mr. Glennon, I am going to have to ask you to leave."

"No!" Gin cried. "Please, Richie, don't go! I swear, it's yours."

At once appearing frightened and pained and enraged, Moose turned abruptly, storming out the door.

"*No Richie, don't go! Please!*" Gin sobbed. "*Come back! I'm telling the truth. I swear!*"

The cord was clamped and cut; the baby was laid on Gin's chest. Her eyes, tormented and flooded with tears, instantly softened. The pain etched on her face was replaced first with a faint smile, then a broad grin. Some mixture of a laugh and a sob erupted from her throat. She pulled the towel back, her eyes lingering over every inch from head to toe as she clutched the baby to her breast.

She winced from time to time as nature took its course, the afterbirth spilling out. She was in a haze, the room and the figures around her fuzzy but the bundle cradled in her arms in crystal clear focus. Ten minutes passed, or maybe five, perhaps thirty, she couldn't tell. She nuzzled and cooed at the baby, softly caressing tiny fingers and toes, drawing a mouth the size and shape of a small coin to her swollen nipple. Looking down at the baby in her arms, tears began streaming down her cheeks again.

CHAPTER 3

AS GIN'S HEAD CLEARED, HER MIND RACED, fumbling through thoughts like a strand of prayer beads. *Will he leave me? When can I go home? Will he be there? Will the boys? Am I imagining things? The baby's dark-skinned. Am I losing my mind? Did any of this really happen? I should call home.*

Gin picked up the receiver from the phone next to the bed, momentarily drew a blank on the number, hung up, then successfully placed the call. No answer. A sinking feeling set in. Her mind went to racing again. *Why is no one home? Who has the boys?*

The next call Gin made was to her sister, who thankfully answered.

"Grace, it's Gin. Can you come get me? I need to get home."

"Whoa, hold on. What are you talking about? Where are you?"

"I'm in the hospital."

"Has the baby come? Are you all right?"

"I had the baby. I'm fine. The baby is too. But something's not right."

"What is it? You sure you're okay?"

"Don't worry, there's nothing wrong with me," Gin said, pausing to draw a deep breath. "The baby's different."

"What's that supposed to mean?"

"It's not, you know ... I mean, it's not white."

"You're scaring me, Gin. You know what drugs they gave you?"

"It's not drugs. The baby is dark, Grace."

There was a faintly audible gasp, the line fell silent.

"I need to get home."

"Wait, how'd Moose react?"

"Never mind about that."

"What happened?"

"What do you mean what happened?"

"C'mon, I'm your sister. Your secret's safe with me. Who got you pregnant?"

"No one! I mean, I don't know!"

"Remember when we went out drinking and dancing with Jim Slater and his teammate while you were staying with me after Annie was born? Thad Mosely. The outfielder."

Gin gave a nod accompanied by a dirty look before it dawned on her Grace couldn't see the gestures.

"Nothing happened."

"You were drunk."

"A little tipsy maybe. So were you. But not falling down drunk."

"There's no chance you might have, you know ..."

"What?"

"Done it with the guy."

"Good God no," Gin blurted out sternly, clearly miffed. "We had some drinks. Danced. Talked. Had a nice time. Nothing else happened."

"You were flirting with him. Not that I blame you. He's definitely lustable."

"I wasn't flirting ... and besides, flirting doesn't make a baby. They went back to their hotel. I went back to your place, I was with you the whole time, remember?"

"That's right ... You're right. Well, there has to be another explanation. Some other guy. A different time."

"There hasn't been another."

"You didn't pick up where you left off with Thad Mosely ..."

"No! I'm telling you, there's been nobody else."

"So, you and Moose made a black baby. That's your story and you're sticking to it," Grace said sarcastically with a laugh she quickly stifled.

When Gin said nothing, Grace dropped the sarcastic tone.

"Like you said, I was with you that whole night. You never were alone with him," she said earnestly before the sarcasm made a reappearance.

"Just say he did manage penetration during one of them slow dances without anyone noticing ... who conceives on the first try?"

Gin remained expressionless. "Gracie honey, I've got to go."

"Hey wait, when do I get to see the baby?" There was a click on the other end of the line, then a dial tone.

Gin hung up the receiver, let her head fall back against the pillow, exhausted. One of the nurses came in to check her blood pressure.

"We're going to keep you here for an extra day or two until your blood pressure returns to normal and is stable. Doctor Gray has put in the order."

The nurse noticed Gin appeared groggy, her eyelids growing heavy.

"We're going to take the baby to another room so you can get some rest. Don't worry, dear. We'll be right through those doors, will come back when it's time for feeding."

Gin drifted off to sleep but a short while later was nudged awake for breastfeeding. After the baby's appetite was satisfied, the nurse came once again to relieve Gin of her motherly duties so she could rest. Before she could fall asleep, a figure appeared in the doorway.

It was Moose.

He tentatively approached the bed without speaking.

"Where are the boys?" Gin inquired nervously.

"At home with the maid."

"Maid? What maid?"

"The Lewandowskis offered to have their daughter move in with us to watch the boys, help with the house."

"They offered to do what? What made them think that was necessary? I'll be home in a day or two."

"I'm telling everyone the baby didn't make it, you nearly didn't survive the delivery, will be away for a spell while you recover. I haven't told the boys yet but will when the time is right."

Gin laid there, stunned, head spinning.

"Why are you telling people this? Why can't I come home?" she asked beseechingly. "The doctors say I should be able to go home tomorrow. The day after at the latest."

"That ain't gonna happen."

"Why not?"

"Lisa will be there to look after the boys, help with meals, keep the house together until we get things straightened out."

"Lisa's a junior in high school," Gin said dubiously.

"She's a senior in the fall and is free for the summer. It was her parents' idea, but I've talked with Lisa myself, she's up for it. I could tell if she was feeling put upon. She's been babysitting since she was 11, been lording over that younger brother of hers for years. Everything'll work out fine."

"How long is this arrangement supposed to last?"

"Ella and Bert didn't put a time limit on it. Just said as long as we need. Awful generous of them."

Moose's back straightened, his expression stiffening.

"This is how it's got to be. The baby is given up for adoption, once that's taken care of you come back home, we get on with our lives."

Gin laid there in stunned silence, staring off into space.

"It's for the best, Gin."

She shook her head, almost imperceptibly at first, then more vigorously as tears welled up in her eyes.

"Can't do that, Richie."

"What can't you do?"

"Give the baby up. I can't do that."

"Course you can. It's the only way that makes sense."

"I can't. I can't do it."

Moose's temper flared. His face flushed, he glared at his wife with icy contempt.

"You got no right to say one way or the other after what you done," he said, holding up his hand to silence Gin when she started to speak. "I'll be damned if I'm bringing home some bastard child from the hospital. I'm not having people sayin' I was cucked."

"I never cheated ... never. I know you don't believe me, but I swear I didn't," Gin claimed, willing herself to hold back tears.

"Oh, spare me!"

Several tense moments lingered between them.

"I won't give up the baby. I'm not doing it."

"You'd rather have everyone know you committed adultery? You want your mom and dad and sister to know that about you? You want Mark and Stevie to know that? You want to bring home this living proof of what you couldn't say no to? Can't you get it through your thick skull? I'm giving you a way out. I ought to throw you out with the trash, but I'm trying to spare you being disgraced. I'm trying to spare our boys the humiliation of having a two-bit slut for a mother."

"You're more worried about your reputation than mine!" Gin spat back bitterly.

"*Of course I'm worried about my reputation!*" Moose bellowed. "Yours and mine both! I'm thinking of our whole family!"

"I'm not giving up the baby."

Moose put both hands on top of his head, looked to the heavens, heaving a sigh of exasperation.

"All right, all right … okay, here's how it's gotta to be. You and the baby go stay with your sister in the Cities. If Grace won't take you in, I'll rent you an apartment there, somewhere far enough away from Uncle Chuck and Aunt Margie so they don't find out."

Moose paused, held up a hand again, buying himself time to work out the details of the plan.

"After a proper amount of time has passed, I'll let everyone know we've adopted a child to fill the hole left by the loss of our baby. You two will come back home."

"You can't do this," Gin said, shaking her head vigorously.

"There ain't any other way."

"You can't take me away from Stevie and Mark. They need their mother."

"You should've thought about that before you … The boys will get by. Far better off than they'd be knowing what you did."

"I beg you. Don't do this Richie. Please, don't do this."

"You made your bed; you lie in it. You don't go along with this, so help me God I'll divorce you on the spot and take sole custody of the boys. What self-respecting lawyer anywhere near here is going to represent someone who's disgraced herself the way you have? You know damn well any judge within a hundred miles is going to look at what you done and take my side. You'll be left with nothing but the mongrel. Are you totally blind? This is a way for you to come back to your family. A way to wash away this whole stain. A way for you to keep the God damned spook without it being seen as illegitimate."

Gin wept uncontrollably. Moose impassively turned away, walking out of the hospital room without looking back.

CHAPTER 4

AFTER HER STAY IN THE HOSPITAL ENDED, Gin was in a fog. She robotically breastfed, bathed the infant, changed diapers, eating barely enough to keep up her strength while going days at a time without a shower or change of clothes. She begrudgingly went along with Moose's story, not because she was comfortable with the ruse but rather because she couldn't think of a plausible alternative for the life of her. She stayed with Grace for a week and a half while Moose checked with people he knew in the Cities about available apartments.

Once a suitable place was found—the top floor of a two-flat—Moose came to move her in. He left Mark and Steve behind with the girl, which greatly distressed Gin. She missed them desperately and demanded to know when she would be able to see her boys.

"Don't worry, I'll bring them next time I come," he said reassuringly. "I just don't want them to see the baby."

He kept his word. Days after settling Gin into her apartment, he brought the two boys to see their mother. He returned with them every week or two, but never to her new home. Each time Moose suggested an out-of-the-way place to meet, insisting Gin not have the baby with her, keeping the encounters frustratingly brief. Each time Moose and the boys were accompanied by the girl, making things awkward.

Lisa Lewandowski was a mere child in Gin's eyes but in truth was more woman than girl. She was large framed and a good bit taller than Gin—five-foot-nine or five-ten by the looks of her—with wide hips and pronounced bottom, a prominent bustline showcased by the crop tops she favored. Ample thighs strained the seams of the tight-fitting jean shorts she wore on most warm days.

Only her plump face looked her age, velvety smooth skin, high cheekbones, sparkling dimples framing even the faintest of smiles. Flowing brown locks splashed over her shoulders. It wasn't the girl's outward appearance, however, that produced a visceral reaction in Gin. It was how naturally she took to caretaking of the boys that bothered Gin most.

Lisa was kindly to Gin—too kind for Gin's taste. That she was pleasant and likeable made it all the harder for Gin to watch the girl climb back in the car with her husband and two boys for the ride back to Faith. As much as she yearned to see her sons and hold them in her arms, each successive visit plunged her more deeply into a state of depression.

She gamely tried to lift her own mood by reminding herself things would change at summer's end. The girl would go back to school. That, Gin told herself, would be the logical moment for her to return home with a newly adopted addition to the family. The nightmare, over. Weeks passed before their next visit. Moose kept having to reschedule. When a mutually convenient time was found and the day came, he broke news that dealt a crippling blow to Gin's already fragile state of mind.

"Lisa is going to be staying on with us after school starts," he announced with the two boys squirming in front of him, the girl to their immediate right. Moose's hand rested on her back as though he was presenting a prized heifer to judges at the county fair. "She's gone above and beyond the call, cooking and cleaning, looking after Mark and Stevie, helping out a ton at the store. She's doing such a great job I'm making her assistant manager after she's done with school."

Gin's head was swimming, her emotions reeling.

"I haven't decided yet for sure if I'm going back for my senior year," Lisa piped up. "I'm checking to see if my class schedule can be arranged so I can work outside of school. Part of me wants to graduate with my friends. Part of me just wants to get on with life."

"Sounds like you have some big decisions to make," Gin said in the girl's general direction before shifting her eyes to Moose. "Richie, can I have a word?"

Moose made a gesture that Gin took as a signal that whatever she had to say could be said in front of everyone. She glared back at him, motioning with a subtle tilt of her head for him to follow her. He stubbornly stood frozen for a moment, but eventually told Lisa, Mark and Steve he'd be right back.

Once out of listening range of the others, Gin rounded on Moose.

"What the hell happened to your plan? I assumed this whole charade wouldn't continue past the end of summer," she cried in something of a whispered shout.

"Why'd you assume that? It typically takes months to adopt a child, sometimes years. If you two suddenly show up after just a few weeks, no one is going to believe we adopted."

"A few weeks? It's been months! I can't do this anymore."

"You damn well better. This whole mess is your doing. If we don't handle it right, everybody'll put two and two together in no time."

"I keep having to tell my folks not to come and see me. That I need time to rest. How much longer am I supposed to carry on like this? They're worried sick and starting to wonder what the hell is really going on."

"I'm not saying you can't see your parents. You just can't come to Faith to visit them. And they can't see the baby. You're going to have to figure this out for yourself."

"Mark and Stevie."

"What about them?"

"They need a mom. I can't take being away from them any longer."

"Look Gin, none of this is ideal. If you'd have given that baby up for adoption, none of us would be dealing with any of this crap. The boys've got me. And Lisa takes good care of them."

Those last words were like salt rubbed in Gin's wounds. She teared up, her voice trembled.

"Is she actually considering dropping out of high school? Must drive her folks mad. They must be thinking she's lost her mind."

"That's none of our business. That's between her and Bert and Ella."

"Are you encouraging her to drop out?"

"I ain't saying anything to her one way or the other."

"But you want to keep her around."

Moose dropped the hushed tone. "Well, there ain't a whole lot of good options, are there? I was handed shit and am supposed to make supper out of it."

Gin hastily drew an index finger to her lips, shushing him. Moose lowered his voice.

"You fucking cheat on me, go and have an illegitimate child, then refuse to give it up. Lisa and her folks have helped me hold everything together. I have no idea what I'd have done without her."

"You have feelings for her."

"What's that supposed to mean?" he said quite loudly, this time ignoring Gin's reaction.

"Do you sleep with her?"

"You're a fine one to ask that! You cheat on me, then assume I must want revenge?"

"You didn't answer my question. You're a man. You can go without only for so long."

Moose staggered backward ever so slightly, jarred. He quickly gathered himself, leaning in close to Gin's ear.

"Think what you want but you'll see different in the end. I ain't divorcing you. When the time is right, I'm taking you back, against my better judgment. I'm even going to accept your baby as my own as long as we're known to be adoptive parents. Why can't you accept that?"

Gin pulled back so she could look up into his eyes. Anger, doubt and a measure of embarrassment swirled inside her, but it felt like a cloud was lifting. She could see light at the end of the tunnel.

"I can," she muttered. "I mean, I do."

Her path at least somewhat clearer, Gin phoned her mom, setting a time for her parents to come visit. She arranged a babysitter for Ray—that's the name she'd chosen—and made sure baby things were confined to a back bedroom in her flat to conceal any sign of her situation. Summer gave way to autumn and winter was on its way, that season of nature's impending wrath. Discarded leaves tossed about, strewn across lawns here, forming curbside dunes there.

One visit from Gin's family became two, then three. By the third time they got together, the story of needing time to recuperate from a delivery gone wrong had worn thin. Gin told her parents that the loss of the baby threw her and Moose for a loop, the emotional strain drove a wedge between them. They decided taking a break from each other might be best for their family. She assured her parents the separation was only temporary. There were no plans to divorce.

Gin's mother looked askance.

"Absence makes the heart go wander," she told her daughter grimly. "Why aren't Mark and Steven with you? They belong with their mother."

Her mom's words summoned all of Gin's insecurities but she soldiered on, assuring her parents that she was seeing the boys regularly, lying convincingly that her mental state after losing the baby convinced her and Moose that she was in no condition to do proper parenting, that it would be good for her to get away from Faith for a little while.

"Did you know the Lewandowskis' daughter moved into your house?"

"Of course I know. Richie and I discussed everything, worked it all out together. It was good of the Lewandowskis to offer to help. Please respect our wishes and keep this within the family."

Gin's father nodded but her mother started protesting again before her daughter cut her off.

"It's all temporary. Everything will work itself out."

The next time Gin saw Moose, she told him how she'd explained things to her parents. He started telling everyone in Faith his wife had suffered a mental breakdown after losing the baby, was receiving treatment but likely would be away longer than initially expected. As word spread around town, concern and sympathy for Moose's plight grew.

Even Gin's parents seemed oddly soothed by the rapidly disseminating news as condolences and well wishes came streaming in. They offered to watch the boys any time Moose needed. He took them up on the offer countless times as Lisa did return to school for her senior year and graduated with her class. Moose continued welcoming their help as he made Lisa assistant manager at the grocery store and later when she started a two-year accounting program at Chippewa Valley Technical College's nearby satellite campus in Neillsville, the county seat. She planned to eventually assume bookkeeping duties at Glennon Realty.

That Lisa was still living in the Glennon household did not escape notice among the locals, giving rise to suspicions that Gin would not return and had effectively been replaced. There were murmurs around town that Lisa surely must be sharing Moose's bed by now, leading to speculation about when he would make it all official. The talk was kept very hush hush, though, out of respect for Moose and recognition of the unspeakable tragedy of losing a child and wife in one fell swoop.

Months melted into a year, then another, and five or six more. Gin's parents couldn't help but conclude that their daughter's marriage was over. What puzzled them to no end was the absence of any legal finality and the fact that their grandsons remained with Moose. Many more times than once, they tried broaching the subject with Gin, but she diverted or shut down the conversations.

For her part, Gin had pretty much given up trying to press Moose for a timeline for her and Ray to come home to Faith. She wasn't even sure she wanted to go back. It irked her that Moose never asked about the baby's gender or showed even the slightest interest in being involved in choosing a name. The position he'd put her in, the choice she had to make, angered her even more. Forgiving was next to impossible, forgetting out of the question.

Shortly after being exiled, she found employment as a receptionist at a medical clinic not far from her flat. No dream job, but she enjoyed the place, the people, the pace. She liked the Cities, how big everything was, how fast things moved, how different people were. Ray seemed fond of their neighborhood, was making friends, attended a good school within walking distance, loved playing Little League baseball. What kind of life could Faith offer by comparison?

Still, Mark and Steve were in her heart and on her mind daily. They didn't like dropping everything to talk on the phone and found her regular calls something of a nuisance. For Gin, they were a lifeline. She visited the boys every chance she got, leaning heavily on Grace to hold things together for her so she could make the trips. She returned the favor and then some ... child care, free taxi service, a meal in a pinch, a workout partner, a sister to confide in, a shoulder to cry on.

Gin's life was full to the brim, yet there was a hole that had her thinking of pursuing a relationship. She dated some but didn't let it get serious with any guy. She had plenty of willing suitors. At 36 going on 37 and after having three children, Gin still had a svelte figure, radiant features and effervescent personality. But any time she was close to saying yes to the next proposition, she'd try talking to Moose about whether it was time to formalize their separation. He'd short-circuit the discussion as quickly as she put a stop to her parents' inquiries.

She recalled once thinking she could see light at the end of the tunnel but all these years later could hardly believe how interminably long the tunnel turned out to be.

Just when most everyone had pretty much moved on emotionally, Faith was in for a shock.

COUNTY
Q

CHAPTER 5

JUST AS THE LAST OF THE WINTER'S SNOW MELTED and the ice went out on the mill pond, word spread like wildfire. Lisa Lewandowski was moving into a house of her own on the Hill. Gin Glennon was coming home. And those weren't the only surprises. Gin arrived with a child in tow, soon to be nine years old, cream-colored patches salting a swarthy complexion, coarse dark hair cropped close on the sides and misbehaved on top.

"This is Ray," Gin repeated dozens of times as locals welcomed her home in the days following her reappearance. They looked her up and down as if to confirm it was really her, shooting Ray furtive glances as though afraid to be caught staring. Noticing their uneasiness, Moose was quick to set the record straight and put minds at rest.

"It's been quite an ordeal, getting Gin home. After losing the baby, the two of us have been working on adopting Ray for several years now, but didn't want to share the news until we were sure everything was in order. He's bounced from one foster home to another, needs some stability. I couldn't be happier and couldn't be prouder to add to our family in this way."

Many in town let Moose know he'd done the community proud, showing remarkable strength and patience amidst all the whispers. Several made a point of how those pathetic few who spread rumors should be ashamed of themselves. After they palavered sufficiently, some tried delicately turning the topic of conversation to Ray. Moose graciously explained they'd found Ray in the Cities with the help of an adoption agency.

"What's the deal with his skin?"

"The doctors call it vitiligo. Can happen to anyone, but it's rare. Most noticeable in dark-skinned people."

Not to worry, Ray will fit right in here, one neighbor reasoned, likening the youngster's hide to a Holstein cow's. Moose laughed heartily. Gin was not amused. She already missed the Cities, although that feeling was no match for the joy of being reunited with Mark and Steve. *Everything will work out for the best. It has to*, she kept telling herself.

Gin had a harder time imagining how trying and painful some of the adjustments would be after a nine-year absence. Relations with her husband were starting over from scratch. Gin felt like she did on a first date. Sharing a bed again after nearly a decade of sleeping alone felt not only awkward but premature.

Mark and Steve were now 15 and 13. They'd done a lot of growing up without their mother around. In many respects, they were strangers. The boys were experiencing the jolt of suddenly inheriting a new, half-grown sibling. Ray had to get used to a strange new school and make new friends, as well as try two brothers and a father figure on for size.

The transition was not smooth. Gin quickly grew bored with life in Faith. She missed her job at the medical clinic and the people she worked with there. Her sister Grace seemed half a world away. Gin no longer felt as close to her parents as she once had. Moose worked incessantly, wanting little to do with Ray when he wasn't busy. Mark and Steve were standoffish.

Ray felt like a zoo exhibit at school and invisible at home. Gin tried her best to make up for it, but paying attention to Ray had the unfortunate side effect of driving a wedge between her and her two teenage sons. Then she would overcompensate until Ray was suffering the consequences.

The Glennons were not exactly one big happy family.

Time healed wounds as it tends to do. Moose, Mark and Steve began at least going through the motions of acknowledging and accepting Ray. Gin gradually felt less repulsed by Moose, more relaxed in his company, more responsive to his touch.

As hard as it had been for her to reacclimate to life in Faith, Gin was acutely aware that adjusting to the place was far more challenging for

Ray. There was no public swimming pool in Faith. No amusement park. No playground equipment. No zoo. No shopping mall. No summer camp. Nowhere to skateboard.

Ray did find simpler pleasures—skipping stones on the mill pond or making an unauthorized climb partway up the water tower. Other days might include hide and seek at Faith's only Protestant church. Less than half the size of St. Mary's Catholic Church across town, the plain white-sided building with a peaked roof looked very much like many of the houses in Faith, except for the oversized stained-glass windows. It was always left unlocked, and its basement had a kitchen and dining room that doubled as a play area. Local kids had the run of the place when services weren't being held.

When the church was in use, a favorite pastime was figuring out ways to enter and explore abandoned buildings, like the one that once housed Faith's movie theater. That could last for hours, until a local merchant or sheriff's deputy caught wind of the mischief and chased everyone out.

Wide open spaces were another thing in plentiful supply. There were woodchucks and muskrats to stalk, skunks to steer clear of. Wasp nests to jab with sticks before taking off running to avoid getting stung. Grasshoppers to inspect and dissect. Wild raspberries growing alongside the road out of town, picked for fun and an impromptu snack. Somebody's parents would dispatch kids to collect asparagus or rhubarb, work to be avoided at all costs. Gathering up hickory nuts from under a tree and flinging them at fenceposts was vastly preferable.

There was fishing to be done not far outside of town to the northeast in the south fork of the Popple River—more brook than river, to be truthful. An even smaller stream passed under a rickety bridge made of weathered wood planks sided with rusted iron trusses. That's where Main Street turned back into the county trunk road headed southwest toward Loyal. Countless hours were spent scaling the beams and wading in that stream. There was an unstructured, carefree quality about all of this that suited Ray.

Despite finding so many endlessly enjoyable ways to pass the time, Ray still struggled to fit in, feeling noticeably foreign. This agonized Gin to no end. It didn't help that there was no organized youth baseball in Faith. Ray dearly missed Little League games, resenting Faith for not having so much as a ball diamond. The closest thing was a large dirt lot adjacent to the elementary school called the "battlefield."

There were always enough kids around for spirited games of tag, keep-away or dodgeball. When it rained the game of choice was smear. A football was tossed up in the air; whoever had the gumption to grab it was chased down, tackled by the rest of the group, forced to surrender the ball. Over and over some brave soul scooped up the football, tried outrunning or dodging the others, only to be caught and piled on. Anyone not covered with mud from head to toe after six or seven rounds was ritually wrestled to the ground, dragged by the arms and legs through the mud.

Ray joined in regularly but brought a bat, ball and glove just in case a game of workup could be pulled together. That rarely happened. Ray guessed there had to be a ballplayer or two living on the Hill, but those kids didn't hang around the battlefield. A few had backyard swimming pools and preferred having friends over. Ray wasn't invited.

Kids on the other side of the mill pond were more interested in hunting and fishing. Even when Ray managed to convince a battlefield regular or two to throw around a ball, it usually didn't take long for playing catch to degenerate into pelting some playground weakling. After not too long, Ray stopped bothering to bring along baseball equipment.

One aspect of life on the battlefield oddly comforting to Ray was the incessant name-calling. Being called a jerk or sissy or dork or twat or fairy or dog breath or numb nuts always stung a little, but Ray understood that everyone on the battlefield was called names like that at one time or another. No one escaped unscathed. Some got it worse than others, but Ray didn't feel singled out because the insults were one size fits all, making for equal opportunity torment.

That is, until one day after school, when a seemingly innocent playground skirmish escalated into a nasty give-and-take ending with two combatants lobbing jeers in Ray's direction. *Half breed! Zebra!*

Ray ran from the battlefield in tears and kept running, not stopping until reaching the edge of town. Out past the old Morger place along the main road was the town cemetery. It sat there lonely, an acre and a half, maybe two acres, a single tree of maybe 50 years in the middle. The whole thing was surrounded by a low chain-link fence with a gate that no longer latched resting open a foot or so. Ray pulled the gate open another few inches, slipped through sideways, continued on through the graveyard.

Rows of markers lined a narrow foot path, names and years engraved on the gravestones. Looking one direction, there was Boniewicz next to Palzewicz, then Tetzlaff. Boyle. Kaczmarczyk. Meaney. Arciczewski. Czerniak. On the other side of the path, another had Slater carved in it. Cash. Szymanski. Lewandowski. Mientkiewicz. Two markers in one row caught Ray's eye, each bearing the name Morger. Not far from that row was another with considerably larger gravestones. Those belonged to Glennons.

Ray's gaze lingered there for only a brief moment before shifting to the woods beyond the cemetery where two slender pines stood next to each other towering over the forest's thick canopy, a good 15 or 20 feet higher than any of the surrounding trees. Those pines were something of a landmark around Faith, known to the locals as the twin steeples. A narrow, deeply rutted lane bordered on each side by four-strand barbed-wire fence led to the edge of the woods.

Rather than return to the gate at the front of the cemetery, Ray climbed over the rear fence and headed for the alley. A desire to be alone trumped concern about being caught trespassing. Upon reaching the end of the lane, Ray traversed what appeared to be an overgrown pasture and started negotiating the forest's thick underbrush in the general direction of the twin steeples.

Thirty feet in, Ray came upon a winding cow path through the bushes and densely clustered trees. After 50 yards or so, the thicket grew seemingly impenetrable. Burrs clung to shirtsleeves and pant legs as Ray pulled back branches, carefully stepping through the slenderest of passageways before hearing a faint trickling sound.

It was slow going, but 20 yards more produced a welcome opening in the thick vegetation, revealing the tiniest of streams, a burbling brook no more than six feet across. Three almost perfectly spaced rocks the size of large pumpkins rested in the water. Stepping confidently across the rocks and jumping to one of the dry mounds of spongy bog on the other side, Ray's well-worn sneakers sunk into the soft ground at the water's edge.

"Crap!"

Trees on the other side of the stream were taller and thicker at the trunk, but the underbrush was no less tangled. The cow path did not pick back up, leaving Ray to search for the route of least resistance. The ground rose for roughly the next 20 yards, then leveled off before dropping off again. At the swale's bottom, bushes and shrubs were even more ensnarled.

Ray had hoped to reach the twin steeples, but the view from the forest floor made it exceedingly difficult to identify which of the countless pine trees those might be. Aborting the expedition seemed more sensible with each step. Just as the idea of turning around had gained the upper hand, Ray saw a most unexpected and peculiar sight: what appeared to be an archway in the wall of undergrowth.

Through this entrance, the tree canopy formed a vaulted ceiling. On the ground in this open space, only pine needles blanketed the floor, no weeds or shrubs or bushes. The room that this unnatural arrangement of vegetation produced was more or less circular, somewhat longer than it was wide, close to 30 feet deep, maybe 20 feet across. Ray gaped at the discovery, marveling at its form and features, reluctant to blink for fear it may disappear. Then without warning a man's voice assaulted the solitude, startling Ray.

"Didn't you see the signs marking this land as private property?" the voice called out sternly from just outside the archway.

Limbs frozen, heart pounding violently, Ray proved unable to speak.

"I say, didn't you see the warning? Violators will be shot, and survivors will be shot again."

Ray's eyes darted desperately, seeking a means of escape, before settling on a figure in the archway.

The voice lowered and softened.

"I see you found the cathedral." The man standing before Ray was slender, about average height, with crooked teeth and unshaven stubble on his face. He ran his hand through his grizzled hair. Under a weathered tan canvas jacket, he wore a blue flannel shirt tucked into faded blue jeans. On his feet, mud-splattered work boots known to the locals as shit kickers.

"You must be Ray."

Ray stood stock-still, saying not a word.

"Didn't mean to scare you. Was just fooling about the business of shooting trespassers. I'm sorry, that was no fit way to introduce myself. I'm Morger."

Morger paused for an instant, the child in front of him visibly unnerved.

"Why'd you wander back here?" he inquired.

"You called this the cathedral," Ray said nervously after drawing a deep breath.

"Indeed."

"Why's it called that? Who made this?"

"No one made it. Been this way as long as I can remember."

"Couldn't have always been like this. Someone must've made it," Ray protested.

"What can't be explained is magic," Morger replied.

Ray didn't look satisfied. "Is this your land?"

"It is. Insofar as it belongs to anyone," came the answer. "Been in my family for generations."

"Your family's name is on gravestones in the cemetery."

"One's for my mother and father. The other is for Gramma and Grampa Morger."

He held out his arm, the outstretched hand summoning Ray to leave the cathedral. "How 'bout we head back. Your mama's worried about you. She's calling around, afraid maybe you've run away from home."

"Is that why you followed me back here?"

"Guilty as charged. Besides, I've been wanting to meet you. I can take you up to the house, introduce you to Colette."

Ray followed Morger through the alder thickets, across the stream, along the cow path leading back out of the woods. Soon the graveyard was again in sight though it was nearly dark. In the dim light Gin could be seen standing just outside the fence waiting for them. Ray was relieved to see her there, making it unnecessary to continue on to Morger's house.

CHAPTER 6

SHOULD YOU HAPPEN UPON FAITH TODAY, the Morger place looks much like it did close to 30 years ago when Ray first wandered into their woods. You won't find Morger or his wife Colette, they've been gone six or seven years. Seems hardly anyone knew the old man's first name. He preferred it that way. Morger and Colette lived on the outskirts of town, not a quarter mile from the boarded-up A&W root beer stand, the first thing visitors see after the "Welcome to Faith" sign and before the first cluster of houses. They kept to themselves, rarely if ever seen in a store much less at town gatherings.

Their homestead is still there, off the main road. To the left is a small shed that has the look of a garage. To the right is the house, nicely shaded by old trees in the yard. Farther down what passes for a driveway is an old windmill on a cement slab overgrown with weeds. The water pump at the base wasn't operational for most of the years they lived there; it didn't even appear to be connected to the windmill. Beyond that is an old barn with a cement silo at its side. Tall weeds surround both. Neither seemed to be in use when the Morgers called this place home, and look even more neglected now.

With one exception, all the buildings were unpainted then and remain so today, leaving the exposed wood a drab, weathered gray color. The sole outlier, an outhouse not far from the barn. Its white paint was badly peeling back in the day, exposing a faded red coat of paint underneath. Both the top layer and undercoat are half gone now. The latrine's door is missing entirely, making it clear to any who pass by that it's a two-holer.

Because a paintbrush hasn't touched the house in years, it appears uninhabited. The one and only sign of life when it was the Morger residence was a sizeable garden out back of the house. Several rows of sweet corn flanked bushy tomato plants, sprawling melon and squash vines, yards of mounded soil inside of which potatoes surely were growing, meticulously tended rows of carrots, sweet peas and green beans. Any given day during the warm months Morger or Colette could be seen tending that garden.

No one alive in Faith today can remember it, but Morger was raised on that farm, the only son of third-generation Irish immigrants. There was some dispute whether the family was originally from Wales or Scotland, but Morger's parents told him the family migrated to Ireland, settling there for some years before fleeing in the mid-1800s during the potato famine. Morger spent his youth in Faith before volunteering for the service. After basic training at Camp Claiborne in Louisiana, he shipped out for the D-Day invasion. When the war ended, he returned to Faith with Colette. He left with her shortly thereafter, taking advantage of the GI Bill to attend college.

Five or six years later, Morger and Colette were back in Faith. They made periodic brief trips to France presumably to visit family, then went away for the better part of two years in the late 1980s. No one around town knew where they'd gone, or if they knew they didn't say. In their later years, Morger worked as caretaker of the cemetery and the town dump. Colette cleaned houses on the Hill and was a lunch lady at the elementary school in Faith until it closed and then at the high school in Colby. That's what the Morgers did to keep busy and make ends meet. It wasn't their purpose.

Ray was told about the Morgers immediately upon arriving in Faith at nearly age nine, and stayed away for the better part of two years. The word around town, at least among Faith's youth, was that the place was haunted. Kids will be kids, but Moose also warned Ray to steer clear of the Morgers. That was harder to discount. Plucking up the courage at 11 years to approach mysterious strangers at a creepy-looking place was no small thing. Ray was steeled by the fact that the one encounter with Morger had proved harmless enough.

Ray took the neatly tended garden alongside the house as further evidence that it must be safe to approach. Besides, no kids had assembled on the battlefield after school, leaving nothing to do, supplying ample reason for throwing caution to the wind that day. Across town Ray walked, passing the boarded-up root beer stand, turning down the dusty driveway, now nearly creeping as if sneaking up on someone. Three untrustworthy steps led to a small porch bordered by a weathered balustrade with several missing columns. The porch's floorboards creaked as Ray approached the screen door, which afforded a glimpse inside the single-story house as the solid wood inner door with a tarnished brass knob was wide open. Ray knocked on the crooked wood frame of the screen door, taking a step back to wait for a reply.

A woman's voice answered. "Come in!"

Ray lingered outside the door.

A slender, stylish-looking woman with a chiseled jawline and cheekbones softened by a warm smile appeared on the other side of the screen. Her graying hair was pulled back into a ponytail, she wore a loose-fitting sleeveless blouse and carefully creased knit dress slacks. This must be Colette, Ray thought.

"Vien, vien," she said, motioning for Ray to enter. "Come in."

Inside the screen door, a cramped entryway. Well-worn linoleum—once tan but yellowed by the years—covered the floor. On the wall, two portraits, one of Jesus knocking on a door, the other a black and white photograph of a soldier in uniform standing with his arm around a woman in a knee-length dress underneath a sign saying Boulangerie, whatever that meant. The woman in the picture had the same severe features as the one who answered the door, only more girlish with unruly dark hair falling on her shoulders, a necklace of pearls resting on her bosom.

A rounded doorway led from the foyer to what looked like a time capsule. The living space was meager, the furnishings spartan. A dining area with a table barely big enough for four chairs. On the stained laminate top, a bowl of apples and a tea kettle. Behind the dining room an open kitchen. Near the sink and stove, yellow metal canisters lined the wall underneath a row of cabinets.

Beside the canisters was a white ceramic jar in the shape of a rotund woman. Her lower half formed the jar's base, draped in a yellow-trimmed apron adorned with poinsettias, a single pocket near her globe-shaped waist. The lid was the woman's upper torso. She had solid black eyes, prominent eyebrows, bright red lips. On her head a red bonnet, a red ribbon tied in a bow at her neckline. In her arms a wicker basket full of red, yellow and blue flowers adorned with green leaves.

Through another arched doorway was a sitting room. Faded and uneven hardwood floors mostly covered by a trampled throw rug. Furniture, old but not collectible. A matching couch and armchair upholstered in threadbare, washed-out orangish-brown. A coffee table in the middle of the room with a wooden rocking chair nearby. Four-decker shelves lined one wall, half full of books, the rest cluttered with knickknacks. A television sat on a wood cabinet nestled against the unadorned adjoining wall. A hallway led from the sitting room and kitchen to bedrooms and the toilet.

Ray's eyes darted, surveying each room, returning again and again to the jar in the kitchen. The woman couldn't help but notice.

"Would you like a biscuit?" She spoke with some kind of foreign accent and could see a puzzled look cross Ray's face. "Cookie."

The woman grasped the jar's lid by the red bonnet, lifted it off, tilted her head to invite Ray to take a look inside. "Macarons. My husband calls them macaroons, but he is mistaken. Those are coconut. These have shells that are a little like meringue, made with egg whites and almond flour. Vanilla buttercream filling. Try some."

Ray reached in, plucking out a cookie.

"You can take more than one," the woman said gently, a warm smile matching a twinkle in her eyes.

"Mmm," Ray murmured between bites, before reaching back into the jar for a second.

"I know you," the woman said, then paused for Ray to look up so their eyes met. "You are Virginia's child. My husband and I know your secret."

A half-startled, half-frightened look darted across Ray's face.

"There's no need to be afraid, you are always welcome here," the woman said reassuringly.

"Where is your husband?" Ray asked.

"He is away but will return soon. You can get to know him better the next time you visit. I hope that will be soon."

It was quite a while before Ray again visited the Morgers. This time it was after dinner one crisp, cool evening. Looking through the screen door it was apparent that both were home, so this time Ray entered without knocking.

"Butter cookies. Fresh baked," Colette said, gesturing toward the cookie jar. Ray made a beeline for the jar, lifted the lid, removing two.

Morger was in the sitting room. No announcing of presence or introductions were done. Ray started up conversation with a question.

"That portrait on the wall. That's you and Mrs. Morger, isn't it?"

"It surely is," Morger replied.

"You were in the war."

"I was."

"Which one?"

"The big one, double-u double-u two."

"Why don't you have any guns? Don't you hunt? Everyone else around here does."

"I know what it's like to be hunted."

"Did you kill anyone in the war?"

Morger pursed his lips, a pained expression washing over his weathered face.

"It was kill or be killed."

Ray wanted to know more, but thought better of probing further on the subject after seeing that look. Colette broke the silence.

"Ray, did you know that we once spent a year living in Africa?"

"Uh-uh."

Morger looked grateful for the change of subject, jumping back into the conversation.

"Colette and I did a church mission in Mali back in the mid-'80s. To be honest, I'd never heard of Mali. Any idea where it is?"

Ray shook no.

"My guess was that it was some island in the Pacific. Had to check a world map. Found it in western Africa. I look at the map closer, see Timbuktu. Didn't even know it was a real place. Always thought it was make-believe."

"Why did you go *there*?" Ray inquired.

Morger lowered his voice in hopes that Colette wouldn't hear his answer from the kitchen.

"Colette wanted out of here. She wanted to go back to France, or just someplace different. I suppose I was looking to make up for the war. Next thing you know we're packing two big duffle bags with prett-near a year's worth of things we were sure couldn't be found where we were going. Even took several bags of peanuts in the shell. Thought they'd travel well, we'd for sure have something to eat. Stupid thing to do. Peanuts are a staple crop in Mali."

The host chuckled to himself at that thought, gazing up at the ceiling as if he could see his memories up there.

"There's a lot I can't remember about our time there, and some things that are so vivid it's like they happened yesterday."

Morger looked back at Ray. "One thing I remember is when we landed at the airport in the country's capital. Guess I expected to see sand. Looked more like the Dakotas."

He again fixed his eyes on the ceiling. "Night had fallen by the time we cleared customs. Left the airport in a beat-up old pickup truck with a canvas top. Close to a dozen of us were cheek to jowl on wood benches in the back, along with our bags, sacks of grain, bundles of wood, bowls of fruit and vegetables, pots and pans. A couple of young men gave the truck a push to get it started. As it got up to speed, they climbed aboard, perching themselves on the tailgate. Was sure they were bound to lose their grip and fall."

Ray noticed Colette had removed her apron and gone outside.

"Where did Mrs. Morger go?"

"Aw, probably just wanted some fresh air. She's a free spirit, that one. Comes and goes as she pleases," Morger said before continuing with his story.

"It was pitch black all along the route. Ruts in the road like craters on the moon. Crumbling cement buildings along both sides. Looked like sheds of some kind but had signs on them with handwritten French lettering and telephone numbers. Turns out they were shops of one kind or another. People sat outside around kerosene lanterns or small campfires."

A question occurred to Ray but it felt like the wrong moment to interrupt. Morger looked lost in thought.

"We reached what we were told was a high school campus that would be home for our first few days in the country. The place was empty, except for the mission staff who welcomed us. First thing they told us was not to drink from the taps, pointing out barrels containing drinkable water. We were led to a dimly lit hall that reminded me of military barracks. Cement floors and walls. Peeling yellow paint. Rust-colored louvered metal windows. No glass, no screens. Corrugated metal roof. Not much for furnishings, just rows of foam mattresses on bamboo bed frames with four poles attached to accommodate mosquito nets."

If Ray had left, Morger would not have noticed.

"Across the way were toilet stalls, sinks and a room with probably two dozen shower nozzles. Didn't say for women or for men. The room was stifling hot, I could've used a shower after the long trip. Colette is Bohemian, you know, doesn't give a second thought to baring herself. But modesty got the best of me. It was late, I was exhausted, splash some water on my face, brush my teeth in one of the sinks, crawl under the net into bed. Fell off to sleep in the clothes I traveled in. Didn't wake 'til daybreak, to the sound of roosters crowing and donkeys braying. Here we are, in the capital city, the first sounds I hear are those of the farm. Damnedest thing. Next thing I hear is a faraway voice chanting words I could not understand over a loudspeaker. Mission staffers are going from bed to bed waking people up, one of them says it's a town crier issuing the call to prayer. That became a familiar sound. Heard it five times a day."

Morger again cast his gaze skyward and his voice rose, mimicking the crier. "*Allahu Akbar! Allahu Akbar!*"

He looked back down, his eyes meeting Ray's. "That's Arabic. Means God is great."

Ray sensed an opening to show curiosity.

"Are the people there Christians?"

"No, mostly Muslim. Seems silly now that I think back on it, but at the time Colette and I—mostly me—thought we could help people there by bringing them Jesus."

"What color are they?"

"Quite a bit darker than you, Ray. Black as night."

Morger seemed distracted, taking a moment to gather his thoughts. A suppressed laugh turned into a wry smile on his wrinkled face.

"I remember trying to be discreet that morning about undressing and pulling on fresh clothing. I knew right then and there I made a mistake not showering when we arrived, when it was darker. The few bulbs lighting the dormitory were covered with grime, left most everything in shadows.

Those shadows were now gone. Must've been about 20 people in our group, half men, half women, give or take. The mattresses were too narrow to sleep two, so Colette had a bed to the right of mine. A bewitching young thing was disrobing right at the foot of my bed."

This turn in the story piqued Ray's interest.

"A woman closer to my age looks away when she sees her neighbor getting naked, shoots me a dirty look when she notices me looking her way. I turn my back to her while also trying to face away from what was transpiring at the end of my bed. Still trying to preserve my dignity, but I'm telling you the effort was futile, more women were just a row or two from me. Dropped my trousers and briefs first, wrapped a towel around my waist before removing my shirt. All the while kicking myself for not doing this at night."

Ray grinned.

"You can imagine how alarmed I was to see six or seven towels on a wood bench outside the doorway to the showers. Held tight to my towel, poked my head in, saw right away why the towels had been left outside. No stalls, no hooks for hanging anything next to the shower nozzles. I look around the room, hoping for a spot somewhere in a corner, those were taken. The young woman who'd slept at my foot was in there. So were a couple other women and several men, all naked as jaybirds. I'm considering turning tail, forgoing cleanliness. One of the women is glaring at me. Oh lordy, if looks could kill. Must've thought I was getting my thrills eyeing up those showering. I sheepishly back out of the doorway, find a spot on the bench for my towel, bare my paunch, my farmer tan, the meager evidence of my manhood to my fellow missionaries. That was one *very* brief shower."

Ray laughed to the point of crying—as much at Morger's telling of the story as its contents.

"All I know is we all got to know each other real good that first morning, prett-near in a biblical sense ..." Morger chuckled as his voice trailed off.

"Why do you figger they put a church mission group up in that place, all intermingled like that?" Ray asked, still dabbing at tears.

"Colette thought it probably was the only place they could get their hands on. She figured it must have been tough for a Christian mission to gain acceptance in a Muslim country. I had the feeling maybe they were trying to break us the way the military does. Push us out of our comfort zone, get us ready for what was to come."

Morger cupped his hand over this mouth, peering up again at the ceiling. Then he returned his gaze to Ray.

"That's what's done to soldiers?" Ray asked.

"You know, it's getting late. Better leave this here for now," Morger answered.

"You mind if I come back tomorrow?"

"Don't mind at all, so long as I'm not boring you."

Ray shook no and headed for the door.

"Good night, Mr. Morger."

From the doorstep, Ray noticed that Colette had returned.

"Good night, Mrs. Morger."

"Bonne nuit, Ray. À demain!"

CHAPTER 7

SEVERAL DAYS PASSED BEFORE RAY RETURNED to the Morger house. The front door was open as usual. Ray peered through the outer screen door, calling out to see if anyone was home. No reply immediately came, but the smell of baking bread wafted out through the screen. That was sign enough, the screen door letting out a pronounced squeak as Ray pulled it open to enter. It banged loudly upon closing again. From a back room came Morger, carrying a photo album.

"You might want to check the jar," Morger said, motioning toward the kitchen. "I think you'll find your favorites."

Ray moved swiftly to the kitchen and lifted the lid. Inside were crunchy shortbread cookies with fudge stripes, the store-bought kind. One of Ray's very favorites, just like Morger said. A mischievous smile crossed Ray's face, broken momentarily by another bite of cookie.

"So, what happened after you were naked with all them people you barely knew?"

Morger laughed so hard he shook.

"Thought you might like to see pictures of the place." Morger placed the album on the dining room table, opened it, flipped several pages, turning it to face Ray.

"This is the school," Morger said, pointing to a photo of what appeared to be a cement block warehouse at the top of a hill. There were pictures of the Niger River that Morger said could be seen below the school's tree-lined dirt courtyard. Men fishing in narrow wooden boats. Bare-breasted women bathing in the river, washing clothes by hand. Crumbling cement houses with rusted sheet-metal roofs lining deeply rutted dirt paths that snaked through the city.

The faded images showed streets teeming with people, goats, dogs, chickens. Small children playing in the trash littering street corners. The dwellings looked bombed out. Morger said one of the mission leaders who lived in the capital called his street Beirut Boulevard. Ray wasn't sure what that meant but was studying the photos too intently to ask.

"All these are shots of Bamako. You know what the word means?" Morger asked. Ray shook no. "Crocodile River."

"There are crocodiles in the river?"

"Imagine so. Was careful not to go in the water. You get schistosomiasis if you do. Nasty disease. Caused by parasitic worms. Penetrate your skin, get into your bloodstream. Messes up your insides real bad, from what I hear."

Ray grimaced but inquired no further. Once the photo album was set aside, Morger returned to Ray's original question.

"We were taken to the heart of the city to look around. First thing that hits you is the smell. Like dust and smoke and the stench of open sewers all blended together. I remember going to a huge open-air market. An army of merchants, all aggressively beckoning you to check out their wares. Women hawk cloth, tend vegetable stands. Show even the slightest interest, they start negotiating a purchase price. Lepers sit next to them with tin cans hung over their stumped arms in hopes of getting a small coin or two. Cripples drag themselves down dirt alleys by their hands. Young boys guide blind men through the market's maze. None of those children ever looked bored or put upon. You remind me of them, Ray."

Ray said nothing.

"At that time, I'm guessing Bamako was between a half million and a million people. On the surface it's an ugly place, filthy and decayed. You see men relieving themselves on the sides of walls. No wonder people here think places like that are shitholes. Look at it through American eyes, you assume people must be full of despair. Look below the surface though, you don't see despair. What you see brings on cognitive dissonance."

Now Ray looked perplexed.

"Aw, that's just a fancy term for thinking two things that don't fit together, one that contradicts the other. People were living on less than a dollar a day, the place is infested with diseases that were eradicated here generations ago. Yet they can't seem to resist smiling. They laugh easily and often, way more than we do here. They sing and dance more too. There's a togetherness that's missing here. I'd gone there thinking this was a godforsaken place that needed saving, but it didn't look or sound or feel forsaken to me. That's cognitive dissonance."

Morger shifted in his chair.

"By the third day, I tell you I was the one in need of saving. That's when the dysentery started. Vomiting and diarrhea, the likes of which I never experienced before or after. Nasty cramps, fever of 103. Colette had the same thing, worse if anything. You know what got us?"

Ray shook no almost imperceptibly.

"Brushing teeth. With tap water. Made us so sick, thought I was going to die."

"How long did you stay there in the capital?"

"Only four or five days. The plan was to be there only long enough to get oriented, then be dispatched to posts around the country. By the time we were feeling better, we were shipping out."

"Where's Mrs. Morger?"

"You know, I'm not completely sure. I think she said she was heading over to your mom's to help can vegetables." Morger paused, then spoke over Ray. "Funny it's called canning. They put everything in glass jars, not cans. By rights it should be called jarring, not canning, don't you think?"

"Why doesn't the Moose want me coming over here?" Ray blurted. "Mom don't mind."

"She wouldn't," Morger replied.

"So why does the Moose have a problem with it?"

"I can't read his mind or look into his heart, but my guess is he doesn't think Colette and I are adequately worshipful."

"What do you mean? You're the most Christian people I know."

Morger had been looking down at his hands, but raised his gaze, peering at Ray over his reading glasses.

"Christian is no longer a title I am altogether comfortable with. Let's just say your dad and I don't exactly see eye to eye on what to worship."

"The Moose ain't my father."

"Not your biological ..." Morger started to say, stopping to recalibrate his answer.

"Not in any way," Ray shot back.

"Be that as it may, Colette and I always enjoy having you here, consider you a part of our family."

Fall gave way to winter and winter to another spring. Time kept its relentless beat, six more seasons slipping by almost unnoticed. Ray was a teenager now and paid the Morgers impromptu visits more and more frequently. Morger and Colette found it odd that anyone Ray's age would spend so much time with an aging couple listening to their stories. But they weren't about to look a gift horse in the mouth.

Ray's reasons for wanting to stay away from home as much as possible weren't really that curious. Mark graduated high school, going off to college to study business administration, with intentions of returning to take his place in the family enterprises. Steve was nearly done with high school himself and was plotting a similar course. Neither brother cared much for baseball; both were avid golfers. Steve lettered in both football and basketball. Moose worked long hours, immersed in his businesses. When he was home, he lectured Ray on the need to set career goals, trying every chance he got to kindle an interest in commerce. His frustration with Ray's seeming lack of initiative simmered, occasionally boiling over.

Ray found solace at the Morgers. Walked across town even on bitter cold evenings in the dead of winter, always welcomed like a long-lost friend. Invariably the cookie jar's lid was lifted; its contents did not disappoint.

"Is something troubling you?" Morger asked one day, noticing Ray's disquiet, offering a seat at the dining room table.

"Naw, just tired."

"Sleepy tired, or tired of something?"

"A little of both I guess. Tired of hearing that I'll never amount to anything unless I set goals. Make a plan. Get serious about my future."

A pained expression crossed Morger's face.

"Can I give you some advice?"

Ray nodded.

"Don't set goals. Find a purpose."

"That's not what the Moose keeps saying."

The same anguished expression revisited Morger's visage.

"You have to find your own way, Ray. Your own truth," he said. "It's not easy. Truth is an orphan."

"Whadya mean by that?"

Morger pondered the question for a brief moment. He could tell Ray was furiously processing his counsel, letting it sink in.

"Sometimes when you let truth be your guide, people abandon you. That's what integrity is all about. Being true to yourself, even as the world is trying to make you something else. As you're finding out, integrity is expensive."

Tears welled up in Ray's eyes.

"I wish I was someone else. I wish my skin wasn't like this, all blotchy."

Ray's lips quivered; tears spilled down. Morger rose from his chair. "I want you to listen to me." Ray's head and shoulders slumped. "Beauty is like a seed. The most valuable part is on the inside."

Ray looked up at Morger.

"Don't you ever forget that."

The old man sat down again but pulled the chair closer to Ray.

"Yiri kurun men o men jee la, ah tay kay bama yay."

Ray's expression morphed from torment to puzzled curiosity.

"African proverb. No matter how long a log stays in the water, it doesn't become a crocodile. Their way of saying, be yourself."

Colette had been listening in on the conversation and sensed an opening.

"We learned a lot the hard way over there," she said. "Did you ever tell Ray how you talked with them about farming?"

Morger's eyes lit up, a chuckle bubbled from his throat at the memory.

"Most of our time there we were stationed in larger market towns. Home base was Kati and later Koulikoro, a little north of Bamako not far from the capital. Spent a fair amount of time in Baguineda too. Same region but off to the east and a bit south. Stayed a while in Bandiagara and Douentza, probably a good 800 clicks east of Bamako. That's where the Dogon people live. Cliff dwellers."

"Clicks?" Ray said quizzically.

"Kilometers. Sorry. To this day I fall into using the slang. Eight hundred kilometers is something like 500 miles, give or take."

Morger's eyes met Colette's, who without speaking commanded him to pick up the pace.

"I'm gettin' to it," he said in her direction, slightly annoyed. "We also fanned out to the west of the capital maybe 250 or 300 miles, where we had an extended stay in Bafoulabé and surrounding villages in the Bafing River delta. So far as I know, the people in that area are mostly Malinke. Had a devil of a time understanding what they were saying. Their language is similar enough to the Bambara we were trying to speak that they could understand us, but we couldn't understand them."

Colette made a circular motion with her index finger as she brought the cookie jar over to Ray for seconds. Morger pretended not to notice her mimed message.

"Wherever we went, it was hard finding a good time to meet with people during the planting and harvest seasons, they were so busy. Got to know some families in Dialakoroba to the south of the capital on the goudron, visited from time to time."

"Goudron?" Ray interrupted.

"There I go again. French for paved road. It was rainy season, probably about the middle of July. The time of year when families are still planting their crops. Every morning, nearly everyone in the village heads out to the fields to work, even young children who tend the oxen. Women work with babies bundled on their backs. A few women stay behind to prepare huge bowls of tô they would carry out to the fields on their heads, often a mile or more from the village."

"They eat toe? Toe of what?"

"Ha!" Morger blurted. "Nah, tô is a thick paste made of pounded millet. You scoop some with your hand, shape it into a ball like you do with cookie dough, dip it in a sauce. Some of the sauces are made of tree leaves. One is made of okra. We called that one snot sauce because it was so slimy."

Ray grimaced.

"What's millet?"

"You're getting me off on another tangent ... It's a grain. About the only thing it's used for here is bird seed. There it's their staple food. Ate a lot of it in our time there. Saw how it was grown. We'd go out to their fields with them every chance we had."

Morger checked the time before continuing.

"One of the young men we got to know was Mamadou. Madu for short.

He asked me in Bambara if I knew how to use a daba."

"What's that?" Ray asked.

"A short-handled hoe they use to dig the soil. I told him I did and was handed one. Madu stopped working to watch as I joined in. The millet was only about ankle high, barely visible among the grasses and weeds that had sprung up around it. I stooped low, worked up the ground around each plant, uprooting weeds and grasses, working them back into the soil. The ground was soft thanks to rain the night before, making the work easier. Still, I stopped every few minutes to stretch out my back. After taking three or four breaks, one of the men tells me: 'There are machines to do this work in America. You don't work with a daba.'

"I wanted to tell them how we cleaned calf pens with pitchforks, stacked hay bales in the loft of our barn, unloaded hundred-pound sacks of cow feed from the truck, but I didn't know how to say it in their language. After being bent over for almost two hours, my back was sore and blisters on my hands had broken open. They were dumbfounded by the sight of a white man doing manual labor. Madu was the only one who didn't try stopping me. He asks if we grow millet in America. I didn't know the word for oats, had trouble thinking of a way to describe hay, so I tell him we grow corn to feed our cows and sell the milk."

Morger mimed looking aghast.

"He says, 'you give your corn to cows? Your animals eat better than our people.' I didn't have the words to say anything back. Besides, he was right, our animals do eat better than a lot of their people. Had a hard time imagining how my mission was possibly going to do anything about that."

Ray seemed to be pondering the story but said nothing.

"A young fella named Moussa is listening to me and Madu. He'd been standing off to the side, kind of sizing me up. Come to find out he could speak a little French. Asks how much milk American cows give. My French wasn't a whole lot better than my Bambara, Colette was a quarter mile away working in the women's field, so I was on my own. Plus, I had to do the metric conversion to liters for him. Took me a while to do the math and find the words, finally I tell him 40 or 50 a day. A good cow right after she gives birth. He looks shocked, tells me one of theirs gives a liter a day, tops."

Morger's eyes grew wide as he mimicked the man's reaction.

"He shakes his head, says 'pah pah pah.' That's what they say when something surprises them or is hard to believe. Then Moussa tells me he heard American farmers use a machine to breed their cows. I tell him no, it's not a machine. Not stopping to think that I was in way over my head language wise, I start trying to explain artificial insemination. Best I could do in French was to say a man breeds the cow. Should've seen the look on that guy's face."

Ray burst out laughing. Colette did too, even though she'd heard the story many times.

"Didn't know the word for semen, was at a total loss to explain the plastic tube used to deposit it in the cow. Moussa says: 'A man breeds the cow? There is no machine?' Only thing I could think of was the French word for thing, so I tell him a man takes a thing about yay long ..."

Morger spread his hands about eight inches apart.

"He takes the thing ... puts it in the cow. Moussa looks at me, says 'pah pah pah.' I'm mortified, the misimpression I've given, without the words to undo what I've done."

Ray dissolved into the kind of laughter that blurs the distinction between pleasure and pain. That set Colette off as well. When calm was restored, Morger and Colette noticed the hour had grown late.

"You mind if I spend the night?" Ray asked. "I can just sleep on the couch."

Colette insisted it would be no problem to make up a bed.

"The couch will be fine."

That wasn't the last time Ray stayed over.

CHAPTER 8

MOOSE GLENNON ALWAYS LIKED TO SAY THAT FAITH ain't in a class by itself when it comes to nicknames but it don't take long to call the roll. Slapping monikers on people is a time-honored tradition, largely because so many of the locals' last names are a chore to pronounce. Most of Ray's school chums had them. Polish surnames, that is. And nicknames. Some innocuous. Others on the clever side. A few were humiliating or offensive or both, depending on your point of view.

Nobody called Kenny Kaczmarczyk by his given name. He was Kaz to everyone who knew him. Brian Mientkiewicz was Mint. Tom Arciczewski was Archie. Doug Palzewicz was Palsy. Rich Boniewicz was Boner. Not being Polish didn't mean you were spared. A heavy-set girl, Eileen Schneider, was Hoss. Lisa Wagner was Hill, partly owing to where she lived but mainly because every boy wanted to climb on top of her. Everett Meaney, an adopted Native American, was Chief. His adopted sister Linh was called by her Vietnamese name but everyone spelled it Lynn.

Ray was a good student but didn't care much for school. Gym class was a personal favorite but also an unending source of anxiety. Loved playing sports, kickball, flag football, wrestling, soccer, even wiffle ball, though it was a lame substitute for actual baseball. Hated having to change into gym clothes. Hated showering afterwards even more. Ray's strategy was to wear the gym outfit as underclothes to avoid having to fully undress. Classmates certainly noticed the undue modesty. Opinions varied widely about the cause.

"I bet he hasn't hit puberty yet and's got no pubic hair," Mint told Palsy and Boner, buttressing his claim with the visual evidence of a face without so much as peach fuzz. "He ain't even close to shaving yet."

Archie was alone in cutting Ray some slack.

"He's got all those weird patches, like the top layer of skin is scraped off. Maybe it prevents whiskers from growing."

Kaz was having none of it.

"Bet you any amount he's got a dick the size of a Jujyfruit."

In the boys' locker room, towel snapping and the occasional wedgie were par for the course. None of that kept anyone up at night. Problem is, hijinks could become hazing in a heartbeat. Ray figured out quickly that the best protection was a low profile. Kids with big mouths were big targets.

Nobody had more trouble keeping his mouth shut than Boner. Far from being outwardly embarrassed or ashamed of his nickname, Boner reveled in it. More than once he paraded around the locker room, proudly displaying an erection. But every once in a while, his mouth got him in trouble. What started as fairly innocent razzing one day after gym class escalated, as these things almost inevitably do, and got Boner's goat, prompting him to invent a nickname for Nick Szymanski.

"She-Man!" Boner crowed. He wouldn't let up. "What's wrong? You dish it out but can't take it, huh She-Man?"

He couldn't have chosen a target more unwisely. Nick Szymanski was not only the doctor's son but also the ablest clique builder in their class by a wide margin.

Nick wasted no time seeking revenge. He and three friends—all Colby jocks—pulled Boner out of the showers naked, dragging him back to the supply room beyond the last lockers. He screwed the top off a white plastic jar containing a bright orange cream. Ray had seen the jar sitting on a shelf but had only heard tell of its use for hazing purposes, for what was known as the treatment.

In bold blue letters on the jar were the words Atomic Balm. Above that in smaller letters the contents were described as analgesic ointment, whatever that is. While the others held down Boner, Nick plunged a wooden tongue depressor into the jar and slathered a thick layer of the jell on a white school-issue towel. As his victim cursed and struggled to free himself, Nick smeared the balm on poor Boner's genitals.

Boner howled in pain as the ointment's effects became noticeable. As the heat intensified, his face was contorted in agony, tears streaming down his face. Delighting in the suffering they'd inflicted, the four attackers proceeded to drag Boner to a rear exit opening to the back parking lot, hurling him into a deep snow bank. Boner scrambled in an effort to get back inside before the door slammed shut but didn't make it. He yelled for help, pounding and yanking on the door, to no avail.

"Anyone who tries letting him in will get the same!" Nick announced loudly upon returning to the locker room, jumping up on a perch in front of his locker—a bench engraved with years' worth of juvenile depictions and profane references to the opposite sex. Ray already was at Boner's locker gathering up the victim's clothes. This caught Nick's attention and he wheeled around, fixing Ray with a menacing glare. "*Are you deaf?!*"

Ray thought impressively fast.

"I was gonna hide them in another locker so he can't find them when he gets back in."

Ray headed for the end of the locker room farthest from the rear door. Most pleased with himself, Nick scanned the locker room in search of the orange-stained towel used to slather up Boner. He disappeared around a bank of lockers. With Nick no longer in sight, the coast appearing to be clear, Ray reversed course, making a beeline for the door with the clothes. Just then, Nick and one of his Colby friends emerged from the bathroom where they'd been washing the evidence of their handiwork from the towel.

"Give him the treatment, Nick!" a voice called out from the dozen or so students lingering in the locker room to watch the drama unfold. "Come on, do it Nick!" another voice cried, egging him on. A bell rang, signaling the need for all students to proceed to their next class. The towel clutched in Nick's hand still bore a conspicuous orange stain but would need to be loaded up again with balm for a repeat performance.

Without hesitation after hearing the bell, Nick dropped the towel, ripped the clothes from the much smaller classmate's arms and thrusted his hand between Ray's legs, securing a tight grip at the crotch and squeezing with all his might. Ray's reaction to this maneuver all the kids at school called grubbing was not the usual one, surprising everyone, especially Nick. Every boy watching had been hit in the balls. Everyone knew even the most glancing of blows were enough to double you over in pain. Those who'd been grubbed knew that having your testicles manually crushed was excruciatingly painful; those who hadn't yet experienced it could well imagine the severity of the torture, grimacing at the mere thought.

At first Ray seemed caught off guard, then affronted by the forcible violation. But there were no tears, no screams, no pleading for mercy. Nick's angry scowl dissolved into a confused look, replaced in short order by one of fright.

"Hey, somebody's coming," one of the Colby friends shouted. "Let's get out of here!"

Nick released his grip, turned and fled with his friends. The boys who remained in the locker room stood there in stunned silence. No one thought to call for help or check if Ray was all right. They stood frozen, mouths agape, as Ray retrieved the clothes from the floor and headed for the rear door. No one followed. Judging from the looks on their faces, they weren't impressed by Ray's actions; they found coming to Boner's aid unimaginably unwise and wildly risky. Boner had run his mouth, he had it coming.

Ray threw open the heavy metal door and stood in its path to keep it propped open, the frigid outside air flooding into the locker room. "Rich, come on, get in here!" Boner was sprawled next to a large snow bank, still naked, still clutching his groin. He had packed snow around his inflamed genitals. A sizeable audience of students in the parking lot gawked and jeered at the unclad freshman.

"I can't come out there and get you ... the door will close behind me and we'll both be locked out."

"My goddamn pecker is on fire!" Boner cried as he pulled more handfuls of snow between his legs, tears still streaming down his face.

"Rich, the burning will go away. You'll get frostbit down there if you keep doing that," Ray cautioned. "You want it to fall off? Get in here!"

"I'll get that prick. He's gonna fucking pay for this!"

"Come off it, Rich. I'm not waiting here forever."

Boner finally complied, making his way to the door amidst hoots of laughter. Ray draped clothing across Boner's privates, quickly ushering him to the bathroom. The next class—juniors—was filing into the locker room. It didn't take them long to put two and two together.

"He must've got the treatment," one said to nods and sniggers around the room.

"What'd you do to deserve that, dipshit?" another barked in Boner's direction.

Moaning in pain, Boner was too preoccupied with finding relief to pay any attention to the taunts. Once inside the bathroom, he immediately started splashing water on his nether region. "Do you want me to go get the nurse?" Ray asked sympathetically. Boner shook his head as a second bell rang out announcing the start of the next class.

"You need to get dressed so we can get to class. We're late already."

"Holy shit it burns so bad. She-Man'll get his."

"Don't be a fool. When're you gonna learn?"

Boner started pulling on his clothes, an opportune time for Ray to leave.

Tardiness on account of helping a classmate injured in gym class did not move the algebra teacher to sympathy. Ray was instructed to go back and get a permission slip from the gym teacher excusing the infraction. It took half the class period to secure the slip and return to class. Ray couldn't help but think the other kids were right—Boner brought it on himself— and nothing was gained by intervening on his behalf.

When the bell rang again at the end of the day's algebra lesson, Ray rushed from the room, enveloped by a hallway full of passing students. Kitty-corner from the math classroom, Nick Szymanski held court detailing his locker room exploits, how he'd given Boner the treatment, how after administering a good grubbing he was convinced Ray's balls must be the size of marbles or maybe haven't even dropped yet. The crowd around Nick—mostly boys but also a couple of girls—laughed zealously.

"Hey dickless!" he called out upon spotting Ray. "Don't worry, you won't be a hen forever. Someday you'll grow into a rooster. Who knows, maybe you'll even start shaving by the time you're 25!"

Among those making no effort to conceal their glee at Ray's expense were Archie and Kaz. That stung ... leaving Ray feeling utterly forsaken.

Ray kept a brave face, enduring the rest of the school day before boarding the bus for the half-hour ride home. Instead of waiting to be dropped off on the Hill, Ray jumped off as soon as the bus made its first stop near the edge of town, walking back in the direction of Colby. Past the Morger farm, along the front of the cemetery, down the lane now blanketed with a good foot and a half of snow.

Bundled in a down-filled coat but without a proper hat or boots, Ray plodded through the snow toward the twin steeples, turning away from the stinging wind. The edge of the forest provided a windbreak, welcome relief from the biting cold. Sneakers, however, offered little defense against the frozen ground.

Ray wound through the naked underbrush, across the frozen stream to the entrance of the cathedral. The thick canopy of evergreens prevented snow from reaching the forest floor. Ray plunked down on the carpet of pine needles. Tears poured from stricken eyes, freezing before they cascaded off hollow cheeks. Ray's chest heaved with each sob. Loneliness, anger and self-pity gushed out in convulsive gasps, drowning out the sounds of snapping branches and crunching footsteps in the snow beyond. Once Ray fell silent and looked up, a woman stood under the thick cluster of branches that formed the cathedral's entrance.

"Mom?"

"Hey Rage." Gin used that nickname only when they were alone. "Colette told me she saw you heading this way."

"You know about this place?"

"Been here a time or two, yes."

An awkward silence fell. Each expected the other to speak, each expectation was dashed.

"I heard what happened," Gin finally said. "One of the girls in your class told me about it."

"Prolly Eileen Schneider. She knows how it feels."

"I'm so sorry you have to deal with things like this, Rage."

"What'd you hear about, what happened to Rich Boniewicz or to me?"

"Both."

"In the locker room and then later in the hallway?"

"I have no idea if I got all the details, but yes."

"Rich had this flaming hot goo smeared on him; you know where. Then they locked him outside, naked. I tried helping him, got grabbed."

"Grabbed where?"

"Here," Ray replied, pointing.

"It was that Szymanski boy who did it?"

Ray nodded.

"I'll talk to his parents and the principal."

"Don't. It won't help. Prolly just make things worse."

Gin frowned, started to protest, but stopped.

"I was told you stood up to him."

Ray shrugged.

"What happened in the hall?"

"Got razzed. Everyone was laughing at me, even my friends. Got called names. Have a feeling one of 'em is gonna stick."

A pained expression covered Gin's face; tears welled up in her eyes. She peered at Ray inquiringly.

"Just names. Don't make me repeat them."

Gin lost her composure.

"Why do kids have to be like this?" Ray spluttered, trying to ward off tears.

"Honey, a lot of grownups are like this too," Gin replied. "They're just more polished at it because they've had so much practice."

Gin paused for an instant, steadying herself.

"Do you think it was a mistake for me to bring you back here?"

Ray shook no.

"Would you rather go somewhere else now? Do you want me to take you away from here?"

There was less conviction in Ray's no this time.

"I've made such a mess of things," Gin said, looking up away from Ray. "My problem is I've always done what others told me to do. About the only time I didn't was when you were born. With the way things are turning out, maybe you'd be better off if I'd have given you up for adoption like I was told."

"Don't say that. You're my mom. You taught me to be brave."

"How's that?" Gin asked skeptically.

"You stuck with me even though you have to put up with people thinking you went crazy."

Gin's composure betrayed her again. She apologized as she struggled to regain it; Ray responded with a gently dismissive gesture.

"I remember the precise moment I knew I was pregnant with you. I don't know how, but I knew. As soon as you were born, it's like a voice inside me was telling me I needed to keep you no matter what. I knew deep down you were going to be very special and do remarkable things. You were a gift from God and I knew in my heart I couldn't give that gift away."

"I'm glad you didn't," Ray said, falling into Gin's arms, embracing her fiercely.

"Don't make the same mistake I made so many times, Rage. Do what your heart tells you is right, no matter what others think."

Gin sniffled, heaved a sigh, then removed her woolen mittens. "Your hands are freezing. Take these." Ray held up a bare hand, open palm facing Gin. "No, take them. Get your hands warm." She removed her stocking hat, handing that to Ray as well.

"I keep telling you to take boots to school with you. We can try swapping," she said, pointing from her fur-lined boots to Ray's sneakers.

"We're not the same size," Ray replied.

"Shall we head for home?" Gin's eyes were still misty but she managed to smile.

Ray nodded.

"Christmas break is almost here. Being away from school for a month will help settle things down." She drew Ray to her in a smothering hug. "The Slaters invited us to a Christmas party they're having next week. You don't have to go if you don't want, but I'd like to connect you up with Jim to talk baseball. I don't think he knows what a big fan you are. It'll be fun."

CHAPTER 9

**RAY WAS RIGHT. THE NICKNAME STUCK. HEN GLENNON IT
WAS.** It didn't take long to figure out that the slightest sign of annoyance
or discomfort with it only made the kids at school use it even more, so Ray
pretended not to care. That proved effective. When kids couldn't get a rise
out of one target, they quickly moved on to the next.

Despite the season, the Christmas spirit didn't exactly permeate the
high school. Between raging hormones and adolescent insecurities, the
place was a juvenile jungle. The pecking order was as complex as it was
cruel. Colby kids felt superior to those from Faith or Unity. Kids from the
Hill were several steps up from those in other parts of Faith. Farm kids
were below everyone unless they were jocks. That status boosted their
standing to some degree.

Then there were the druggies. A strange designation, considering
that drinking was practically endemic, with everything from weed to
hard drugs readily available and commonly used in and around school.
Those not partaking were the exception, those who did, the rule. Still, the
druggies were largely ignored by their peers, as though they didn't have
a social station. They weren't assigned nicknames. They weren't asked to
join anything or invited to parties. It's like they didn't exist.

Katy Cash was teased mercilessly for being the preacher's daughter. She
overcompensated by trying to come across as loose—sort of half hippie,
half harlot—both in how she dressed and acted. Farmers' sons like Jeff

Czerniak, Bruce Boyle, Tom Tetzlaff and Royce Ackerman—known as Punk among those he hung out with—were looked down upon by the town kids and ritually taunted. The least imaginative of their tormentors called them hicks or rednecks. As for the more creative slurs, bestiality was a popular theme. Those on the receiving end sought to deflect unwanted attention by making life miserable for someone they deemed a rung or two below them on the school's social ladder, joining forces with town kids to emotionally batter those unfortunate souls.

No one got it worse than Mike Driscoll. It was his fate to be the whole school's punching bag. He lived with his family out in the country between Faith and Unity but they weren't farmers, a fact which dropped his social status beneath even the farm kids. His folks were dirt poor, living in a decrepit single-story shack with peeling white paint at the intersection of two gravel roads.

Mike's father was good with his hands—the yard was littered with old cars he was forever fixing up—but he had a hard time finding steady work. Odd jobs he managed to find here and there barely kept food on the table and eviction at bay. As far as anyone could tell, all the mother ever did was drink.

Ray had something of a crush on Mike's sister Chris, who was two years older and fully blossomed. Poor grooming drew the eye away from a strikingly pretty face; hand-me-down clothes cloaked a seductive figure. She was even more endowed above the shoulders, sharp as a tack with a bewitching smile and needling wit, yet did poorly in school. Her brother was every bit as smart and funny, but his disheveled and unsightly physical appearance overshadowed those attributes.

Barely a year earlier, Mike had been badly disfigured and nearly decapitated in a ghastly accident while riding his family's rattletrap snowmobile. A nearby farmer, upset by locals riding through his back forty without permission, strung a single twisted strand of barbed wire across a makeshift trail. Traveling at a considerable speed with the machine's single headlamp dimly lighting the way, Mike Driscoll never saw what hit him. The wire passed just over the low windshield that mostly shielded the driver's hands from the bitter cold, hitting Mike square in the face. The force of the blow drove him straight off the back of the sled, the wire ripping through his mouth, knocking out several front teeth, gashing him from ear to ear.

Locals almost unanimously sided with the farmer, reasoning he was well within his rights to make his property off limits, showing little sympathy for young Driscoll. They told each other they hated to see anyone get hurt, but the boy had no business on land that wasn't his. Mike heard none of it, as he was lying in traction in the Marshfield hospital with a neck injury. Doctors sewed him up as best they could and implanted acrylic replacements for his missing teeth.

After the wounds healed and stitches were removed, he was left horribly scarred. The kids at school, taking cues from their elders, coldly concluded he had been in the wrong and had no one to blame but himself. The bulbous scar tissue that formed between his cheekbones and jawline on both sides of his face inspired classmates to start calling him Chico.

He hated the nickname. To be sure, it was no term of endearment. It was a grim and insensitive reminder of the trauma he'd endured, a cruel affirmation of where he stood among his peers. Unlike Ray, he couldn't conceal his irritation with the name-calling, often lashing out in anger, sometimes with his tongue, other times with his fists. Each outburst was like blood spilt in a shark-infested pool. Kids were kicked hardest when they were down, Chico was a case in point. Every eruption prompted humiliating retaliation, a sort of adolescent death spiral.

Days before Christmas break, Ray noticed a circular scar on Chico's forearm and asked about it. "My brand," Chico replied nonchalantly, explaining he had burned his own skin with the bowl of a marijuana pipe. "Everyone around here brands me. This one's my own. Chose it for myself."

What happened next was decidedly not of Chico's choosing. It's impossible to know for sure how it started, but something said or done in the boys' locker room got under Chico's skin and he wouldn't let it go. The next thing anyone knew a plan had been hatched to shut Chico's mouth. Volleyball nets used for gym class were strung to long metal poles imbedded in cement poured in the center of old car tires, making them easy to wheel off the gymnasium floor when not in use. Nick Szymanski enlisted Tom Tetzlaff and Punk Ackerman to round up a couple of other strapping farm boys and ambush Chico, who was standing in front of a locker in his underwear. The four quickly overpowered him, peeling off his briefs while onlookers either did nothing or cheered on the assailants.

Chico was carried naked out of the locker room, down a narrow corridor, through a small workout room carpeted with tumbling mats where varsity cheerleaders were practicing routines, then into the now-empty gym. One of the poles was tipped over and lowered to the floor. Chico's hands were secured near the top of the pole, his wrists tightly encircled with thick white athletic tape. His attackers wrapped tape around his ankles near the base, brought the pole nearly upright and wheeled it out into the hallway.

When the bell rang signaling the end of the class period, students flooded the hall to see a nude Chico Driscoll on display. Students hooted and hollered, laughed and jeered, no one lifting a finger to intervene on Chico's behalf. No teachers had yet emerged from their classrooms and the school principal was nowhere in sight when Ray arrived on the scene. Ignoring a few shouted pleas and a couple of tugs on the shoulder to stop, Ray hurriedly unwrapped the tape securing Chico's ankles to the pole, then stood on tiptoe atop the cement and rubber base to reach his wrists.

With Ray clawing at the several layers of tape to start unraveling it, one of the farm boys pulled the rescuer's pants down, much to the delight of the swelling crowd. Fearing underwear would be next, Ray looked down to see who did the pulling. There stood Tom Tetzlaff, who initially sought cover in one of the emptying classrooms after helping to wheel the volleyball pole into position. He'd rushed back to the scene when Ray's intervention threatened his prank.

A hush fell over the hallway. Students tightly clustered around the pole seemed mesmerized, not by the sight of a naked classmate dangling from the pole or his disfigured face, but rather the spindly brown legs that had just been unveiled. All eyes were drawn to the considerably lighter patch of skin running from the left hip down the thigh nearly to the knee, as if a map of South America had been painted over Ray's flesh.

Tetzlaff appeared immobilized. Like the other students his eyes were fixed on this abnormality, but the look on his face expressed shame. It was as though exposure of a pair of discolored legs somehow crossed a line, calling into question what moments earlier had seemed a perfectly justifiable punishment to teach Chico a lesson. Tetzlaff, with his stringy hair, greasy complexion and tautly muscled physique, seemed to shrink on the spot under Ray's glare. Face flushed, Tetzlaff looked bewildered, then alarmed. He reached down with both hands to conceal a change in the color of his jeans near the bottom of the fly, the area becoming darker blue grew larger than his hands.

"*All right, enough!*" a man's voice bellowed from beyond the crowd.

Everyone turned around to see Mr. Mills, the gym teacher who also served as head wrestling coach and football assistant. Several other teachers were emerging from their classrooms.

"Don't you all have somewhere to be?" he barked. "Come on, clear the hall! Get to your classes!"

As other teachers arrived on the scene, demanding explanation, no offender fessed up, no one ratted out the perpetrators. With pants hiked back up, Ray finished freeing Chico's hands, lowering him from the pole. By this time, Chris Driscoll had pushed her way through the crowd seeing it was her brother at the center of the commotion. She gave him a notebook of hers to cover himself and silently mouthed "thank you" to Ray. When their eyes met, Ray's heart leapt.

Tom Tetzlaff wetting himself was the talk of the school. Only a few days remained before the three-week-long Christmas break, which shortened the shelf life of the gossip. He stayed out sick the following day and the next, surely to dodge the razzing.

That reprieve had the effect of shifting the conversation to what caused Tetzlaff to suddenly lose bladder control. One student speculated it must have been something Ray did. Others scoffed, reminding everyone Ray did nothing. Didn't grub him, didn't lay a hand on him. Another wasn't so sure.

"I mean, come on, you saw it. He stares him down, the guy pees his pants."

Just plain coincidence, one boy retorted. The girl next to him agreed, mocking the others.

"Oooh, watch your step or the little freak will put a spell on you. Doo-do-doo-do, doo-do-doo-do."

That comment irritated Brian Mientkiewicz.

"None of you were in the locker room when Boner got the treatment. Hen just looks Szymanski straight in the eye. Shoulda seen the look on Nick's face. First looks like he seen a ghost. Then like he's scared shitless and he runs out of the locker room. Now Tetzlaff. Hen stands up to him and he pisses himself."

"You're so full of shit, Mint," said one of the other boys dismissively.

"You weren't there, moron," Mint shot back.

Such talk continued to swirl around the school for the next several days before being mercifully laid to rest by the arrival of Christmas break. For Ray, school being out for close to a month was a relief.

Reminders of the season were everywhere. Holiday lights and ornaments were strung across Main Street and adorned most every light pole. Virtually every house in town also was lit up to one degree or another, creating a festive mood. Homes on the Hill were the most elaborately decorated, none more so than the Slaters'. With Christmas Day less than a week away, with both Mark and Steve not yet home from college, it was just Moose, Gin and Ray attending the party being thrown that night by Jim Slater and his wife Maggie.

Gin and Moose were dressed to the nines but the red knit sweater and tan corduroys that Gin had in mind for Ray lost out to jeans and a prized black hooded sweatshirt emblazoned with a graphic celebrating the Minnesota Twins as 1991 World Series champions.

When the Glennons rang the doorbell, Maggie answered the door, beaming radiantly as she welcomed them in. Jim already had cracked open a beer and was in animated conversation with three other men Ray didn't recognize.

"Hey Mags, Merry Christmas!" Moose said as he gave her a peck on the lips and handed her a bottle of wine.

"Well, look what the cat dragged in!" Jim crowed at the sight of Moose strutting in his direction with his arms thrust upwards in a V above his head. The others surrounding Jim bellered their greeting—"Mooooose!" Moose drew Jim into a warm embrace. "Merry Christmas, you old scoundrel."

Gin and Maggie exchanged knowing glances.

"Always the peacock," Gin whispered, nodding toward Moose.

In her early 40s, Maggie was easily able to pass for 20-something, slender and fit with long, lustrous brown hair. Moose and Gin were well aware that Maggie had a reputation for promiscuity in her younger days that she had never lived down. She wasn't originally from Faith, but had lived in the community for many years, was well known to the locals. She loved sports and was even fonder of athletes, managing to find work in public relations or sports management that put her in close proximity to teams.

Before settling down with Jim she had been something of a groupie who bedded more than a few professional ballplayers. This knowledge made it all the more amusing to Gin and Moose that Pastor Jeffrey Cash, his wife and daughter were regular guests at the Slaters' parties just as the Slaters regularly attended Sunday services.

Entering the Slaters' sprawling home, Ray spotted Katy Cash standing near her parents in the dining room adjacent to the first of two spacious living rooms. Katy was not dressed at all the way she typically was at school. She wore a red and green plaid jumper over a white blouse with a red ribbon tied in a bow at the neckline. Her usually unruly hair was neatly combed, pulled up stylishly, held in place by a matching ribbon.

"Tell anyone at school about this outfit and I'll kill you," she hissed when Ray approached.

"You look nice," Ray replied diplomatically. "Merry Christmas."

Katy rolled her eyes but returned the pleasantry.

Ray returned to Gin's side upon overhearing her mutter under her breath "I ought to give you a piece of my mind" when she saw Doc Szymanski and his wife. Ray gently nudged Gin's elbow to remind her not to get into any of that messy business, grateful to see no sign of Nick accompanying his parents.

The Slater house was mammoth by Faith standards. The foyer at the front door was a greeting space the size of the Morgers' entire sitting room. Straight ahead an elegant staircase led upstairs. To the left was a cozy study with a fireplace and a custom-made bookcase built by a local Amish artisan. To the right was the front living room with another fireplace, opening to a dining room with an oak table big enough to seat at least a dozen. Off to the side, a well-appointed kitchen with two ovens and a breakfast nook.

In the back of the house was another even larger living room—the family room, they called it—and a den with a billiards table. Beyond that was the room that caught Ray's eye. Glass cases lined three of the four walls. In the cases were an assortment of trophies large and small, numerous souvenir baseballs and bubble gum cards, framed photographs and articles from newspapers and magazines, several baseball caps and jerseys. A plaque engraved with Jim's name and team—the Toledo Mud Hens—as well as the words American Association Pitcher of the Month. Team photos of the Detroit Tigers, Milwaukee Brewers and Chicago Cubs. Dog-eared copies of

Baseball Digest, a paperback publication called *The Baseball Dope Book*, and three tickets to 1982 World Series games.

Ray studied each item, captivated to the point of feeling alone in the room. Lisa Wagner poked her head in the doorway, surveying the memorabilia. "Hi Lisa," Ray said sheepishly, avoiding the name kids at school called her.

"Hello H …," she answered, presumably starting to say Hen before stopping herself, blushing.

Ray fidgeted awkwardly, not sure what to say next. The girl everyone called Hill had that effect on people. She had a lithe, athletic build to go with sparkling eyes, a dazzling smile, meticulously styled hair. Hill was easily the best dressed of the student body, not exactly a difficult distinction to earn, though her clothes did consistently flatter her. That night she wore a form-fitting argyle sweater and black pleated skirt. Ray felt ready to faint.

"You like baseball?" Ray asked her.

"Not really. I don't watch sports much. I do like watching the Olympics. Especially the gymnastics and figure skating."

Ray nodded and resumed fidgeting, three times thinking of something to say, three times concluding it would come off as stupid. Just when fleeing to the bathroom to vomit seemed like a logical next step, Gin salvaged the situation. She entered the trophy room with her hand on Jim Slater's elbow as if guiding him in his own home.

"There's someone I want you to meet."

Slater had a modest middle-age spread around the midsection but was still slender for his age, six-foot-three, maybe six-four, with a thick head of dark hair flecked with gray, a shadow of stubble over ruggedly handsome features, and wire-framed glasses he hadn't needed in his playing days.

"Your mother tells me you're quite a baseball fan," he said, extending a massive right hand to Ray, who imagined a baseball must look like a golf ball in that hand. Ray nodded eagerly, grasping the hand with as firm a grip as could be managed.

"You play?"

Ray grinned, nodding again.

"What position you like best?"

Ray shrugged indecisively.

"Not much of a talker," Slater said, looking down at Gin. "That's okay. Nothin' wrong with strong, silent types."

Ray seemed paralyzed, incapable of speech.

"So, you're a Twins fan," Slater said, pointing at Ray's sweatshirt. "You must've been on cloud nine in '87 and '91."

Ray nodded absent-mindedly.

"Who were your favorite players?" Slater inquired, obviously enjoying his effect on the youngster. Snapping back to attention, as if emerging from a trance, Ray replied, "Kirby Puckett."

"Everybody loves 34," Slater said.

"Herbie's another," Ray answered. "Number 14."

"Right you are. Fourteen. Hrbek had some major thump."

Gin moved from Slater's side to Ray's. "Do you have any questions for Jim?"

"Um, I was wondering about the Toledo Mud Hens."

"Oh yeah, that's a minor league team I played for when I was coming up through the Tigers system. Toledo was their triple-A team. Final step before the Show."

"You played in the major leagues."

"Got a cup of coffee with the Tigers. Caught on with the Brewers for a spell after that. My timing couldn't have been luckier ... had a chance to be on Milwaukee's World Series team in '82."

Ray's eyes widened. "You got to play in the World Series?"

"Naw, didn't make the postseason roster. Was up and down between the minors and the big-league club. Got a few chances to pitch early in the season, was able to spend time around the team in the stretch drive of the pennant chase but didn't make it on the field."

Slater could tell Ray was spellbound and tongue-tied for the time being, so he carried on.

"That was a hell of a team. Stormin' Gorman. Rockin' Robin. Coop. Molly. Vuke. Rollie Fingers with his handlebar mustache. The team was known for hittin' the long ball, and Harvey Kuenn being manager, they were called Harvey's Wallbangers."

None of this meant a thing to Gin, but she beamed at the sight of Ray enthralled, hanging on Jim's every word.

"Almost won it all," he continued. "Took the Cardinals to seven."

Slater paused, reveling in the memory.

"Stayed in the Brewers organization for part of the next season, then was let go. Had the good fortune to get picked up by the Cubs. Mostly played with the Cubs triple-A affiliate in Iowa, but got called up two different times in '84, pitched in four games. Man oh man, that was a great team. Ryno, the Red Baron, Sarge, Zonk, Bull Durham, the Penguin, Smitty, Rainbow Trout. Should've made it to the World Series. Not sure we could've beat the Tigers that year, but would've loved to see that matchup. A few outs away from wrapping up the pennant against the Padres, it all comes unraveled. Wait 'til next year. Every Cubs fan's motto."

Slater drummed his fingers on the glass of one of the cases, peering through at the keepsakes.

"My arm was pretty much shot; the gig was up. I'd have given my left nut for another chance in the Show. But three, four years of big-league money set me up pretty good. Business connections I made while in the game led to some things that have panned out nicely. If you're not stupid, blow all of what you make playing, you end up having it pretty good."

His voice trailed off, his thoughts drifting.

"Seems like every big leaguer's got a nickname," Ray observed. "Did you have one?"

"My teammates in Toledo started calling me Scrooge when I learned to throw a screwball. The name stuck once it became my out pitch. Some called me Neezy, from Scrooge's first name, you know, Ebenezer. In the story Scrooge is a miserly villain. Liked thinking of myself that way when I pitched. Didn't want to give up nothin'."

"Wouldn't mind being called that. Better'n what kids call me," Ray blurted.

"What's that?"

"Hen."

Slater squinted his eyes, thinking for a moment. Then a smile emerged.

"Hen Glennon, you know what that reminds me of?"

Ray feebly shook no.

"Donn Clendenon, a big ole power-hitting first baseman, played mostly for the Pirates, was with the Expos a while too. When I was about your age he played for the Amazin' Mets, won the '69 World Series. Hen Glennon rhymes with Clendenon ... puts you in mighty good company as far as I'm concerned."

Gin initially thought that was a silly thing for Slater to say. Seeing Ray's reaction, she reconsidered.

"Can I have your autograph?" Ray asked, beaming.

"You bet," Slater replied before rummaging through a drawer below one of the glass cases, pulling out a Topps trading card. He scratched his signature on it, gave it to Ray, who examined it closely.

"This is your rookie card with the Tigers. You can't give this away."

"Got at least 15 of those. It's yours. And I can do you one better."

Slater opened one of the glass cases, reached in, took out a baseball. He inspected it briefly, turned, handed it to Ray. Neat, looping cursive formed the inscription in vivid blue ink: Donn Clendenon 69 Mets WSC.

Ray gripped the ball tightly in one hand, the card in the other, staring at the two gifts in disbelief.

Slater again extended an oversized right hand to Ray, who scrambled to free a hand by holding both the ball and card in one.

"It's been a real pleasure talking baseball with you," he said. "You keep cheering on those Twins, sir."

A puzzled look at being called sir dissolved into a broad grin.

Slater turned to leave and Gin wrapped Ray in a hug. She looked to be floating in a blissful fog, a sparkle in her eyes, joy etched in her dimples. Suddenly her expression went blank. Standing next to the pool table in the nearby den was Lisa Lewandowski chatting with Moose and Maggie Slater. Jim joined them and Gin felt obliged to as well.

Lisa warmly greeted them with outstretched hands, a "great seeing you" and "Merry Christmas." She excused herself from the conversation to join Ray in the trophy room.

"Did your brothers have something better to do, or aren't they home from college yet?"

"They aren't full brothers."

Ray's curt response took Lisa aback. Ray could tell and regretted both the answer and the tone.

"They're still at college for another couple of days. They'll be home by Christmas Eve."

"Tell them I'd love to see them when they get home," Lisa said. She continued, her voice lowered.

"Ray, I've been wanting to tell you something but have been holding off and I feel badly about that. Been telling myself you aren't old enough, probably was just afraid to say it. To be honest I'm still sorta scared, but, um … I want to explain why I decided to move in with your dad and brothers."

"He's not my real dad."

"I'm aware of that. Sorry, I mean why I moved in with Moose and Mark and Steve."

Ray recoiled ever so slightly, surprised and uncomfortable, yet still curious.

"When your mom didn't come home from the hospital, I saw a chance to get away from my parents. They fought constantly, argued about everything … money, religion, me, my little brother, you name it. Listening to them screaming at each other drove me nuts. When they weren't ragging on each other, they ragged on me. To Dad I was some kind of misfit. Constantly lectured me about needing to straighten out. Mom was scared to death I'd never find a good man to marry and would end up all alone. I kept telling her I wasn't looking for a man to marry. Drove her crazy. She'd blame my father for the way I was turning out; he'd yell right back that I was all her fault. I had to get out of that house, couldn't stand living there another day."

"You didn't want to marry the Moose?" Ray interjected. "People say you did."

"I know that's the story that went around. It's just my word against theirs. You have no way of knowing who to believe, but I didn't do any of the things people say I was doing. That's not who I am. I never wanted to marry him. My mom and dad might have wanted that, but not me. Maybe someday I can explain it in a way that'll make it all make sense. But the God's honest truth is I just wanted to get out of my parents' house. I didn't want to hurt your mom … or cause you any pain. It breaks my heart to think that I did."

Tears spilled from Lisa's eyes, cutting a path down her quivering cheeks.

Ray said not a word but reached out and laid a hand, palm open, on Lisa's chest over her bust. She startled, glancing around to see if anyone noticed this high school freshman touching her, a 30-year-old woman.

What happened next surprised Lisa even more than Ray. She brought both hands to her chest and held Ray's hand in place for a heartbeat, then two, three, four, five. Her face relaxed. She drew a deep breath, exhaling something akin to a sigh of relief.

CHAPTER 10

ON THE SHORT WALK HOME AFTER THE PARTY, Gin was in a jovial mood, slightly tipsy from one too many glasses of wine. She smiled warmly at the sight of Ray continuing to examine the ball and trading card as if looking for the slightest imperfections.

"Did you see what Jim Slater gave Ray?" she excitedly said to Moose. He looked unaware, so she took the items from Ray, first the card, then the ball, showing them to him.

"Jim gave you these?" Moose asked Ray, who nodded affirmatively. Moose held Gin's hand steady so he could look more closely at the ball she was holding.

"Donn Clendenon," he read. "Why'd he give you a baseball signed by this guy?"

"He won the World Series with the New York Mets in '69. Mr. Slater told me a story about him and gave me the ball too."

"Better not play with that one," Moose cautioned. "Might be worth a pretty penny someday if you keep it in mint condition."

Ray couldn't imagine ever wanting to sell it and considered speaking up but figured saying anything would be pointless. They had arrived at the front door of their house. Ray recovered the souvenirs from Gin, followed them inside, made a beeline for the stairs.

"Shoes off!" Gin barked. "Don't go tracking snow through the house!"

Ray kicked off both shoes and disappeared. Gin proceeded to the kitchen to put leftovers from Maggie Slater in the refrigerator. When Moose told her he was tired and heading straight to bed, Gin pretended to busy herself for 10 or 15 minutes before going upstairs herself, poking her head in Ray's room.

"Hey Rage, just curious, what did you and Lisa Lewandowski talk about at the party?"

"Nothing much."

"You two talked for quite a while."

"Wanted to tell me she didn't move in here for the reasons everyone thinks. Said she needed to get away, live somewhere else. Couldn't take it there anymore."

"I don't know if I believe *that*," Gin retorted skeptically.

"Told me her parents were nasty to each other and to her."

"I haven't experienced anything in my dealings with them that gives me that impression. They seem like nice enough people."

Ray didn't care to quarrel over this.

"She seemed ... I don't know, stirred up, ready to lose it. I think our talk did her good."

"What'd you say to her?"

"Nothing really. I just ..." Ray mimed the rest, extending a hand to Gin's chest. Gin felt woozy, pretty sure it wasn't just the wine's effects.

"You put your hand on her boobs?"

"Above there."

"Rage, you've got to be careful, honey. You can't just go grabbing strangers."

"I didn't grab her. And she's not a stranger."

"She's not family either. Regardless, if you go touching any woman—*anywhere*—without asking, without her saying it's okay, you can get in big trouble."

"It's only touching girls that's a problem?"

"That's not what I'm saying ... Oh, I don't know ... it depends. Boys are brought up so they're more uncomfortable being hugged than girls are, that can be a problem too. But they've got less reason to be afraid of getting assaulted. It's confusing, I know. Just be careful, sweetheart."

Gin wanted the exchange to end as much as Ray did. She had a sick feeling that she'd done more harm than good. Before saying goodnight, she gave Ray a bear hug.

While Moose was already sound asleep, Gin had trouble turning off her brain. She tossed and turned much of the night. The next morning arrived annoyingly soon, after only a few hours of fitful sleep. When she awoke, the bedroom door was open, the other side of the bed was already empty. She could hear the shower in the bathroom.

When Gin pushed away the blankets, she saw she was still wearing the dress she wore to the party. She unbuttoned the front, wriggled out of the dress first, then her tights, reached behind to unfasten her bra, winced seeing herself in the mirror.

She pulled a pair of leggings from the dresser drawer, improvised a top by throwing on the shirt that Moose had worn to the Slaters, buttoned the middle three buttons, rolled up the sleeves and, forgoing a shower, headed to the kitchen to make coffee. After Moose had left for work and a second cup had soothed her mild hangover, Gin summoned Ray to the breakfast table.

"Sorry about last night. I don't want you spending time worrying about what I said. I feel like I muddied the waters. Don't think on it too much."

Ray looked a little perplexed but nodded in agreement.

"You amaze me, Rage. You've got such a big heart ... I mean, seeing how you treat others good even when they treat you bad. When I see that, especially from someone so young ... it's rare ... catches me off guard, you know what I'm tryin' to say?"

Ray still looked puzzled but nodded again anyway.

"Lisa's never treated me bad."

"I know, but a lot of others have. What I'm saying isn't about Lisa. How you are with people, I love that about you, I never want you to lose that."

"I know you are trying to protect me by saying be careful. Kids at school make fun of my skin and my hair, they think I'm weird. But you make me strong. You let people think you went crazy rather than abandon me."

"I don't know what I ever did to deserve you," Gin said with her back to Ray.

"I could say the same thing. I love you, Mom."

CHAPTER 11

AFTER BREAKFAST, GIN PULLED A GIFT-WRAPPED package out of a cupboard and placed it on the kitchen table in front of Ray along with what at first glance had the look of a tin foil football.

"Could you bring these over to the Morgers?" she asked. "It's a cheese box and some cranberry bread. I've got a long list of things that need doing by Christmas."

Ray didn't dawdle in paying the Morgers a visit, both to deliver the gifts and show off the mementos from Jim Slater. Carrying all the items across town made the walk seem quite a bit longer than usual. About halfway there the prospect of Colette and Morger being away dawned on Ray. Calling ahead, an annoyingly adult thing to do, suddenly looked downright sensible.

Once the old farmhouse was in sight, curls of smoke wafting out of the chimney were sign enough that they were home. Ray bounded up the steps, rapped on the door, heard shuffling footsteps. Moments later the door swung open.

The old man wore a faded blue bathrobe over a yellowed and ragged-looking T-shirt. He stooped more than Ray remembered, his legs swimming in baggy sweatpants. The hair on his head stood up at the back the way it does when you lie on a pillow or recline in an easy chair too long. Behind him was Colette looking considerably sprightlier, sporting tight curls in her freshly permed hair.

Colette beckoned Ray with the familiar portly ceramic woman with the black eyes and red lips, yellow-trimmed apron, red bonnet and basket of flowers. She lifted the lid, held the jar out, tilted toward Ray to display an assortment of Christmas cookies.

"I brought you these," Ray said, handing the presents to Morger. "From our family ... Merry Christmas."

Ray then plucked out a cookie in the shape of a wreath. "Oh, come now, take a big one," Colette scolded.

"Come in and sit for a bit," Morger said.

They sat at the dining room table that was the home's hub. Colette unwrapped the foil package, expressing delight at the contents. "Cranberry bread, thank you so much! Let your mother know how much we appreciate it."

Morger tore open the other gift and surveyed the assorted bricks of cheese and two tubular sausages. "This is wonderful. Thank you!" he said, retrieving a knife, plate and box of crackers from the kitchen.

Before any of the Christmas present was offered, Ray took another cookie from the jar.

"I see where your allegiances lie," Morger said with a wink.

By Ray's calculation, enough time had passed for the sake of politeness, withdrawing first the card and then the ball from a coat pocket.

"Look at what Mr. Slater gave me."

Colette regarded the card before handing it to her husband.

"It's his rookie card from when he came up with the Detroit Tigers. He signed it for me."

Eyes then turned to the autographed baseball.

"Whose signature is this?" Morger inquired.

"Donn Clendenon's. From when he won the World Series with the New York Mets in '69."

The way Morger and Colette looked at the ball clued Ray that the significance of this particular player's autograph needed explaining.

"Mr. Slater was telling me about the nickname his teammates gave him. I told him what kids at school call me and I think he was trying to make me feel better about it. Tells me it rhymes with Clendenon, gives me his ball."

"What on earth do kids call you that rhymes with Clendenon?" Morger wondered.

"Hen."

Morger and Colette both looked befuddled.

"Hen Glennon. Get it?"

"Ah, oui," Colette said with a laugh.

"That's not so bad as nicknames go," Morger added.

"I hate it."

Morger was about to extoll the virtues of thick skin when Colette gently rested her hand on his forearm, signaling him to say nothing further.

"What made them start calling you Hen?" Colette questioned.

"Stuck up for a kid who was getting attacked, got grabbed … here," Ray said, pointing. "The kid who did it told everybody I'm a hen, not a rooster."

Morger started to speak but Colette's subtle squeeze to his forearm stopped him.

"Just name-calling," Colette counseled. "Pay it no mind."

Morger got up from the table, retreating to the sitting room. Ray followed him.

"Can I ask you something?" Ray said to the old man.

"Of course."

"I try talking to my mom, but it makes her cry."

Morger's leathery face, generously speckled with sunspots, was expressionless.

"It was Nick Szymanski who grabbed me there. I didn't scream, didn't cry, didn't yell for help, didn't do anything. Just stood there, looking at him. Then it's like he got real scared. Ran away."

Ray waited for Morger's reaction but there was none.

"Another time a kid got stripped naked, taped to one of them volleyball posts the net gets attached to. They wheeled the thing out into the hall, everyone sees this kid hanging there with no clothes on. One of them who did it pulled my pants down from behind when I was freeing the kid's hands and feet. Everybody's crowding around, laughing, thought I was going to get all my clothes ripped off too."

Colette looked alarmed, but Morger remained placid.

"I don't even know what I was thinking. Tom Tetzlaff's the one who pantsed me. I turn around, stare at him. He starts looking the same way Nick Szymanski did. Then he pees his pants."

Ray thought Colette seemed doubtful and had no idea what to make of the look on Morger's face.

"I'm not making this up, he peed his pants, right there in the hall."

Silence.

"Why did Nick run away? Why did Tom wet his pants? I didn't do nothing." Morger finally spoke.

"We've been hearing of this. Colette and I don't get out much, so for us to hear about it means you must have the whole town talking, Ray."

"Talking about what?"

"You know what I say, what can't be explained is magic. The kids at school can't understand what happened. Some must've told their parents; they can't explain it either. That spooks them."

"Some of my friends are saying they think I can put spells on people or something. If I could, don't you think I'd know how I do it?"

"I'd say you do know. Not in your head yet, but your heart already knows how or you couldn't do what you did. The kids at school and people around town think it's magic because they can't figure out what else it might be. I could be wrong, but I think there's an explanation for what you made happen. The power is real, Ray."

Ray eyed Morger, absolutely baffled. "What power?"

"It isn't one thing, it's a combination of things. You didn't hurt anybody; you didn't do anything deserving of punishment. It's hard to punish someone who doesn't have it coming. You came to someone's aid when others were being cruel. You were willing to be victimized yourself to spare a victim. Innocence and sacrifice together make a force more powerful than fists and guns. I don't have any idea how you came by it, Ray, but you have it."

"How'd you figger all this out?"

"I was your age once. I wish I'd known then what you already instinctively understand. I had to do a lot of living before I could make sense out of these things. You seem to come by it naturally. You have a gift, Ray."

"I wish I had grandparents who want to spend time with me," Ray said, abruptly changing the subject. "I mean, I have 'em, they just don't really want to have anything to do with me."

"You have us," Colette proclaimed gently but firmly.

Ray thought about that for a moment. Yes, that'll do just fine.

"Okay, Gramma and Grampa, Merry Christmas! I should get back home.

Do you mind if I take a cookie for the road?"

"Be our guest," Colette replied. "Wait, let me wrap up a few for you to share with your family. Remember to give your mom our thanks for the gifts."

Ray smiled, grateful for the lifted mood and lightened heart that came from his visits to the Morger place. Ray's walk home seemed shorter.

Ray returned to an empty house and assumed Moose was working and Gin out Christmas shopping. Turns out Gin was at her parents' house. She had decided it was time for a heart-to-heart. She took a seat on the living room sofa.

"I have something to tell you … been wanting to tell you for a long time," she began.

Her parents braced for bad news.

"I don't know how to say this, so I'm just going to, uh … Ray is not adopted. I ask you to keep this between us."

"What do you mean, not adopted?" Claire Barber said, gaping at her daughter.

"Ray's mine. When I went to the hospital and gave birth, my baby didn't die. I didn't have a breakdown. Richie and I separated when I refused to give Ray up for adoption."

"Well, then, who exactly is the father?" Butch Barber demanded, looking stunned, sounding angry.

"I don't know," Gin answered.

"What in heaven's name do you mean, you don't know?" Butch shot back. "How the hell many of them black bucks you been to bed with?"

"None."

Gin's father threw his hands in the air and harrumphed, "Obviously at least one's had you. No sense denying it. The kid sure ain't Moose's!"

Claire tried calming him, to no avail.

"How the hell am I supposed to react? I just found out our daughter is a no-good tramp and the whole story we were fed about our adopted grandchild is a God damned lie!" he spat, his arms flailing.

"Butch, don't, *please* settle down," Claire pleaded.

"Don't tell me to settle down! Our daughter let a godforsaken ni …"

"*Butch!*"

"She's a married woman and goes off and gets herself …" he raged, his eyes ablaze, his words dripping with contempt. "She don't even know which one it was!"

"*Stop!*" Gin screamed, her cheeks flushed, lips quivering. She gathered her emotions, lowered her voice. Butch spoke over her. "I always thought you were the good one, was sure you'd never do anything like Grace did, having that child out of wedlock. Come to find out you did even worse."

"Don't interrupt me! This is why it's taken so long for me to tell you."

"Let her finish, Butch," Claire commanded.

Butch made a gesture of resignation.

"I've not been with anyone but Richie the whole time we've been married. I swear to God."

"Don't lie to us," Butch fumed.

"I'm not!"

"You're hiding something. Why tell us the baby's yours, then turn around and claim you have no idea who's the father?"

"I wanted you to know the truth, who Ray really is."

"It appears now he's a bastard, that's who he is!"

"How can you say that? Richie's the only one who could be the father."

Butch burst out in derisive laughter. "*Come off it*, the one and only thing for sure is that Moose ain't the father! He's light. You're light. Two light people can't make a dark baby. For some reason you can't bring yourself to come clean about who the father is."

"I don't know how I got pregnant!"

"Do we have to explain the birds and the bees to you? You got pregnant by breaking your wedding vows and climbing into bed with some darkie."

"You're such a hypocrite," Gin exclaimed spitefully.

"*I'm* a hypocrite? I kept *my* vows!" Butch roared.

"You spew this racist bullshit, go sit in church every Sunday, worship this lily-white figure above the altar who had to've been dark-skinned in real life. Your Bible tells you your savior is the result of a virgin birth ... you swallow it hook, line and sinker. Joseph wasn't the father, that's the word of the Lord! Do I have to explain the birds and the bees to you?"

"How dare you talk to your father like this!"

"Damn right I dare! You set one foot outside church and, all of a sudden, the Bible stories don't apply anymore and you're calling Ray a bastard. Ray is mine. You don't accept your own flesh and blood."

"T'ain't my flesh and ain't my blood!"

"Ray is *my* flesh and *my* blood. You stand there all high and mighty, a man of the law and a man of the church, and call your own daughter a no-good tramp."

"Get out of my sight," Butch spouted bitterly.

Gin sprang from the couch and rushed out the door, slamming it behind her. Once behind the wheel of her car, her whole body started shaking. She sat there for several minutes before starting the engine, still trembling when she backed out of the driveway heading for home. When she got there, she pushed open the front door, walked dazed toward the kitchen. She flung herself down in a chair at the dining room table and started sobbing. Moose wasn't home yet. Ray heard the commotion.

"Mom, what's wrong? What happened?"

It took Gin several moments to regain her composure and answer. Her voice was still shaky when she did.

"I went to see your grandparents ... on my side. I sat down with them, told them you aren't adopted, that you're mine. It got really ugly. Dad demanded to know who your father is. I fear they'll never want to see me or you ever again."

"Who *is* my father?" Ray asked softly.

"I honestly don't know. That's what I told them. It's not an answer they want to hear."

Ray accepted the answer far better than Butch Barber did.

"I wanted my parents to know the truth about you. I should have left well enough alone. All I've done is make things worse for both of us. I'm so sorry, Rage."

"It's okay, Mom. It's *okay*. You've got nothing to be sorry for."

"Oh, how I wish that was true. I've screwed things up so bad."

COUNTY **Q**

CHAPTER 12

WORD TRAVELED FAST WITHIN THE BARBER FAMILY. The very next morning, Grace called Gin.

"Holy hell, what happened? Mom says you had a big blow-up with them and it's best not to get together for Christmas."

Gin's heart sank.

"I told them Ray's mine ... that everything else was made up. I figured they should know the truth at some point. Maybe I thought there was nothing to lose anymore. Guess I thought wrong."

"Jeezus, you burst an awful lot of their bubbles all at once," Grace said. "They never had to worry about you. I was the one who kept them up nights. This must really throw them for a loop. But looking on the bright side, it's got to boost my standing with them a little."

Gin wasn't quite sure whether to apologize or say you're welcome, so said nothing.

"Barber family Christmas is no great loss," Grace said. "Can't remember the last time I enjoyed it."

"We'd love to have you and Annie here for Christmas."

"Moose'll be okay with that?"

"Won't ask him. I'll wait 'til we're leaving church to let him know, tell him you're already on your way."

"You sure about this?"

Gin smiled and nodded; answers Grace couldn't receive over the phone.

"Sorry ... of course! I wouldn't invite you if I wasn't sure."

"I'll bring wine to drown our sorrows. This'll be good. Won't have to worry about feeling like a disappointment just being in the same room as Dad and Mom. Always wondered how you could manage to seem so comfortable being the sheriff's daughter."

"What makes you think I was comfortable?"

"Always seemed like it. Me, I couldn't stand the taste of beer but drank anyway just because I wasn't of age. Didn't like getting high all that much either, but smoked a shitload of pot for no reason other than it was illegal. Otherwise, doubt I would've touched the stuff. Half the boys I went out with turned my stomach, but I still let them feel me up or finger me because I knew they'd brag about it the next day in school. Only way I could think of to get the law enforcement stink off me. Being Butch's daughter, always being expected to keep your nose clean ... might as well spray yourself with friend repellent."

Gin let out a laugh. "You think I never partied?"

"*You?*"

Gin rolled her eyes, oblivious to the fact Grace couldn't see the gesture over the phone. "So, no one told you about the time Dad caught me and Richie in his car?"

"You're shittin' me!"

Gin let out a dramatic sigh, feigning insult.

"We're parked on a side street just off Main. One thing is leading to another, pretty soon he's got my shirt off. He's fumbling around, trying to unfasten my bra, can't get it unhooked. I give a little help, pull it down around my waist. We're caught up in the moment, not noticing if anyone's around. All of a sudden a flashlight is shining on us."

"Dad! You're seriously not making this up?"

"I don't know that he recognized Richie's car. All he sees at first is some girl with no top and a boy with his hand down her pants. Then he aims his light up to our faces, sees it's us. I'm screaming at him to turn the light off, trying to zip up my pants and get my bra resituated. Next thing I know he's got me out of the car, marching me down the block towards his squad car, I got no shirt, it's like he's in some kind of hypnotic state. All of a sudden, he stops dead in his tracks, leaves me on the side of the street, goes back to Richie's car. He stands there for the longest time bent over with his head stuck through the driver's side window. You know how it is, probably wasn't more than a minute but seemed like an eternity. I mean, I'm standing there without a shirt."

"What'd Dad tell him?"

"Threatened to get him kicked off the football team. Said he'd make a steer out of him if he got me pregnant without marrying me first, which is funny because I was already pregnant when we got married."

"Were you grounded?"

"I was sort of past grounding age when we were planning the wedding."

"I meant when he found you two jumping each other's bones."

"Not in so many words."

"That is so bogus. They grounded me at the drop of a hat."

"Dad must've thought embarrassment would be the best punishment. Made me ride back home with him in the squad car shirtless. You must've been out getting into trouble, or you'd have seen the whole thing ... he made a big production out of it."

"I can't believe I never heard about this until now."

"Yeah, you'd think Mom or Dad would've ... or Richie ... can't believe you didn't overhear him bragging about it ... Whoa, look at the time! I should get going. Hey Grace, nice talking. Look forward to seeing you and Annie. We can talk more then. Love ya."

"Love you too."

Faith's various schisms are always visible enough, but never more gallingly pronounced than at this time of year. On Christmas morning the Slaters had four cars parked in their driveway, four or five more on the side of the street outside their home. Presents piled at the base of an elaborately decorated tree flowed like lava across the floor. The Szymanskis welcomed guests to their somewhat smaller but equally bounteous celebration. The Wagners too.

Lisa Lewandowski and her housemate killed time at home, dreading the thought of spending a few hours with Lisa's parents but looking forward to seeing her younger brother. Morger and Colette walked arm in arm down the snow-covered, fence-lined alley leading to the woods. Archie, Kaz, Boner, Palsy and Mint all looked like dead boys walking as they stood in line with family members at St. Mary's waiting to take communion.

Tom Tetzlaff, splattered with manure, was in the barn finishing the morning chores, scattering straw in stalls to soak up urine and crushed limestone in the aisles between the stanchions to cut the odor. Chico Driscoll—a year too young to hold a driver's license, six years from being legally permitted to purchase alcohol—was behind the wheel of his family's rusted-out Ford pickup on orders from his mother to pick up a couple of bottles at the liquor store, a transaction consummated by the clerk behind the counter without questions. Chico's sister Chris sat coatless on their hovel's fractured cement stoop bawling in the aftermath of her father asking her to give him a Christmas present.

Grace Barber was on the freeway from the Cities on her way to her sister's, with daughter Annie in the passenger seat beside her. Claire and Butch Barber were in church. Gin Glennon sat five rows behind them, Ray to her left, Moose to her right. Mark and Steve, home from college, sat next to their dad listening to Pastor Cash. To hear him preach was to be assured everything was as it should be in Faith.

Most days, the minister's message emphasized that favor would be bestowed on believers, that prosperity was heaven sent. Quite often but not on this day, he professed his church's belief in divine healing, spoke of the rapture at the bodily return of Christ to earth, and extolled the virtues of church missions to seek and save all who are lost in sin.

This being Christmas, traditional hymns were sung—"Away in a Manger" and "Hark! The Herald Angels Sing"—before Linh Meaney was invited to the altar. Her voice didn't boom like Pastor Cash's. Congregants strained to hear. The diminutive teen recited, exactly as scripted. Joseph and Mary in Bethlehem. A baby wrapped in swaddling clothes, lying in a manger, for there was no room in the inn. Shepherds keeping watch over their flocks. An angel of the Lord appears, fear not, with good news of great joy for all people, a savior, 'tis Christ the Lord. Glory to God in the highest, on earth peace to men on whom His favor rests. Exactly as scripted. Wise men from the east. A guiding star. Gifts of gold, frankincense and myrrh.

Pastor Cash thanked Linh for her reading and took the pulpit.

"Merry Christmas! Today we celebrate the miracle of creation. Glory to God in the highest, and on earth peace to men *on whom His favor rests*," he said, his voice rising at the end. "Hold in your hearts the gospel of Matthew: This is how the birth of Jesus the Messiah came to be. His mother Mary was pledged to be married to Joseph, but before they came together, she was found to be pregnant through the Holy Spirit. An angel of the Lord appeared to him, saying 'Joseph, son of David, do not be afraid to take Mary home as your wife, because what is conceived in her is from the Holy Spirit. She will give birth to a son, and you are to give him the name Jesus, because he will save his people from their sins.' When Joseph woke, he took Mary home as his wife but did not consummate their marriage until she gave birth to a son. And he gave him the name Jesus. This is the word of the Lord. This is the miracle of Christmas."

At these words Gin couldn't help but cast a glance in her father's direction. Butch's head was bowed prayerfully. He did not flinch, showed no reaction whatsoever. Unaware of the tension between two in his flock, Pastor Cash unwittingly poured it on.

"Hold in your hearts the gospel of Luke: 'How will this be,' Mary asked the angel, 'since I am a virgin?' The angel answered, 'the Holy Spirit will come on you, and the power of the Most High will overshadow you. So, the holy one to be born will be called the Son of God. Even Elizabeth your relative is going to have a child in her old age, and she who was said to be unable to conceive is in her sixth month. For no word from God will ever fail.' Mary answered, 'I am the Lord's servant, may your word to me be fulfilled.' This is the word of the Lord. This is the miracle of this holiest of days."

Gin again looked up, her eyes drawn to the two seated figures five rows ahead. Butch and Claire Barber remained attentive, but neither moved a muscle or gave a hint of emotion. Pastor Cash pivoted to his scripture of choice.

"We celebrate today the birth of the Holy Spirit's progeny, he who came to relieve us of our sins, he who said I am come that they may have life and that they might have it more abundantly. On this Christmas Day, hold in your heart what the gospel proclaims: My God shall supply all your need according to his riches in glory by Christ Jesus. Though he was rich, for your sake he became poor so that you through his poverty might become rich."

Pastor Cash tied it up with a Christmas bow.

"No word from God will ever fail. May all of us be moved to be the Lord's servant, and may His word to us be fulfilled. That is the promise of Christmas."

More formalities were performed, more hymns—"Silent Night" and "Joy to the World"—were sung, after which those assembled headed for home. Butch filed past Gin and Ray without a word or gesture and left Moose's greeting unanswered. Claire smiled weakly, almost apologetically, but kept pace with her husband as he made for the door.

Ray was used to feeling more or less invisible to extended family, but still was jarred by the brusque treatment. Not wanting to say anything in Moose's presence, Ray waited until they returned home.

"I guess you were right, Mom. Grampa and Gramma don't want anything to do with us," Ray said in a private moment in the back of the house.

"It appears so," Gin replied.

"That sucks."

"Maybe they'll come around. Don't worry about it, honey."

"I'm not worried, it just sucks."

The conversation was prematurely ended by the sound of Moose hollering from somewhere near the front door.

"Grace and Annie just drove up. I didn't know they were coming."

"Forgot to tell you, totally slipped my mind. I invited them to have Christmas with us since we're not going over to my folks' house."

"Would've appreciated a heads-up. And what's up with your folks? You guys not speaking or something?"

"It's a long story. Just be good, it's Christmas." The doorbell rang and Gin shot Moose one last stern glance before opening the door. "Hey, Sis! Merry Christmas!" Gin exclaimed, hugging her sister before drawing Annie into a warm embrace. "Annie! Did you get a nice haul this morning?"

Annie smiled and nodded, showing her aunt shiny new earrings she was wearing.

"Those are beautiful!" Gin raved as she took their coats. She noticed but chose not to comment on the heavy mascara and black lip gloss Annie wore. Moose came forward to give Grace a peck on the cheek. She recoiled ever so slightly, then was visibly self-conscious about her reaction.

"Welcome to the wild frontier," Moose said. "You forgot your blaze orange. Not to worry, we can loan you some when we go huntin' later."

Moose's eyes met Gin's. "*Kidding*," he quickly added. "Hey guys, get off the couch and come say hi to Annie and Aunt Grace."

Mark and Steve didn't budge, their eyes glued to the television set, not even noticing Annie standing right behind them.

"Who's playing?" she asked.

"Bulls-Heat," Steve answered curtly without breaking his concentration on the screen.

"Game hasn't started. This is just the pregame show," Mark added without turning around to acknowledge the source of the question.

"Heat? Where're they from?" Annie said, gamely trying to make conversation, unconsciously twirling her long straight hair with her fingers.

"Miami," Mark and Steve answered at once.

"Who you rooting for?"

"Chicago," Steve said without missing a beat. "Definitely the Bulls," Mark agreed.

"How's college life?" Annie inquired, changing the subject, hoping to get their attention.

"Liking it. A couple of classes I had to take busted my balls. The GPA took a hit," Mark replied.

Annie grimaced at his imagery, but quickly rallied. "What's your major?"

"Business administration."

She knew she should say oh how interesting or something along those lines, but couldn't bring herself to do it. To Annie, there couldn't be a more unappealing course of study. She couldn't think of a single other thing to say, so she gave up and their attention returned to the game, which was about to tip off.

Ray hung back, melting into the woodwork, watching Annie watch Mark and Steve watch the game. Gin and Grace kibitzed in the kitchen as Moose left the table half set to join his sons in the living room. The first quarter wasn't quite finished when Moose's mother and Old Dean arrived along with Young Dean and Paul and their families. Ray half expected an auction to break out.

After a ham dinner—timed strategically for halftime—attention turned to the tree. The household's gift exchange had been done first thing that morning before church, but the supply of presents under the excessively adorned branches was replenished upon the extended family's arrival. Packages were ripped open, wrapping paper was strewn about, gifts were admired, thanks were given, updates on the score were announced, some grumbling ensued about missing most of the third quarter.

Ray was mostly seen but not heard through it all. The game ended. Those who hadn't been paying attention asked the score; those who'd watched announced to all within earshot—Bulls 90, the Heat 80. Steve told no one in particular that Jordan had 24 and Toni Kukoč 19.

"How about Pippen?" Ray asked so Steve would think someone was listening.

"Didn't play. Was on the bench in street clothes. Hurt foot."

With the game over and the crowd around the TV breaking up, the bottle of wine Grace brought and several liqueurs were broken out, along with eggnog and apple cider for the underage. Glasses were passed around and toasts made, first by Old Dean, then Moose, followed by Gin.

Annie found herself standing near Ray and extended her glass. Ray did the same, clinking hers. "Merry Christmas, Ann. How's school going?" Annie winced, then rolled her eyes.

"I've got senioritis, and am not even a senior yet. Most of my classes suck, but I do like my English teacher. Just got done reading *Animal Farm*. You know that book?"

Ray shook no. "The last books we read in English were *The Call of the Wild* and *The Yearling*. And a Shakespeare play. Oh my God, it was like a foreign language. I couldn't understand what it meant."

Steve was listening in nearby and chimed in.

"If you ever go beyond introductory Orwell, read *1984*. Assuming it's not banned in your school. Predicts big government meddling in everything, taking away freedom, exactly what's happening now."

"What's happening is more like *Brave New World*," Annie interrupted. "Freedom's given up without a fight, without even realizing it's gone. All they have to do is keep us distracted, entertain us to death."

"Maybe you'll give it up without knowing it, but anybody with half a brain won't," Steve blurted, a hint of a wry smile flashing across his lips. "Figures they have you reading that Aldous Huxley crap in the Cities."

"Didn't read it in school. Found it on my own. And it's not crap, it's a classic."

With Steve there, Ray hesitated to add anything to the conversation. When Steve moved on, Ray was left alone again with Annie.

"That was rude, sorry about that," Ray said to her. "He can be a jerk sometimes."

"No sweat ... Hey, I didn't ask you how school's going for you. Do you miss living in the Cities?"

"Yeah, I miss it sometimes. School here's okay, I guess. It's just a little hard fitting in looking like me."

Annie fidgeted, not knowing quite how to respond to that. Ray noticed her discomfort.

"Everything's cool. It's just, I don't know, why does high school have to be like ..."

"*Lord of the Flies*," Annie finished. Ray looked bewildered but intrigued.

"Just another book. I read a lot of books. I guess that makes me a nerd."

"Reading doesn't make you a nerd, it makes you smart."

Annie threw her arms around Ray, surprising herself more than her cousin, who reciprocated the gesture by holding her in a tight embrace, lasting so long that Annie was a little creeped out. A clear violation of adolescent protocol, but it felt good. She was self-conscious about her chest, embarrassed to have it pressed against someone else, even if that someone's a relative. On second thought, being relatives somehow made it worse. But it was nice, no denying it. Part of her was mad at Ray, another part of her was mad at herself for initiating the whole business, then being weird about how it played out. It did feel good. Really good, actually. So confusing.

CHAPTER 13

THE MORNING AFTER CHRISTMAS, Gin paused at the door to Ray's room on the way to hers after showering, wrapped in a towel.

"Grace told me Annie had a nice time yesterday, was glad they came here for Christmas. Grace was surprised," Gin said.

Ray's only response was a smile.

"I'm surprised too," Gin went on. "I've always gotten the impression Annie can't wait to leave when she's here."

"Mom, if I tell you something, do you promise not to tell Aunt Grace or Ann?"

Gin knit her brow, nodding her agreement after some hesitation.

"Ann feels more like my sibling than Mark and Steve."

Gin clutched her towel with one hand and ran the other through her still-wet hair.

"I have a hunch Annie feels the same way you do. Grace mentioned she was talking about you in the car on the way home."

Ray's eyes lit up.

"It's just that we're close to the same age and she lives in the Cities, so we've got that in common too. I lived there longer than I've lived here."

Ray paused for an instant before continuing.

"She's super smart, thinks that makes her a nerd, says she doesn't fit in. I know what not fitting in is like, although not cuz I'm smart."

"Don't sell yourself short, kiddo."

Gin walked from the doorway to where Ray was seated on the bed and sat down on the far corner.

"It's cool to see you two hitting it off more and more as you get older. Are you sure you don't want me to tell Grace what you said?"

"You can't! You promised!"

"Don't worry, won't say a word. I'm just happy for you."

"Mom, can I tell you something else?"

"Course you can."

"It's nice having someone who's like a sister and all. But eventually I'd like to find someone to be with, you know, to marry." Tears welled in Ray's eyes. "I don't know how that will ever be possible, I'm just so…"

"Oh honey, you are …"

Ray held up a hand, stopping her mid-sentence.

"Don't tell me beauty is on the inside. Nobody can see what's inside. All they see is what's visible. Looking like I do, no one is ever going to want to marry me. I don't think I'll ever be able to have kids."

Gin tried to fight back tears, but quickly called off the battle. She slid over on the bed, putting an arm around Ray. She regretted not dressing before stopping to talk, but was not about to excuse herself at this juncture.

"Ragin, someone is going to come along who sees you as I do, beautiful inside and out. It's just a matter of being patient and finding the right person. But it'll happen, I promise you … Listen, kids can be mean. And you know what? Look at me … honey, look at me."

Ray looked into her eyes.

"The meanest ones are the most insecure. They don't feel good about themselves, so they knock others down to build themselves up. I know that high school seems like your whole world right now, but chances are you'll never see most of your classmates ever again once you graduate. You'll have a clean slate, meet people who see you the way I see you. You'll find just the right person, get married, have kids together. It'll happen if that's what you want."

She gave up on modesty, releasing her grip on her towel and taking Ray in her arms. Ray tried re-tucking the unfurling towel, making them both laugh through tears.

"I better let you get dressed, Mom."

"Things have a way of working out. It just takes time. It's going to be okay," Gin said softly.

Christmas break came and went. School started up again, the second half of the scholastic year evaporating fast. Ray made a point of laying low, trying mightily to avoid another confrontation like the ones with Nick Szymanski and Tom Tetzlaff.

As the weather improved and the snow melted, Ray spent increasing amounts of time during non-school hours breaking in the new baseball glove received for Christmas. Hours were spent bouncing a nearly napless tennis ball off the church's cement foundation or the brick wall of the school. When not fielding grounders or working Vaseline into the leather to soften the mitt, Ray tried to hit stones all the way across the mill pond with an old wooden bat. Some skipped across the water before sinking into the pond. Others soared high and far, but never quite made it to the other side before splashing down. So many stones were smacked that the circumference of the bat's barrel was whittled down to roughly the same as the handle.

About the only respite the glove and bat ever got was when Grace would bring Annie to visit, or when Gin took Ray to visit them in the Cities. On those occasions, Ray and Annie just walked and talked, becoming better and better friends. Sometimes the subject was books, or TV shows, or things going on in the world. Other times it was boys in Annie's school or girls in Ray's.

Toward the end of the school year, ground saturated by the spring thaw dried sufficiently to allow gym class to move outside. One week was devoted to playing softball, which Ray had been looking forward to for months. Students wanted to choose up sides, but the teacher did it for them, rotating students from position to position so everyone got to play both infield and outfield.

In the second of three games that week, Ray got to bat twice before class ended, hitting a line drive up the middle for a single the first time, later splitting the gap between left and center, circling the bases for the game's only home run. In the field, only two balls were hit in Ray's direction. The first was a lazy pop fly that was easy to catch. The second was a screaming liner over the shortstop that, with a perfectly timed leap, Ray snagged for the out.

When the class period was almost over and equipment was gathered up to be hauled back inside, the gym teacher approached Ray.

"Are you trying out for the baseball team?" Mr. Mills asked.

"Wasn't planning to. Everyone thinks I'm too small."

"You don't have to be big to play baseball. Only thing that matters is how good you are. You should think about it. There's only the varsity team because there aren't enough kids going out for baseball to have a JV squad. But I think you might have a chance to make the team as a freshman. You should give it a shot. I coach wrestling and football, but even I can tell you're good."

"Not sure my family would let me. I'm expected to help with the businesses."

"You're only a kid once. I'm sure they wouldn't stand in the way of you playing."

"Not sure I want to, but I'll think about it."

Mr. Mills let the subject drop but, unbeknownst to Ray, the gym teacher had a word with the baseball coach, who in turn talked to Moose. The interest in Ray trying out for the team took Moose by surprise, and he brought it up at the dinner table.

"Jim Slater called me," Moose started, looking across the table at Ray. "He thinks you should go out for baseball. Tryouts are after school tomorrow and the next day."

Gin looked excitedly over at Moose, then to Ray.

"There's no freshman team or junior varsity. I'd have to beat out upperclassmen."

"They need bodies. Improves your chances," Moose reasoned.

"Honey, nothing's lost by trying out," Gin said. "Who knows, maybe some of those older kids haven't played that much and aren't as good as you. Even if you don't make the team this year, it'll be good experience and you can try again next year."

Ray shrugged. Moose looked disgusted by what he took as further evidence of Ray's lack of initiative. Ray expected him to launch into a lecture, but for some unknown reason, he held his fire.

The next day after school, Ray didn't show up for the first tryout. Supper was a haphazard affair that evening. With Moose working late, Gin running errands, and instructions for Ray to heat up a frozen pizza, there was no dinner table conversation on the subject. The following day Ray skipped the final tryout, instead going straight to the bus after school let out.

Instead of waiting for the stop on the Hill, Ray got off the bus at the first stop as it rolled into Faith, walking past the boarded-up root beer stand and along the edge of the highway. With the cemetery in sight, Ray turned down the gravel driveway, up the creaky steps to the weathered old screen door that wasn't quite flush. With the warmer weather, the inside door was wide open.

"Mind if I come in?" Ray called out.

"Door's open!" came the response.

Ray stepped inside, immediately moving to the plump woman with the bonnet and apron on the kitchen counter and lifting the lid. Inside were chocolate chip cookies, still soft and faintly warm. Between bites Ray could hear a cadenced beat from a single snare drum wafting out of the sitting room. The sound came from a vinyl disc spinning on a dated and dusty turntable. First a solitary man's voice accompanied the insistent beat, then a chorus.

> *Fighting soldiers from the sky*
> *Fearless men who jump and die*
> *Men who mean just what they say*
> *The brave men of the Green Beret*
> *Silver wings upon their chest*
> *These are men, America's best*
> *One hundred men will test today*
> *But only three win the Green Beret*
> *Trained to live off nature's land*
> *Trained in combat, hand-to-hand*
> *Men who fight by night and day*
> *Courage take from the Green Berets*

Colette gestured for Ray to go in and take a seat.

> *Silver wings upon their chest*
> *These are men, America's best*
> *One hundred men will test today*
> *But only three win the Green Beret*
> *Back at home, a young wife waits*
> *Her Green Beret has met his fate*

He has died for those oppressed
Leaving her his last request
Put silver wings on my son's chest
Make him one of America's best
He'll be a man they'll test one day
Have him win the Green Beret

Morger sat silently in his shabby upholstered armchair, a handkerchief in one hand.

"Were you a Green Beret?" Ray asked.

"No, but I fought next to them on a few occasions."

"What kind of soldier were you?"

"Not a very good one, I'm afraid."

"I mean ..."

"I know what you meant. I was an army grunt in a tank destroyer battalion. Did most of our fighting with the 1st Infantry. The Bloody 1st."

Ray had countless questions but no idea where to start. Morger was lost in thought.

"You know, everybody hears a song differently. Some like the melody and ignore the lyrics. Some listen to the lyrics and interpret them one way, others interpret them another way. That song came out in the mid-'60s if I recall correctly. A lot of people took it for Vietnam War propaganda. To me, it wasn't about Vietnam, or even the Green Berets. It's just about fallen comrades, the sacrifices made in war. Been a long time since I listened to it," Morger said, absent-mindedly folding, unfolding and refolding his handkerchief.

"Don't really understand why, but that song was always a comfort to me. Maybe it gave me a way to justify things I did, or just a way to think of those I served with who didn't come home. Don't get me wrong, I believed in what we were doing over there. What Hitler was doing was evil. Had to be stopped. To this day, not sure there was any realistic alternative to going to war. I'd like to think there might have been another way, a way that didn't involve all that killing and destruction ... All I know is I would never wish that on my own son."

"You have a son?" Ray asked, sitting down on the couch.

"Naw, being blessed with children ... that's something that was never meant to be for Colette and me. But if I'd ever had a son, I wouldn't have wanted to watch him go off to war. Of course, nowadays it could be a daughter just as easily as a son. I'm all for equal rights, but if killing's a right, it's a right I wouldn't wish on anyone. It's a right I wish I'd never had."

Ray was morbidly curious about the killing, and Morger could sense this.

"You see, our job was to knock out the German tanks, clear the way for the infantrymen. The German tanks were better than ours, more powerful guns, better armor. Our strategy must've been quantity over quality, just keep running waves of tanks at them. The Germans tanks would blow up one of ours, we'd throw another at them … like sheep to slaughter. When we were able to knock out one of theirs, couldn't really see who we killed, it was done at a distance. But I saw who *they* killed up close. One minute I was talking to a buddy of mine. Next thing I know I'm diving into a ditch. When I look back to where my friend was, he wasn't there no more. Found him 20 yards away with his head blown clear off. Seeing that made me realize every time one of our shells hit our target, some German soldier was right there next to his buddy who was blown to bits."

Ray winced.

"Sorry for being so graphic. Don't mean to give you nightmares. Had enough of those myself. I wasn't much older than you are now when I was over there. Saw a lot of guys about my same age killed right next to me. Lost count how many. At the beginning I thought it was sheer luck I wasn't dead. After a while, it sure seemed like a higher power was looking out for me. If I didn't believe in God before the war, I sure did by the time it was over."

Ray couldn't think of what to say; words wouldn't come.

"God never puts more on you than you can handle," Morger continued. "Whenever I thought I was at my breaking point, when I was sure I couldn't take any more death and destruction, there would be a lull in the fighting, like it was heaven sent. We'd roll into some small village, get a hero's welcome cuz we weren't the Nazis. We'd trade cigarettes for fresh laid eggs or bread straight out of the oven. Or we'd find a tavern where we could relax for a moment, have a beer. The love of my life came to me in one of those villages."

Ray looked quizzically in Colette's direction as Morger continued his story.

"We landed in Normandy the third week of the invasion, fought our way south, then east across France. We came to a village not far from the German border occupied by the Nazis. It looked the size of the towns around here. Couldn't tell how many survived the occupation, but the place had been reduced to rubble. Met a beautiful young girl there. Homeless ... traumatized. She spoke almost no English, I spoke almost no French, yet there was this magical connection. Damnedest thing ... we could communicate without really knowing each other's language. Spent the better part of three days together. Can't speak for her, but three days was enough for me to know. After the war ended, I went back for her. Had no way of knowing if she'd still be there or how to locate her if she wasn't, but we found each other. Been together ever since."

"I never thought he would come back for me," Colette added, her accent dulled by the years but still subtly evident.

"You left your family there?" Ray asked her.

"I didn't have much family left. My mother and father were both killed during the bombing. My brother joined the army, was captured and killed. My sister left for Paris. She is still there; we visit her from time to time. But right after the war, there wasn't much reason to stay, there wasn't much left. Our house was destroyed, my family was gone."

"Was it scary leaving home, coming to America?" Ray inquired.

"It was very different, but no, not scary. It was free of war. So big. Wide-open spaces like I'd never seen, so much land for farming. Morger's father and mother were still alive, farming right here, living in this house. We stayed with them for a few months, helped with the farm, but Morger had the opportunity to use his military benefits to go to the state teachers' college in Eau Claire. We lived there for four years. I was surprised to find a place here with a French name. Was a small reminder of home."

"Eau Claire is French?"

"Means clear water. I found Eau Claire to be a charming place. I didn't have employment right away. My job was to learn English and get pregnant. I did one better than the other, as you can tell."

"It wasn't for any lack of trying that we didn't have children," Morger said with a wink. "We never did get to the bottom of what was the matter. Colette sure wasn't frigid. Most likely I shot blanks."

Colette's furrowed eyebrows said all that needed saying about Morger's indelicacy.

"Aw come on, Ray's plenty old enough to know the ins and outs of procreation. Besides, you're always remarking on how people here in this country are so uptight about their bodies, have so many hang-ups about sex. Remember in Mali, how you teased me about being bashful at bedtime because we always seemed to have an audience."

"*What?* Gotta stop you right there," Ray interjected.

"Privacy as we know it doesn't exist there. You are in the presence of others every waking hour. People live in such close proximity, in large extended families. At first, I'd get annoyed when some old lady would pull straw off the roof of one of our huts to make a broom, or when strangers would break off branches from a tree in our yard to use as toothbrushes. Came to realize that there was no such thing as strangers, nothing belonged to us in their eyes. It was not our tree, it was not our straw roof, it was not our right to be left alone."

Morger continued: "At night we'd be in bed under the mosquito net, you could hear people walking through our compound like it's a train station or something. Quite often you'd see four or five little heads peering in at us through the screen door of our hut. It was like we were on display, an irresistible exhibit, especially for the kids. When we did make love, it was the talk of the market the next day. Colette took it in stride. Gave me a hard time for turning on the BBC's classical music broadcasts—full volume—on amorous evenings. We'd hear them saying 'Adama and Hawa were playing music again last night.' Had a bit of a chilling effect, you might say."

Ray smirked, tickled by the business about playing music. "Pah pah pah."

Morger laughed mirthfully, admiring both Ray's memory and wit.

"Adama and Hawa? That's what they called you?"

"Indeed. Those are the Malian names they gave us."

Colette warmed to the discussion and joined in.

"Remember what Aminata said to us?" she asked Morger.

"About what?"

"About working."

A glimmer of recognition shone in Morger's eyes, prompting a chuckle.

"We were sitting one afternoon with a woman named Aminata who lived next door to us," Colette began.

"To set the mood properly," Morger interrupted with a twinkle in his eye. "She lays out a mat for us to sit on, another for herself. Before she sits, she takes off her top. I'm trying to keep my composure with this woman sitting there in front of us bare breasted. Not something you see in your average living room here. Commonplace there."

"We haven't been talking long and Ami says to us '*ow yay bara kay suro wa*,'" Colette related.

"What does that mean?" Ray asked eagerly.

"She asked if we worked last night," Colette explained.

When Ray looked perplexed, Morger again felt the need to supply context for humor's sake.

"Colette goes '*Ami!*' Just about pushes her over. Ami's prett-near doubled over laughing. I wasn't following."

Colette picked up where Morger left off.

"Among the women, the word for work—*bara*—is slang for sex. That's what she was asking about. She already knew the answer, was teasing us about it."

"Says a lot ... not only about the lack of privacy but also their view of lovemaking," Morger interjected.

"That's the sad part of all this," Colette said. "Sex—like just about everything else in a woman's life in those small villages over there—is an obligation, not a choice. She has no choice when her body is mutilated at puberty, she doesn't get to choose who she'll marry."

"How were they mutilated?" said Ray, looking aghast.

"When a girl there is coming of age, she goes through a rite of passage where parts of her genitals are cut out. I was surprised to find that village women were among the most vocal supporters of the practice. Some even believed if it wasn't done a girl would not become a woman and couldn't bear children. The women I met didn't appear angry about it. They told me it hurt, but accepted it. Didn't see that they had any choice."

"That's horrible," Ray exclaimed.

"You first have to meet freedom to ever miss it," Morger chimed in. "I'll tell you this, if there was any relationship whatsoever between wealth and how hard you work, every African woman would be a millionaire. Ain't nobody anywhere in the world works harder, from before the sun rises to well after it sets. When I hear rich people say poor people just need to work harder, it about makes me upchuck. Most of what the rich have is inherited, the rest they get sitting on their backsides, watching their money make more money. They ain't never met an African woman, or they'd know hard work is hardly the secret of affluence."

Soaking it all in, Ray had lost track of time, then noticed the clock.

"Hey, could one of you call my mom and let her know I'm here? She's prolly worried."

"Of course," said Colette, taking her leave. Awaiting her return, Morger and Ray killed time with small talk, the weather, favorite flavors of ice cream, then ...

"Your wife ... er, Colette ... I mean Mrs. Morger ..." Ray stammered.

"You can just call her Gramma."

"She said you went to the teacher college in Eau Claire. You were a teacher?"

"I was. For over 25 years."

"What did you teach?"

"Social studies at the high school. History, among other things. Mostly U.S. history."

"I bet you were a good teacher."

"Some thought I was, others thought I wasn't. Isn't that the way it always is with teaching?"

"Why'd you stop?"

Before Morger could answer, Colette came back from talking on the phone with Gin.

"All taken care of. I asked your mom if it's all right for you to stay for supper. If you want. She's okay with it."

"I'd love to. Thank you."

"You accept the offer even before you know what's on the menu?" Morger teased.

"Beef bourguignon," Colette announced, then noticed Ray looking puzzled. "Beef stew."

"Sounds good to me."

Sparse fixtures produced the ambience of dining by candlelight. Colette placed an ornate tureen full of steaming stew in the middle of the table alongside a long, slender loaf of bread on a cutting board and a large bowl of mixed greens topped with shaved radish. Three wine glasses, porcelain dinner plates and silverware flanked the food.

"Na yan dumunikay," Morger said. "Come and eat."

"Bon appetit," Colette said once everyone was seated. "Help yourself, Ray. I hope you like it."

"Would you like some wine?" Morger asked Ray. "We also have milk if you prefer. Or water of course."

"I'll try some wine," Ray answered sheepishly.

Morger poured three glasses, raising his in a toast.

"Here's to our guest and the blessing of good company."

Three glasses clinked. Ray took a tentative sip, Colette and Morger awaited a verdict.

"Good," Ray proclaimed without great conviction.

"Ray, we so love having you as part of our family," said Morger. "When you get to be our age, it's natural to want to pass along favorite stories. Trouble is, not too many are interested, especially those as young as you. Old people's lives bore them."

"What we talk about isn't boring. Not to me."

Morger's eyes glistened. Colette looked down at her lap, then cleared her throat.

"Ray, I don't mean to pry, but your mother gave me reason to suspect you might be here because you don't want to be at home," Colette uttered softly. "Something about the baseball team."

Ray stiffened.

"You don't need to tell us if you don't want to. Just know if you'd like to talk about it, you can."

Plates were filled and cleaned, filled and cleaned again, except Colette's. Glasses were filled and drunk, filled and drunk again, except Ray's. When supper was over, Colette started to clear dishes from the table.

"We were playing softball in gym class. The teacher told me I should go out for baseball, said he thinks I'm good enough to make the team as a freshman. Tryouts were yesterday and today after school. Decided not to go. The Moose thinks I'm either afraid or too lazy to try. I don't know what Mom thinks. Could be that she doesn't know what to think. She knows I love to play."

Morger listened intently but didn't say anything. Colette gently invited Ray to continue.

"What made you decide against it?"

"It's not that I'm afraid of not being good enough. If I am, I am. If I'm not, I'm not. That's not it. It's something I can't tell the Moose. I'm not even sure I could tell my mom."

"Could you tell us?" Colette asked as reassuringly as she could.

"There's nothing I love more than playing ball. I'd love to be on the team. But I don't want to be a jock, part of that crowd. They're such jerks. I don't want to wear a letter jacket advertising that I'm a jock. How could I tell that to the Moose? He'd take it personally. I know he would. It'd be ugly."

Both Morger and Colette seemed to be forming their thoughts, measuring their next words.

"The other thing ... if I'm on the team that means being in the locker room not just during school hours but after school too. I hate that place. With everything that's gone on, I don't know how much more time I can spend in there before something really bad happens. It's like playing with fire."

Ray started to say more but then hesitated before starting again.

"You told me once that you know my secret. I thought if you do ..."

"We do," Colette affirmed. "Oh Ray, I am so sorry. I wish we could help you think of a way to solve all this so you could do what you love. I'm afraid there's no simple way."

COUNTY
Q

CHAPTER 14

AS THE SUN BROKE OVER THE HORIZON, a thick quilt of fog clung to the ground as though the land clutched it tight to ward off the chill of the morning air. The rays piercing the lolling mist produced a hazy glow, like a halo hovering over the countryside. As the fog lifted, the sunlight kissed the heavy dew that coated every blade of grass, making them glisten like polished emeralds.

Ray awoke to the sound of coffee percolating, looked around, groggy and disoriented. The couch's faded and shabby upholstery was bathed in light pouring through the undraped sitting room window.

"Bonjour, Ray!"

Wearing a lavender housecoat with a floral print and suede slippers of the same color with faux fur lining, Colette busied herself setting out cups and plates on the dining room table along with a tray of muffins and pastries.

"Morger is taking his morning constitutional," she said. "Sometimes he picks raspberries when he's out walking. Perhaps we'll be lucky this morning."

Shortly, Morger let himself in. He was carrying a newspaper but no berries. After washing up in the bathroom, Ray made straight for the front door to make a quiet exit but was summoned to the table and offered coffee.

"Sit yourself down," Morger commanded. "You need to eat something before you go."

Ray declined the coffee but accepted a glass of milk, apple muffin and sweet roll. After snarfing down breakfast and lingering for a teenager's idea of a sufficient amount of time to show appropriate gratitude for their hospitality, Ray headed for the door.

"Got to get to school, but have to stop home first to change clothes, so I better get going."

Morger lifted his gaze from the newspaper long enough to wave. Colette accompanied Ray to the door. "Bonne journée!"

"Have a nice day, Mrs. Morger," Ray replied politely.

There was no meandering on the way home. Ray slipped into the house unnoticed, changed clothes, and was nearly at the front door to leave when Gin heard the footsteps.

"Rage, is that you?" came the voice from several rooms away.

Being called that signaled Moose either had already left or was not within earshot.

"Hi, Mom! On my way to catch the bus."

"I can give you a ride. It's on my way and there's plenty of time. Just have to be in Abbotsford by nine."

Gin appeared from one of the back rooms, hair done up, smartly dressed in a sleek navy pantsuit and heels.

"Why you all dressed up?"

"Meeting. Some issues with business registrations. The county assessor's office has questions."

"Sounds important."

"No big deal. Pretty boring actually. Come on, let's go."

They weren't in the car but a minute when Gin's curiosity overtook her instinct to leave well enough alone.

"Why did you skip tryouts? You love baseball. You must want to play."

"Just tryin' to give the Moose heartburn I guess."

Gin sighed, threw Ray a glance, half amused and half scolding.

"Come on Rage, I know you'd give anything to be on that team."

"Not quite *any*thing."

"So, what's stopping you?"

"Use your imagination, Mom. Think about who you're talking to here."

Gin took her eyes off the road, looking over at Ray. She knew.

"Look, I love playing ball. I wish I could. I wish for it more than I wish for anything. But wanting to doesn't make it smart. I've had some close calls at school, been dumb about things. What do you want me to do, go looking for more trouble?"

"Standing up for others isn't dumb. Risky, yes. I get your point ... I do. I'm sorry, I shouldn't have brought it up. You think things through better than I do."

"It sucks, but that's life, right? Just wanted you to know it has nothing to do with what the Moose thinks it is."

"I already knew *that*, honey."

She was about to drop the subject and drive in silence, but the urge to amend her earlier thoughts proved irresistible.

"You know what? I'm not saying you should go looking for trouble, but if it comes, it comes. If everything's brought out into the open, so be it. It's a relief not having to pretend anymore with your grampa and gramma, not having to live some ridiculous lie. If they hate the truth, and hate me for it, so fucking what."

She immediately threw a hand over her mouth, first to mime disappointment with herself, then to suppress laughter. Ray laughed too.

"Sorry, I should watch my mouth. I don't set a very good example, do I?"

Ray didn't answer right away. "What are you saying, Mom? You wouldn't mind if the kids at school knew? As soon as they know, the whole town will know. You wouldn't mind if everyone knew ... you know, the real me?"

"I'm not telling you what to do. All I'm saying is you shouldn't have to live a lie on my account. When the time is right ... if the time ever feels right ... I want you to do what you think is right, what's best for you without worrying about me. It doesn't matter what people think of me. I care more about what you think of me than what everyone else thinks."

Ray pondered this, peering out the passenger's window at the passing farm fields.

"Rage, you can tell me ... do you think your gramma and grampa are right about me? Never mind, that doesn't matter ... I mean, are you ashamed to have a mom who doesn't know who your father is?"

Ray shook no.

"Do you think I'm immoral? I can take it if you do, I really can."

"I love you, Mom."

Gin took that as a yes. Tears streamed down her cheeks. Ray could read her face.

"Mom, if you are immoral, then I have no idea what moral is. You accept me the way I am. Hardly anyone else does. The Moose doesn't. Mark and Steve don't. My grandparents don't. Kids at school just know I'm not like them and most of them have a problem with that. You accept me. If that's immoral, someone's going to have to explain morality to me."

Gin looked in the rear-view mirror, horrified to see how her tears made her makeup run. "Oh my God, I look like I'm melting."

"I'll trade you faces any day," Ray said with a sardonic smile.

Gin pulled into the school parking lot, parking well away from the line of buses and cars.

"I'll let you out here. Don't want anyone seeing the scary clown who gave you a lift," she joked. "See you tonight, honey."

That day and those that followed, school bullies left Ray alone, apparently wary of possibly experiencing the same fate as Tom Tetzlaff or Nick Szymanski. With time, however, classmates egged each other on, one daring the other to prove Ray had no magical powers. Steering clear of empty hallways and melting into the crowd only went so far. Older kids took to jumping Ray when opportunities arose. Sometimes the assaults resulted in a bloodied nose or torn clothing. Others left no visible signs, only a battered psyche. Ray didn't fight back. Didn't report the abuse. Pounding on Ray without consequence was in vogue.

Killing time after lunch, waiting for the bell summoning them to their next class, students milled about outside the school, soaking up the sun on a gorgeous spring day. One small group threw a frisbee. Another formed a circle, kicking around a golf ball-sized bean bag. Others stood around talking. Ray walked along the sidewalk in front of the school, finishing a peanut butter sandwich and carton of milk. Kaz and Boner stood at the far corner of the building, motioning to come.

Ray looked around to see if they were hailing someone else. They motioned again. As Ray walked over to join them, they disappeared around the corner. When Ray reached the edge of the school and looked around the corner, there was Katy Cash out back taking a drag from a joint before passing it to Kaz, who took a hit before handing it to Boner.

"Wanna get high?" asked Kaz.

"No thanks," Ray answered, turning to leave.

"Don't be a dork," Boner said, inhaling deeply, holding the smoke in for several seconds before coughing it out.

"Afraid of getting caught, or don't you like to party?" Katy taunted.

Then she recoiled as Kaz reached around from behind to fondle one of her breasts. She wheeled around and smacked him on the arm, a reaction that struck Ray as more playful than punitive. Kaz was undeterred. He drew in close and ran both hands from her shoulders to her waist, giving her buttocks a squeeze.

"Come on, don't be a spoilsport," he pleaded. "How 'bout a little peek before the bell rings?"

Katy's demeanor changed from nonchalant to alarmed and then frightened as Kaz groped for the tab to the zipper on her jeans and yanked it down. She screamed, pushing his hands away as he fumbled to unfasten the button securing the pants at the waist. As she rezipped her fly, Kaz thrust his hand up her shirt, pulling at her bra. She let out another yelp, pulling at his arm with one hand while clutching her chest with the other in hopes of keeping her bra in place.

"Knock it off!" Ray yelled at Kaz and stepped between him and Katy. *"Stop it!"*

Ray and Kaz wrestled briefly, Kaz quickly gaining the upper hand, flinging Ray to the ground, the full weight of his body grinding Ray's head into the dirt. Ray desperately tried to wriggle free without success. Then, just like that, Kaz released his grip, raising a hand to his forehead. He felt lightheaded, close to fainting. His skin grew clammy, his heart pounded violently. He drew rapid, shallow breaths, panting. He fell back off Ray onto the ground, dizzy, an itchy sensation in his throat, like his windpipe was closing.

"I can't breathe!" Kaz sputtered frantically. "Everything's spinning."

Katy implored Boner to go fetch the school nurse, but Kaz shook his head vigorously. Boner speculated that maybe there was something in the weed sending Kaz on a bad trip. Katy was thinking panic attack, Boner countered he might be having some kind of seizure. The two argued over whether to bring Kaz some water or try getting him to his feet and helping him inside. Kaz laid back, covering his eyes with both hands, his breathing still labored. Ray knelt beside him, putting one hand under Kaz's neck and resting the other on his chest.

"It's gonna be okay," said Ray soothingly. "Try to take deep breaths."

Kaz lifted his head ever so slightly, alarmed to see red splotches now covering his arms.

"What the hell is this?" he splurted, holding up one arm.

"Oh my God, you're breaking out in hives," Katy told him. "See, this *is* a panic attack."

Boner's first thought upon seeing the rashes was that Ray's condition had somehow rubbed off on Kaz, maybe it was infectious, but Boner kept that idea to himself.

"P-panic, my ass," Kaz protested. "Boner's right, there must be something in the weed that didn't agree with me."

The bell rang, summoning students back inside.

"Not a word about this to anyone," Kaz demanded as he slowly rose to his feet. "Seriously, not one word."

Ray sure didn't tell anybody. Whether it was Katy or Boner who spilled the beans is anyone's guess—each blamed the other—but the story spread like wildfire. Kaz did his best damage control, insisting he'd had an allergic reaction, but whispers still circulated widely. What happened with Nick Szymanski could have been an isolated incident. Tom Tetzlaff pissing himself could be explained away as an odd coincidence. But three strange things happening when Ray got bullied was too much to dismiss out of hand. Some kind of threshold had been crossed. Something about Hen Glennon made these things happen. Nobody beat up Ray the rest of that school year.

Ray welcomed the reprieve but was as unnerved by what had transpired as anyone. Perhaps even more so, due to happenings the kids at school knew nothing about, like the whole business with Lisa Lewandowski at the Slaters' Christmas party.

The last day of school before summer vacation, Ray eagerly waited outside for the bus after the final bell, as there was much to look forward to. First, a week in the Cities at Aunt Grace's house to see Annie, play video games, hang out at the mall, go skateboarding, take in a Twins game or two. Then Annie coming to stay in Faith for two weeks. Lost in those happy thoughts, Ray didn't notice Chris Driscoll standing nearby.

"Is it okay if I sit with you on the bus?" she asked to Ray's great surprise.

"You want to sit with *me*?" Ray replied incredulously.

"If that's okay."

"Won't you be embarrassed sitting with a freshman?"

"The year's over and I'm probly not coming back, so it's not like I'm going to have to deal with any of these losers next year anyway."

"What do you mean you're not coming back?"

"Likely dropping out. Might change my mind, but as of now I'm pretty sure I'm done with school."

"You're smart, you should stick it out so you can graduate."

"If I'm so smart, how come I flunked two classes and barely passed the others?"

"Not caring for school don't make you dumb."

"The way things stand today, if did come back I'm not sure there's a way for me to get enough credits by the end of the year to graduate ... Anyway, do you mind?"

"Mind what?"

"Mind if I sit with you. I want to talk to you about something."

That prospect made Ray's heart pound and palms sweat. Chris stood there, waiting for an answer. When the bus for Faith arrived, Ray got on first, went back a few rows before taking an open seat, sliding all the way over to the window making a place for Chris to sit. She sat down on the edge of the seat, leaving a good foot between her and Ray. She remained silent until everyone made it onto the bus and the bus driver swung the door closed.

Chris promptly slid over next to Ray, so close their legs touched. She turned her back to the aisle, hunching over as though she was about to show Ray something illicit. She spoke in a voice so soft that Ray strained to hear her.

"I heard what you did for Katy Cash and what happened to that sleazy little prick who was running his hands all over her," she whispered.

"Who told you?" Ray said a little more loudly before being shushed.

"Never mind how I know. What I heard is the same as I've seen for myself. I saw what you did when those assholes were fucking with my brother, I saw you make that Tetzlaff creep piss his pants."

"Those things just happened. I didn't *do* nothin'."

"Horseshit. He didn't just piss down his legs by accident. I saw the look on his face. Like he'd seen a ghost. Katy saw the same with what's-his-face.

You scared the crap out of him."

"Katy told you that?"

Chris nodded before clutching Ray's arm so firmly it hurt.

"Don't you go and narc on her. Not to your friends, not to nobody."

"I ain't got no actual friends."

"Me neither. Just don't tell nobody. Promise me."

"Don't worry, I won't."

Chris released her grip. She seemed to be struggling with what to say next. Tongue-tied, Ray was unable to bail her out. After an awkward silence, she brought her hands together, fingers intertwined, as if in prayer.

"I don't know what you have going on later or ... or, I mean, do you have to get home right away?" she said nervously.

Breathing suddenly became a considerably more taxing chore for Ray, quite incompatible with speaking. Chris looked close to aborting the conversation and moving to another seat, but gathered herself.

"Could you ... um, would you stay on the bus when we get to your stop and get off with me when we get to my house?"

"Ah ... sure. Why?"

"I want to tell you something, but not here. We have to be alone."

Ray felt like vomiting, hoping against hope for nerves to calm and heart rate to slow. The ride's last 30 minutes felt like 90. When the bus reached the intersection of the two gravel roads where Chris lived, she rose from her seat before it came to a full stop, staggering slightly. She strode swiftly down the aisle and out the door, offering no farewell to the driver and receiving none in return. Feeling a bit wobbly, Ray moved more deliberately toward the exit to avoid any parting calamity, saying a quick "thank you" and "see you next year" to the lumpy, gruff man behind the wheel.

Ray negotiated the last step without incident and followed Chris, who did not proceed up the driveway to her house but instead to the rear of a ramshackle shed with a wheel-less Chevy Camaro next to it nearly shrouded by overgrown weeds. Chris plopped down on the ground with her back against the wall of the shed, out of eyesight and earshot of the house. The shed had the same warped clapboard siding and peeling white paint as the house, and identical moss-covered asphalt shingles at least a decade overdue for replacement.

A wasp nest clung to the soffit just above where Chris was now sitting.

Ray saw it but decided against suggesting a change of location, joining her amidst the tall weeds. She took a pack of cigarettes and a lighter out of her shirt pocket, held them out, returning them to her pocket when Ray declined her offer.

"I won't if you don't," Chris replied. "You shouldn't have to breathe my smoke."

Ray looked warily up at the procession of wasps coming and going.

"I don't know how you done what you did," Chris continued. "But I wish you could do that to my old man."

"Why?"

"He ... um ... he does shit to me, things that no man should do to his daughter," she said with a shaky voice, tears filling her eyes and beginning to spill over her cheeks.

"Like what?"

"Um ... oh Christ ... I'm sorry," she said, her lips quivering.

Ray took her hand, squeezing it. "What's he do?"

"He c ... he cu ... he comes in my room, in the middle of the night when he thinks everyone's asleep, or in the middle of the day if he thinks no one else is around," she said, steeling herself. "When Mom's not around, he pulls me into their bedroom or into the toilet. He has me do shit to him ... and does shit to me."

"Sexual stuff?"

Chris nodded shakily.

"In here too," she said, rapping her knuckles on one of the clapboards that looked like it had been gnawed by some rodent. She started sobbing. Ray wanted to put an arm around her shoulders but thought better of it.

"Does your mom know?"

"I don't know how she couldn't, but she's drunk out of her mind half the time, so who knows. If she did know, I'm not sure she'd remember. But she must be aware at least some of the time. He's not exactly careful or quiet about it. But she don't say nothin'. Probly figgers if he gets it from me, he'll leave her alone. I think it wakes up Mickey sometimes. I get the feeling he knows, but we don't talk about it."

"Mickey?"

"That's what we've called my brother since he was little. Just within the family. I know that's not what he's called at school."

"Why do you stay?"

"I ain't got no place to go."

"You've got to tell someone."

"I'm telling you."

"I mean someone who can do something about it."

"You can do something. I've seen it. Katy Cash has seen it."

"I don't how those things happened. They just did. It's not some kind of hex or anything. It's nothing I did. It just happened. I was thinking maybe I could ask my mom to talk to my grampa since he's sheriff, but they're not speaking to each other right now. There's got to be someone you can go to."

"I already did, and it didn't do no good. I told our priest back when we were still going to church, and he acted like it was my fault, like I was leading my old man on or something. He told me to say a bunch of Hail Marys and pray on it real hard. Then I told the junior high principal."

"This has been happening since junior high?" Ray said, mortified. Chris nodded and kept nodding, her expression hardening.

"He wanted me to describe what goes on between me and my old man. Asked where he touches me, and if I touch him anywhere. Kept asking me to be more specific, like he thought I was making the whole thing up. Wanted details ... started giving me the feeling the old perv was getting his jollies from it. I mean, I wasn't gonna spell it out for him. I ran out of there. He never came looking for me. Must've figgered I was just trash."

Chris started sobbing again. Ray wanted to offer comfort or at least sympathy but felt paralyzed, more useless with each heaving, retching gasp. Chris abruptly turned away and threw up in the weeds. She wiped her chin with the back of her hand.

"I must look like hell," she said, her eyes red and puffy, strands of disheveled hair glued to her forehead and temples.

Ray nearly said something about longing to look as good as her when she looks like hell, but stopped short.

"Can you help me with my old man?" Chris said pleadingly. "Just say something to him, look at him, whatever it is you do."

"I seriously don't know what happened with Szymanski and Tetzlaff and Kaz. I don't think I did anything."

"I got nothin' to lose. If whatever you did to all those guys doesn't have any effect on my old man, I'll be no worse off than I am now. You can't be any more useless than that priest or the principal."

Ray felt set up to fail, summoned to perform with no idea whatsoever how to carry out the performance.

Chris rubbed her swollen eyes and ran a hand through her tangled hair, a look of gratitude in her eyes.

"I ain't never laid with anyone who didn't try to molest me." She got to her feet, Ray following suit. The two walked back around the shed, past the old Camaro and the Driscolls' Ford pickup, heading toward the house. Ray tried not to look at Chris, but it was hard not to, the way her hips swayed as she walked, her slightly upturned nose and untamed hair. Ray walked at her side, robotically, one foot in front of the other, wondering how to get home since the bus was long gone.

Suddenly a car engine backfired and a male figure emerged from behind the wheel of an early- '70s puke green Dodge Charger. The man—rubbing hands on grease-stained jeans, tugging habitually on the brim of a soiled Goodyear cap—walked briskly in their direction.

"Paul Driscoll," he introduced himself in a surprisingly high-pitched voice, throwing out his right hand at Ray. When the gesture was not reciprocated, he moved to Chris's side, put his arm around her waist, and slid his hand into her back pocket. She hastily removed his hand, looking utterly creeped out.

Ray had seen enough. "I know what you been doing."

"Say that again," Driscoll replied coldly.

"I know what you do to Chris. How you hurt her."

Driscoll's face flushed; he balled his hands into fists. Certain that her father was about to attack Ray, Chris stepped between them. He pushed her to the side but did not advance on Ray.

"I never hurt no one in this house. You have no idea what you're talking about. You got a lot of nerve, boy, comin' here runnin' your mouth like this. You best get your ass off my property."

Ray didn't move a muscle.

"I'll deal with you later," Driscoll said menacingly to Chris before returning his glare to Ray. "You deaf? I told you to get the hell off my property. There's a shotgun right inside that door there. Ain't got no problem using it on trespassers."

Ray stood stock still. Driscoll wheeled around, headed for the house. Chris's face drained of color, the muscles around her mouth grew taut, her eyes filled with dread.

"You gotta get out of here," she shrieked, pushing Ray away. "I'll be okay. Go!"

Ray did not retreat. Moments later, Driscoll emerged from the house with the shotgun. He marched up to Ray, stopping mere inches away.

"I said get!" he shouted.

Ray didn't budge, showing no signs of fear, instead regarding Driscoll with a strangely serene expression. Driscoll aimed the gun to the sky and discharged the weapon. The blast startled Ray and Chris screamed; still Ray stood firm. For an instant Driscoll seemed ready to strike Ray with the stock, then appeared uncertain.

"You've got no right to hurt Chris the way you do," Ray said. "You've done it for the last time."

Driscoll took inventory of his options. *Daring him to stop me comes off as an admission. Does he know everything? What's he fixing to do with what he knows? What am I supposed to do? Beat the crap out of him? Shoot him? Do nothing? How the hell does this end?*

Driscoll broke out in a drenching sweat, panic all over his face. He nervously fingered the gun but kept it pointed at the ground. He broke eye contact with Ray, as though haunted by what he saw in those eyes. Without another word, Ray turned and walked away, up the driveway to the gravel road, toward home. By the time Chris nearly caught up, Ray was 30 or 40 yards down the road.

"I can drive you home," Chris called out.

"No need, I can walk," Ray replied. "I don't think he's gonna hurt you anymore."

COUNTY
Q

CHAPTER 15

THE BETTER PART OF A WEEK LATER, Ray was packing for the Cities when there was a knock on the front door. Thinking it was for Moose or Gin, Ray went right on packing. The knock repeated a second and third time. Slightly annoyed that no one had gotten the door, Ray bounded down the stairs, peeking out the window to see who'd come calling.

Chris Driscoll. Standing on the front steps. Just turning to leave when Ray pulled open the door. "Chris! What are you doing here? I didn't know you knew where I lived. Are you okay? I've been wanting to check in with you but realized I don't have your number. I thought of stopping out at your place, but didn't know if you'd want that or how your dad would react. It's so good seeing you, for real. Come in ... please, come on in."

Ray's initial assessment was that she was fine by all appearances, no visible injuries. Upon second consideration, she seemed better than fine. Her hair was brushed, secured behind her ears with barrettes—unusual—and she wore cut-off denim shorts, a black sleeveless Nirvana T-shirt, newish looking sneakers.

"I hope I'm not interrupting anything ... I had to tell you what happened after your little encounter with my old man." Chris spoke excitedly.

"Don't worry, everything's cool," she reassured Ray, who beckoned her to enter.

"You weren't expecting me ... I don't want to intrude ... I'm sure your folks wouldn't ... wouldn't appreciate that," said Chris, stammering. "I was thinking maybe we could walk around or something."

"Sure, I guess, yeah. But you really can come in, that's not a problem."

"Probly better if I didn't."

Ray shouted back into the house, "I'm going out!" With no sidewalks on the Hill, they walked down the middle of the street. Chris didn't wait for Ray to ask.

"Oh my God, you won't believe what happened. My old man's been in the hospital. You put him there, I'm sure of it."

"What're you talking about? How'd I do that?"

"All I know is after you left, I was sure he'd beat the shit out of me. Instead, he can't stop complaining how bad his back hurts. Then his stomach starts aching. Before you know it, he's puking his guts out. Overheard him telling my mom his dick's burning. Not long after he's screaming in pain every time he goes to pee."

Ray gaped at Chris slack jawed.

"Apparently, he was pissing blood. That's what Mom told Mickey, told him he was running a high fever, had the chills all night. He was in bad shape like that for like three days, carrying on about how it feels like his dick's gonna explode. Mom tries convincing him he should go to the hospital. We ain't got insurance, so he don't want to go, but we're all telling him they've got to take you at the emergency room whether you got insurance or not."

"You got him to go to the hospital?"

"Yeah, he went. Mom was in no shape to drive him, so I took him in, drove him back home after they released him. And here's the good part ... rather than just listen to him moan and groan in the car, I told him what happened when boys at school messed with you, how Tom Tetzlaff pissed his pants, how Ken Kaczmarczyk had like a panic attack or seizure or something. I told him that's why I invited you over to our house. He hasn't laid a hand on me since. You got him good and spooked."

Ray stared at Chris in disbelief.

"Sounds like he passed a gallstone or something. It's not anything I did."

"Kidney stone, that's what the doctors said it was. But he don't know for certain you didn't give him that stone, and that works out good for me."

"You've got to stop spreading stories about Tetzlaff and Kaz. And don't tell anyone about your dad landing in the hospital."

"Like I'm gonna tell anyone what my old man was doing with me. Like I want that getting around. You're the one who needs to promise never to say anything."

"You know I won't."

Without breaking stride, Chris wrapped both arms around Ray's midsection, her cheek resting on a bony shoulder for four or five steps. She let go once she could tell Ray found it cumbersome to walk with her draped like this. As they'd been talking, they came down off the Hill, past the mill pond, down Main Street.

"Can I show you something?" Ray asked. "It's out past the cemetery."

"There's nothing past the cemetery. Just fields and woods."

"It's in the woods."

"You want to take me out in the woods ... hoping I'll show you a thing or two?" she teased.

"Nothing like *that*."

Chris laughed. "And I don't have to worry that you're some ax murderer who's luring me out there just to kill me and cut me into pieces?"

"You got nothing to worry about," Ray shot back, now playing along with the teasing. "Most likely."

"Oooh, sounds like I better watch my back." Chris laughed again—an unencumbered kind of laugh. There was a small measure of buoyance in her demeanor and a bounce to her step that was missing before.

Beyond the business establishments on Main Street—some open, others closed—they walked past rows of houses to the outskirts of town, continuing on as the street turned into a trunk highway. Ray spotted Mrs. Morger in her front yard and waved. Colette returned the gesture.

"You know those people?" Chris asked.

Ray nodded.

"I thought they were supposed to be mean or crazy ... Or both."

"Definitely not crazy, not the slightest bit mean. About the nicest people I know. All the nonsense about their place being haunted, that's not true either."

Chris looked surprised to hear it.

"Where we are going is on their land. They don't mind. They let me go back there whenever I want."

They continued along the gravel shoulder of the highway, skirted the fence of the cemetery. Ray pointed the way to the pocked dirt lane that dead-ended at the edge of the woods. Off in the distance the twin steeples loomed over the rest of the forest.

"See those two pines right next to each other?" asked Ray, pointing.

"Is that what you wanted to show me?" Chris answered, sounding rather unimpressed.

"Nah, where I'm taking you is pretty much right under those trees."

Chris looked skeptical but followed along as Ray plunged into the thick underbrush. Thirty feet later, Ray found the cow path snaking through the bushes, pulled back branches and snapped off twigs to clear the way for Chris, extending a hand to her as they plowed through the thicket. Thorny stems scratched her bare legs, once badly enough to draw blood.

In fairly short order they heard the trickling sound of the stream and reached the tiny tributary moments later. First Ray and then Chris held their arms out to their sides as they stepped gingerly across the rocks that served as their bridge. Ray cautioned Chris to watch her footing as she stepped from the last rock to the peat bog at the water's edge. She accomplished the maneuver like a gymnast on a balance beam.

They trundled on, first up as the ground rose, then down into the swale signaling to Ray the destination was near. A few more steps and there it was, the peculiar configuration of forest undergrowth forming an entryway into the spacious oval room. Thickly clumped trees and bushes formed bizarrely symmetrical and nearly impenetrable walls, overhanging branches creating a generously arched ceiling. On the ground at their feet was a carpet of pine needles, devoid of weeds or tree seedlings. Chris studied the space wide-eyed, as stupefied as Ray had been.

"Morger calls it the cathedral."

"Did he make this?"

"Claims he didn't. Says it's always been like this ... for as long as he can remember."

"You believe him?"

"No reason not to. Can't see any signs that branches were cut or trees planted. Looks like everything just grew this way. Strange, isn't it?"

Chris signaled her agreement.

"I camp out here overnight sometimes," Ray said.

Chris noticed a spot near the back of the space where there was ash instead of pine needles, encircled by softball-sized rocks.

"I was thinking if you ever need to get away from home, you know, to be safe, you could always come here."

"It'd freaked me out to come here alone or spend the night."

"I'd be willing to keep you company."

Chris contorted her nose and puckered her lips the way she did when she was about to poke fun.

"I might have to take you up on that offer."

"It's like my own secret hiding place. I can get away and be alone with my thoughts," Ray said.

As the two sat in silence for three, maybe four minutes, Chris studied Ray. What an odd boy, she thought, but in a good way, so unlike all the other boys.

"Do you want to stop by the Morgers on our way back into town? I can introduce you to them."

"Sure, I guess. You think they'd mind?"

"Not at all. They'd love to meet you."

They left the cathedral, made their way back out of the woods, hopped the cemetery fence, walked through the graveyard, proceeded to the Morger place. Chris hung back as Ray bounded up the stairs onto the porch and rapped on the screen door. No one answered. The inside door was closed but unlocked. Ray opened it with a turn of the knob, motioning to Chris to come in. Once Ray disappeared into the house, she cautiously tip-toed up the stairs and across the porch, stopping at the door to peer through the screen.

"You don't have to stay outside. They always tell me to make myself at home even when they're away."

"So, they leave the house unlocked and anyone can just barge in anytime? Aren't they worried someone will rob the place?"

"I think they figger there's nothing in here worth taking. They got this super old cookie jar, though. Looks antique. Right over here."

Ray brought the white ceramic jar into the light for Chris to see. She examined the black eyes and brilliant red lips, yellow-trimmed apron adorned with poinsettias, red bonnet and wicker basket full of brightly colored flowers. Ray lifted the chubby upper torso that served as the jar's lid. Chris moved in close, peering into the opening to find the container filled nearly to the brim with shortbread. Resting on top of the pile of cookies, however, was a thrice-folded piece of paper.

"What's this?" she wondered, taking the note from the jar, handing it to Ray.

Ray unfolded the single sheet of ruled notebook paper, studying the 13 words on the page with a most bewildered look. The message was handwritten in blue ink but did not appear to be in Morger's or Colette's hand. Ray was familiar with their penmanship and this looked different, a more elegant and exacting cursive than either of them normally produced.

Heaven is not a house you move into. It is one you build.

"What's it say?" Chris asked.

"It says heaven's not a house you move into, it's one you build."

"What do you make of that?"

"Not sure. Weird thing is, I've seen their handwriting, the both of them. Neither one wrote this."

"Then who did?"

"Beats me."

Ray refolded the note, pocketing it. They each took a cookie before Ray showed Chris around the house. They lingered in each room, looking around, only briefly poking their heads in the two bedrooms.

"This place kind of gives me the creeps," said Chris.

"Why?"

"It's like going back in time, everything in here looks a hundred years old. And that message you say neither of them wrote. Like some letter from the grave."

"They ain't dead," Ray answered, sounding a little annoyed. "We just saw Mrs. Morger on our way to the woods, remember?"

"Or you thought you did," she retorted with a smirk.

"Very funny ... Maybe it's a sign. Or a reminder."

"What is?"

"The message. Why else was it waiting for us in the cookie jar?"

"How do you know it was left for us? Could've just as well been left for them. You said yourself neither of them wrote it. Maybe you should put it back."

"I just have this feeling it was meant for us. I'll show it to them the next time I see them, ask 'em where they think it came from."

Chris and Ray let themselves out, closing the door behind them, walking back up the long driveway to the road into town. They made idle conversation on the way to Ray's house on the Hill, mostly about summer plans and favorite rock bands. Ray tried convincing Chris to let Gin give her a ride home, but she was adamant she'd rather walk the roughly three miles to her place. Unspoken was her discomfort with having Ray's mother see where and how she lived. Ray sensed this and let the matter drop.

They said their goodbyes at Ray's doorstep. Chris lit a cigarette, walked across the lawn and down the street. Ray watched as her silhouette grew smaller and smaller, mesmerized by the shape of her, the way those hips swayed when she walked. The trance broke only when a hand plunged into a pocket and happened upon that mysterious note from the cookie jar.

COUNTY
Q

CHAPTER 16

RAY'S MUCH-ANTICIPATED WEEK IN THE CITIES came and went by fast. Annie and Ray spent most of one day riding roller coasters, went to a Twins game one night. Other days they biked, skateboarded, played video games. Grace took them to the Mall of America, where they rode more rides, ate fast food, window-shopped, people-watched. Annie wanted to go see *The Truman Show* at a nearby multiplex; Ray thought *Armageddon* on a big screen sounded better. Grace settled it by taking them to *Mulan*. When Gin came to get Ray at the end of the week, she collected Annie as well to bring her back to Faith.

With far less to do, the first week felt like two, the second like six. Oddly enough, that seemed to suit Annie and Ray just fine. Annie liked coming and going as they pleased, not having any set agenda, bolting out the door after breakfast, not being expected back until suppertime.

Ray was itching to play ball, but Annie wasn't into it, so they negotiated mutually agreeable ways to pass the time. A few times they helped stock shelves at the grocery store, but mostly they were free to make things up as they went along. They went for walks this way and that, rode bikes around town, hung out at the battlefield, where younger kids pulled them into an impromptu game a time or two.

They gathered up used aerosol cans, got a fire going in an old steel barrel out back of the shuttered paper mill, tossed the cans into the drum, turning them into flaming projectiles. That had them scrambling to stamp out a resulting grass fire. They ventured out into the countryside to swim and fish in the Popple, one time lying in the tall grass of a farmer's hayfield for close to two hours talking about much of nothing. Running out of topics, Ray pitched the idea of going to see the cathedral and visit the Morgers. This struck Annie as a fine idea, especially when Ray filled her in about the kids believing the place was haunted and the grown-ups' warnings to stay away.

Remembering how Chris Driscoll had been bloodied by the walk in the woods, Ray recommended Annie wear long pants. Down the Hill they went, to the mill pond, over to Main Street, snaking through the rows of nearly identical houses, out past what used to be the A&W root beer stand.

Continuing along the shoulder of the highway, Ray pointed out the Morger farm but suggested they stop on their way back. Annie thought the place could very well be haunted by the looks of it but kept her assessment to herself. The two continued on to the cemetery just down the road from the Morgers, reminding Annie of a Stephen King novel.

"Which one?" Ray asked.

"*Pet Sematary*. Super creepy. Said himself it was the only book he ever wrote that scared him. Got me listening to the Ramones," she said, calling attention to the graphic on her shirt by pulling it outward and upward with both hands. "A bunch of their songs are mentioned in the book. I s'pose it explains how I got into the whole goth-punk thing."

Ray and Annie entered the cemetery through the broken gate, lingering in front of a few burial sites, then weaving through tombstones to the rear of the graveyard. They climbed over the fence, ambled across the pasture, down the fenced lane to the edge of the woods. Wading through the thick tangle of tag alders and prickly shrubs annoyed Annie, making the well-trampled path coming up on their left a welcome sight.

Moments later they reached the burbling brook. Ray stepped briskly from rock to rock and made the short hop to the soft ground on the other side of the stream. Annie followed close behind. She hesitated from her perch on the last rock and Ray instructed her to aim her leap for one of the grassy lumps protruding from the slough. She missed her mark ever so slightly, the melon-sized mound gave way under her weight, causing first one foot then the other to sink into the muck. She was a good sport about it.

Annie's sopping Chuck Taylors squished as she followed Ray to higher ground, over the crest, down into a swale, making her suspect more marshland was up ahead. Her eyes met Ray's, she held up a hand, drawing a finger to her lips. Ray froze in place. A bird chirped, then nothing. Tree leaves gently rustled, moved by the faintest of breezes, then again nothing.

"What is it?" Ray finally whispered, breaking the silence.

"I'm blown away by how quiet it is. No horns, no sirens. Nothing. Nobody. Barely a sound."

Ray hadn't really thought much about that before.

"Where's this cathedral?"

"Right up ahead. Just beyond that line of trees over there," Ray answered, pointing and tramping on through the woods until a thick cluster of tree trunks and branches forming an archway of sorts was within Annie's sight.

Suddenly, unexpectedly, the shroud of quiet was pierced by the agonized wail of a large animal. Another clipped snort, a deep and prolonged groan, a series of frantic-sounding grunts. Unmistakably a cow bellering, one in considerable distress. The sounds came from just beyond the archway. Ray inched toward them; Annie stayed put. At the opening, Ray peered inside, saw a black-and-white Holstein prone on the pine needles some 15 feet away. The cow let out a higher-pitched moan. Ray turned and waved vigorously for Annie to approach.

"It's a cow calving. Nothing to be afraid of."

"A cow doing what?"

"Giving birth. Come see!"

It only then dawned on Annie that this cathedral Ray had been going on about was nature's doing, not some building erected in the woods by human hands. She proceeded cautiously through the archway, her eyes scanning a dense awning of foliage at least two body lengths high. Ray stood perhaps six feet behind and slightly to one side of the laboring animal sprawled before them.

Annie gave the cow a wide berth, taking a circuitous route to a position behind Ray. From there she could see bloody membrane emerging from under the cow's raised tail. After a mighty heave pale hooves and a pinkish snout resting on twiggy black forelimbs made a bashful appearance before receding back inside. Minutes passed. With another strained push by the mother the hooves, forelimbs and snout again squeezed through the narrow passageway until they could see black hide stretched tightly over a flat face with two dark eyes set wide. Soon the ears were visible, then the neck, the shoulders.

What had been happening in fits and starts gained momentum as the slender barrel of the body oozed out, followed quickly by the haunches. Wiry hind legs unfurled, with almost comically oversized hocks and hooves. The mother lurched and wheeled around, immediately starting to lick the slimy newborn clean. Both Ray and Annie were astonished by how quickly the cow was up on all fours, with afterbirth dangling from under her tail, how in another instant the calf was standing on wobbling legs, unsteady but determined to locate its first meal.

Within moments it was eagerly nursing, impatiently bunting the mother's udder, creamy yellow colostrum oozing from the sides of its mouth, as the doting cow dutifully licked her calf's coat to a lustrous sheen. When all the afterbirth was expelled and fell to the ground, the cow wasted no time in devouring it.

"Gross!" Annie shrieked. "Why's she eating it?"

"No idea," Ray answered. What Ray did know is they should alert the Morgers at once that a calf was just born on their property. Annie wasn't quite ready to leave.

"Who made this?"

"Mr. Morger told me it's been like this for as long as he can remember. Been here a bunch of times, this is the first I've ever seen an animal in here."

"Weird. Doesn't look natural, does it?

"It doesn't, but it is."

"It's what, weird or natural?"

"Both."

Annie's eyes explored the enclosure, surveying the walls, lingering on the ceiling before returning to the nursing calf, then to Ray.

"It does look like a cathedral in a way," she observed.

"We should go," said Ray. "We need to let the Morgers know about the calf. You can meet them."

Annie cast one last glance in the cow's direction before turning toward the archway. The Holstein contentedly murmured to her offspring in a soft, nurturing tone, nuzzling it lovingly. "Mmmm. Mmm."

Ray made haste with Annie doing her best to keep up as they marched briskly up the knoll, down into the marshy trough, across the stream, through the thicket, out of the woods, up the dirt lane, around the cemetery, along the highway shoulder toward town. Ray was nearly at a run when they turned into the driveway, veering off on the narrow path cutting across the yard worn bare by repeated footsteps. Annie caught up to Ray as they reached the steps, their combined weight producing more pronounced creaking in the porch floorboards than usual. Ray didn't bother knocking on the screen door, flinging it open and pounding on the inside door.

"Hello! Is anyone home?" Ray hollered. "You gotta see this! You won't believe it!"

The door swung open just as Ray was fixing to pound on it again. Morger stood there in a faded denim shirt and baggy tan corduroys cinched at the waste by a leather belt, stroked the stubble on his drooping jowls, peering inquiringly over his reading glasses at the visitors.

"What's all the fuss?"

"This is my cousin Ann," Ray began. "I was showing her the cathedral, guess what we saw?"

"Whoa, not so fast ... Pleased to meet you, young lady," the old man said. "Now what's this you've seen?"

"A cow calving."

"You're not pulling my leg?"

"No sir ... Ann can tell you ... she saw it too."

Annie nodded earnestly.

"Must be one of Ackerman's cows got through the fence again. Not surprised she hunkered down there. Nice secluded spot. I'll call him, let him know where she's at. Are the cow and calf all right?"

"They seem fine. Both were up on their feet when we left."

"Always a good sign. Well, come on in, have a seat while I call Ackerman." Morger turned away, calling out, "Colette, we have company!"

Morger excused himself as soon as his wife arrived to greet their visitors.

"This is my cousin Ann. She's visiting for a couple of weeks," Ray told Colette, slightly stooped but still elegant looking, approaching with arms outstretched.

"Delighted to meet you, Ann. Where's home?"

"St. Paul."

"Lovely ... You don't see cows dropping calves there every day."

"Uh-uh."

"Come sit. Let me get you something," Colette said, turning to the kitchen.

Ray and Annie remained standing, hovering near the dining room table.

"We saw the calf come out," Ray said excitedly. "Saw the whole birth. Never saw it happen up close like that before."

"The miracle of life," Colette replied, returning from the kitchen with a tray carrying a pitcher of lemonade, a tea kettle along with several cups and glasses. "Such a wondrous thing to witness. A bona fide miracle."

Colette made another trip to the kitchen, returning with the cookie jar.

"Macarons," she said, holding out the jar, removing the lid, revealing a colorful assortment of delicate sandwich cookies—some yellow, some pink, some blue, some green. "Do you know these, Ann?"

"I don't," Annie confessed. "They look good, kind of like Oreos, 'cept all different colors."

Annie reached in the jar, opting for bright pink, examining the airy wafers and creamy filling before taking a bite. Ray selected a yellow one.

"Mmm, these are delicious. May I have another?" Annie said with her hand to her mouth to conceal her chewing.

"Have as many as you like. Glad you enjoy them."

Annie glanced around, surveying the house.

"Are you cat people or dog people?" she asked Colette.

"Neither. We're country folk, no pets in the house. Morger grew up here on the farm. They had cats out in the barn to keep the vermin down, a dog outside to watch over things, help herd the cows in from pasture. No need for that anymore since we're no longer farming."

"Mrs. Morger, I want to show you and your husband something," Ray interjected. "Remember a couple of weeks ago when I was walking by and waved?"

Colette gestured that she did recall it.

"That was Chris Driscoll with me. We hiked to the cathedral, stopped in here on our way back but you were gone by then. The door was open, so we let ourselves in ... hope you don't mind."

"Course not. You're always welcome, you know that."

"Showed her the cookie jar, lifted the lid, found this," Ray said, holding out the folded note. "Was wondering if you could explain it ... who it's for, who wrote it, what it means. I've seen your handwriting, and your husband's, and it doesn't look like yours."

Colette took the note, unfolded it, studied it carefully.

"This was in the jar?"

Ray nodded affirmatively.

"I've never seen this before and I'm afraid I don't know where it came from. What it means is clear enough. But I don't know how this got in our cookie jar. Maybe Morger will know."

"Know what?" Morger asked from behind Colette as he returned from his phone call.

Colette passed the note to him, explaining that Ray found it in the jar. Morger examined it meticulously, turning it over as though looking for some clue.

"Do you know the handwriting?" Ray asked.

"I do not."

"Have any idea who might've written it or how it got in the jar?" Ray asked.

"None whatsoever," Morger replied tersely. "I sure didn't write it. This is curious, this is."

"That's what I thought too."

"What can't be explained is magic," Morger concluded, still puzzling over the page. "I was right, the cow is Ackerman's. He and Punk are coming over. Will need me to show them where she and the calf are. They'd about given up looking for her. Darnedest thing how cows will go into hiding to have a calf if you don't get them confined to a pen in time."

Annie tried getting a look at the note, itching to ask what the whole conversation was all about, but Morger circling back to the calving piqued her interest too.

"After the calf was born, this slimy stuff was hanging out of the cow. When it dropped to the ground, she ate it. Kinda disgusting to be honest."

"Cows eat the placenta to get rid of evidence of the birth that could attract predators," Morger explained. "Inherited instinct, hardwired in them even after all these years of domestication. It's not something they do only if they give birth outdoors. Even when they freshen in the safety of a barn with absolutely no danger of predators getting to them, they eat the placenta. There's no real need anymore. Just instinct kicking in."

Ray was eager to leave before Punk Ackerman and his dad got there. With Annie distracted and her curiosity sufficiently placated, Ray said goodbye to Colette and Morger, pulling Annie toward the door. Once they were outside, she started peppering Ray with questions.

"What was that all about?"

"What was *what* all about?"

"That note. Can I see it?"

Ray pulled the folded-up piece of paper out of a pants pocket, handing it to Annie. She unfolded the sheet, turning it over like Morger had, searching for something more than the 13 words.

"You sure neither of them wrote this? One of them could be a calligrapher."

"What's that?"

"You've seriously never heard of calligraphy?"

"No."

"It's artistic handwriting. Really beautiful. They might not normally write like this, but one of them could know how."

"They both said it wasn't theirs, you heard them."

"You believe them?"

"Why wouldn't I?"

"So, you buy that this just magically appeared," she said, waving the note at Ray.

"I don't know who's behind it or where it came from. I was hoping one of them could tell me. I don't think he really believes it's magic; he says that all the time, whenever something stumps him."

"You and some girl were snooping around in their house when they weren't home and happened to find this?"

"I stop by to visit all the time; they don't expect me to knock anymore. I was with this girl Chris Driscoll. We're friends, sort of. She just finished her junior year. I wanted to introduce her to them."

Annie looked askance.

"Just friends, nothing more than that," Ray quickly added. "Not even really friends. She had some troubles at home, asked me to do her a favor."

"Uh-huh," Annie mumbled in amusement.

"It's not like that."

"Like *what?*" Annie teased.

Ray protested no further.

"I don't know, everyone around here could be right, maybe that place *is* haunted. You have to admit, this is pretty creepy," Annie muttered, her eyes still fixed on those 13 words.

Ray had no answers, no explanations, no words. Nick Szymanski came to mind. Tom Tetzlaff. Lisa Lewandowski. Kenny Kaczmarczyk. Paul Driscoll. Ray was tempted to let Annie in on those curious coincidences but thought better of it. Might freak her out and drive her away. A risk not worth taking.

At supper, Gin asked Ray and Annie what they'd been up to that day. Annie was eager to talk about the note and the Morgers, but Ray headed her off.

"We saw a calf born ... out in the woods," Ray announced, shrewdly avoiding any mention of the Morgers in Moose's presence. "It was one of the Ackerman family's cows."

"Bet that's the first time you've ever seen that, huh Annie?" Gin said excitedly.

"Yeah, for sure. It was amazing, but also kinda gross. The calf came out all wet and slimy, and the mom ate the sack the calf had been inside."

Both Gin and Moose grimaced a little, both thinking this was inappropriate mealtime conversation, but neither reprimanded Annie.

"School's gonna be starting soon. You been giving any thought to what you might want to do after graduation, Annie?" Moose inquired, more for the purposes of changing the subject than for curiosity's sake.

"Not sure yet, probly go to college."

"Any idea yet what you might want to major in?"

Annie shrugged. "Haven't really given it a lot of thought. I'm only going to be a sophomore, so I have a while to decide. I'm thinking sociology, psychology, English lit—those are my favorite subjects."

Disapproval was written all over Moose's face, and he made no effort to hide it.

"What kind of job you gonna get with a degree like that?"

She shrugged again, sinking a little lower in her chair.

Gin noticed Annie's body language. "There's plenty of time to sort all of that out. It's great that you already have a good idea of what interests you."

Moose couldn't contain himself.

"It's none too early to be deciding what's next after high school," he said pointedly, looking first at Annie, then Ray. "By your junior year at the latest, you should have a good idea which direction you're heading, that's gonna determine which schools you apply to. And you best be thinking ahead about what kind of jobs will be out there in the field you choose."

Ray looked down at the table but could feel Moose bearing down.

"That goes for you too, Ray. If you're not gonna play sports, you ought to have a part-time job outside of school to start gaining work experience."

Ray got up and left the table, leaving behind a half-eaten plate of food.

Moose rolled his eyes, shook his head. His face flushed, frustration coming to a boil.

"Or you can be a lazy good-for-nothing!" he said acidly. "You can make something of yourself or amount to nothing. Your choice, buddy."

```
COUNTY
Q
```

CHAPTER 17

NEARLY THREE YEARS PASSED BEFORE RAY saw Chris Driscoll again. She went through with her plan to drop out of school, vanishing from the scene altogether. Her brother said she was in Wausau. Either didn't know or wouldn't say more than that. Ray was keeping a low profile at school, with a different friend group, hanging out mostly with Ev Meaney, occasionally his sister Linh, and two new kids, Frankie López and Willie García.

Ray started out calling them by their full given names—Francisco and Guillermo—and was among the last to adopt the shortened handles, only doing so when both boys showed eagerness and determination to assimilate, an impulse Ray understood but did not regard fondly.

Ray avoided opportunities to date, even turning down two invitations to go to prom—one from Eileen Schneider, another from newcomer Rosa Vazquez. With gym being optional for upperclassmen, Ray dropped the class, much to Gin's dismay. Moose, on the other hand, took it all as validation of his harsh judgment, as did the fact that midway through senior year Ray had not started much less submitted a single college application.

Many a dinner-table conversation degenerated from small talk to nagging to belittling. Ray let it go in one ear and out the other, but it fanned the flames of marital discord. Gin and Moose barely spoke most days and took to sleeping in separate beds. Despite the deteriorating condition of his marriage, Moose refused to relent, in one breath offering Ray a job, in the next a tongue-lashing for lacking initiative. Gin tried her best to compensate with a sympathetic ear and steadfast encouragement.

The parental seesawing continued for months. Ray proved remarkably impervious to Moose's upbraiding but grew increasingly aware of—and troubled by—the toll all this was taking on Gin. Frequent visits to the Morgers continued, but Ray almost always declined invitations to stay for supper and rarely spent the night there. If they felt snubbed or were hurt by Ray's diminished presence, they hid it well. They sensed that Ray felt an obligation to be at home for Mom's sake.

One day well after the spring melt, Ray spotted a familiar figure walking in downtown Faith and did a double take. The young woman was more made up and provocatively dressed, but Ray still recognized her and called out from a block away. The woman kept walking. Another considerably louder call got the woman's attention, causing her to turn and look.

"Chris! It's me ... Ray."

She hesitated at first, then walked in Ray's direction. As she got closer and her face came into focus, Ray was struck by how her eyes weren't as bright. Her expression was vacant, her appearance haggard. She hardly looked excited to see an old acquaintance, but Ray was undeterred.

"Oh my God, it's been so long. It's great seeing you."

Chris managed a somewhat forced smile but did not immediately speak.

"Mickey told me you're living in Wausau."

"I was. I'm back here now."

"You're living with your folks?"

"Fuck no. I mean, I'm in touch with them, but ..."

"Where are you staying then?"

"Know that place on Pine Street, used to be a hotel called the Hideaway before it closed? It's got new ownership, they rent out rooms by the month now. All I can afford."

"What were you doing in Wausau?"

"Nothing I'm proud of."

"What're you doing now?"

"Nothing to be proud of."

Three years had put quite a distance between them.

"I dropped out of school, had to get out of there," said Chris after a prolonged silence.

"Out of school ... or away from home?"

"Both."

"What took you to Wausau?"

"I knew a couple of people who'd gone there, said it's big compared to here, lots of jobs. Thought I'd give it a try. Was waiting tables, rented an apartment, was working out okay for a while. I haven't been well, the cost of my medicine and rent was more than I could make waitressing, so ... auditioned at a club, got a gig dancing."

"Wow, cool!"

"It's not what you think, not like Broadway or Vegas or anything. Just a dive bar in front of a bunch of scuzzy guys," she said, looking uncomfortable and ashamed.

Ray didn't know what to say. That came off to Chris as clueless.

"You know, a strip joint ... Wouldn't mind tending bar there, tips are good, I could keep my clothes on, but they want me on stage."

"It's good you stopped."

"I didn't. Still drive over there once a week. Dance two or three times a week over in Neillsville, too. Can make four or five hundred at the club in Wausau, sometimes six on a good night. A couple hundred a night at the other place."

"You make that much dancing?"

"Some of it dancing, most of it from tips for doing other shit."

Ray looked at Chris inquiringly. The cosmetics couldn't conceal her pain, but she didn't elaborate.

"Look, I ain't proud of what I do, but it pays the rent, keeps gas in the car. Gotta have my medicine, otherwise my stomach hurts so bad it doubles me over. I get these horrible migraines."

Ray gave Chris a hug, recalled their last time together, released her.

"Remember that note we found in the cookie jar?"

Chris stared blankly, then nodded.

"Heaven's not a place you move into someday, it's one you build yourself, right here, right now. I think I know what we're supposed to make."

"Um ... okay," Chris muttered, now looking half dumbfounded and half amused.

"A shelter ... for kids being treated the way your dad treated you ... for anyone really, anyone needing a safe place to stay," Ray explained. "You can live there too ... get away from what's making you sick. Already have a name for it."

"All right ..." Chris replied barely above a whisper, still puzzled.

"Ebiyan House. Ev Meaney, you know him, he's Native, told me *ebiyan*'s the word for heaven in his tribal language."

"Are you serious?"

"Don't you like the name?"

"No, I mean, are you serious about doing this?"

"Dead serious! Ev's already in ... he's gonna help."

Chris looked down at the ground, then up to the sky, letting out a muffled laugh. She peered into Ray's eyes, then looked away as if she'd stared directly at the sun.

"This is completely nuts, but count me in."

Ray took a step back as though staggered by a punch.

"This is gonna be good, I know it will. I'll be in touch ... Wait, how do I get ahold of you?"

"You've already got ahold of me." A hint of her old smirk appeared. "Don't have a phone right now or I'd give you my number, but you know where I'm staying."

"Right ... This is gonna be good, you'll see."

The next order of business had to be a visit to the Morgers. A rush of adrenaline sped Ray's stride to something of a trot, slowed only by the stairs to the porch. By the fourth rap on the door's cockeyed frame, Morger answered.

"Door's open!"

Ray flung open the screen and turned the knob of the inside door which, sure enough, was unlocked.

"Hey!"

"We're in here," Colette called from the sitting room. Ray found Morger in the armchair, Colette on the sofa. Colette noticed Ray was winded.

"You look exhausted. Come sit down, catch your breath. Let me get you something to drink."

Ray smiled at Colette, then abruptly turned to Morger.

"You told me once don't make plans, find a purpose."

"I remember," Morger replied.

"Couldn't stop thinking about the message Chris Driscoll and I found in your cookie jar. 'Heaven's not a place you move into, it's one you build.' Don't know if I ever told you or if you heard from others, but Chris's dad did horrible things to her. Ev Meaney and I want to build a safe place for kids, or really anyone. Call it Ebiyan House—that's the word for heaven in his native language. Just talked to Chris about it, she wants to help. Hoping we can get her to stay there once it's finished so she can get away from what's happening to her."

"What does she need to get away from?" Colette asked, handing Ray a glass of juice.

"Her dad was abusing her. She dropped out of school, moved to Wausau, waited tables but had a hard time making enough to pay rent. Started dancing nude at some bar. Doing other stuff with customers too, wouldn't say exactly what. I think she's gotten into drugs. Pretty messed up."

"She's back in town?" asked Colette.

"Yeah, staying at that place that used to be the Hideaway Hotel. Apparently, rooms are now rented by the month."

"*Mon Dieu*," Colette muttered under her breath. "She needs to get out of there. You see a steady stream of men coming and going, that's no place for her to be. You go find her, tell her she can stay with us, as long as she wants."

Ray nodded, flashed Colette a look of gratitude, and turned to Morger, who signaled he agreed. When he spoke, he was uncharacteristically brief.

"I always think of what to say. Colette thinks of what to do."

Colette wasn't done thinking.

"You can build your shelter on our land, right along the main road where everyone will be able to see it. I can't think of a better use for the land."

Morger again signaled his consent. Ray wrapped Colette in a warm embrace.

"Never stand up the heart," Morger said, realizing instantly the sentiment didn't register with either Ray or Colette. "Don't delay acting on your dreams," he clarified.

Ray took the advice to heart, bid farewell to the Morgers, headed out to tell Chris of their offer. The walk was a quick one, up the road past the old root beer stand until it became Main Street, a left on Second, down a block to where it intersected with Pine Street. What looked like an unusually long ranch-style home was set back from the street with cement parking stalls in front of each of 10 numbered doors, five on one side of what was labeled the office, five on the other side.

It occurred to Ray that Chris hadn't said which room was hers. Starting at one end of the building, Ray knocked on doors, number 10 first, then 9. No one answered. Hearing the rap on 9's door, someone in number 8 pulled open the drapes a smidge and peered out. It wasn't Chris, so Ray moved on, knocking on the door to number 7. There was movement inside, moments later the door cracked open, just enough to see a middle-aged woman with heavy mascara, wrapped in a bedsheet, peeking out.

"Oh, sorry, wrong door, I guess. I was looking for Chris Driscoll."

"Three."

"Um, thanks. Sorry for bothering you."

Ray proceeded past the office to number 3. A badly rusted silver Chevy Cavalier was parked outside, next to a somewhat newer Ford pickup. One tap on the door yielded no results. After three more in rapid succession, Chris opened the door, stepped outside, quickly closing it behind her.

"Can I come in?" asked Ray.

"Better if you don't. The place is a mess."

"I went to the Morgers to tell them about the plans. They offered a piece of land to build on."

"Great!" Chris said with manufactured enthusiasm.

"That's not the only thing. They want you to move in with them. You've been in their house; it's nothing fancy, but it's better than this place."

"Naw ... wouldn't be right. I can't impose on them."

"I didn't put them up to it, they offered, for as long as you want. What's this, one room? Do you even have anywhere to cook?"

"I have a hot plate and a toaster oven. Those are fine for fixing meals."

"They have that nice big kitchen. Spare bedroom. Got your name on it."

Ray could tell Chris was holding something back.

"Come on, they want to help, and I don't want to wait until the shelter gets built to get you out of here. Who knows how long that will be."

Chris hemmed and hawed, fidgeting with her hair.

"Here's the thing ... um ... I mean, you know, I haven't been well ... um, it wouldn't be fair to them to have me underfoot when I'm in this shape. They shouldn't have to ..."

"They want to!" Ray blurted out, cutting her off. "Look, I'm not blind, I can see how you're living, what it's doing to you. You'll have a bed to sleep in, food to eat, until you're better. You won't have to worry about money, you can stop. Please say yes, please."

Chris's expression softened and her eyes watered.

"Come on, you were the one who said I was full of shit when I told you I didn't do anything to Tom Tetzlaff. You were convinced I brought on that episode Kaz had. You believed I could somehow make your dad stop doing what he was doing. You were sure what happened to him was because of me. Remember?"

Chris looked somewhat defiant, but nodded weakly.

"Your dad used you. All these men who go watch you dance and do whatever with you are using you. The Morgers want to help, *I* want to help, so you don't get used no more. Their house ain't haunted, it's enchanted, I'm telling you."

Ray pulled Chris into a firm embrace, her face buried at the junction of Ray's neck and right shoulder. Ray could feel Chris's heart pounding. Then the beat began to slow, her grip relaxed. She labored to draw a breath as though the air was thin and oxygen was elusive. She pulled away, an almost frightened look in her eyes. She knew what she was going to do.

"I'll pack my things."

CHAPTER 18

COLETTE WAS SURPRISED BUT DELIGHTED when she opened the door. Ray and Chris stood on the porch. Even before Chris's belongings were unloaded from her car and brought indoors, she was shown to her room.

"Thank you for taking her in," Ray said softly to Morger once he returned from the spare bedroom.

"I consider it a blessing. This is about the best thing Colette and I have been able to do since we got back from our mission."

Four sets of hands and Chris's few possessions made for light work. After the last of it was moved in, Colette stayed with Chris to get her situated. Morger returned to the sitting room, planting himself in the upholstered armchair. Ray plopped down on the couch.

"Do you ever think of going back to Africa?"

"Not as missionaries, that's for sure."

"You didn't like being a missionary?"

"I very much enjoyed our time there, but no, I didn't end up feeling missionary work was worthwhile."

Morger paused, but Ray could tell more to the story was coming so said nothing.

"You know, we spent some time in a little hamlet called Gninela, got to know this woman named Djeneba. Beautiful. Smart. Quite possibly the most cheerful person I've ever met. She had this laugh that bubbled up from deep inside her belly, ending with a little whoop that I can still hear like she's right here in this room."

The old man shook his head, absent-mindedly picking at worn-through patches in the arms of his chair.

"We were in Gninela at the time of year when her family's granary ran dry—they call it the hungry season. Djeneba was spending her days making soap to sell in the market so she could buy enough millet or rice to tide her family over. She was only able to provide enough for her children and husband ... you could tell she wasn't eating by how thin she was getting. Yet when a neighbor of hers came down with malaria, Djeneba took time away from her own work to pound the family's millet into flour. Such a good soul."

He picked again at the fraying upholstery, staring blankly at the wall, seemingly oblivious to Colette and Chris joining Ray on the sagging couch.

"One afternoon Colette and I hear yelling and screaming coming from Djeneba's compound, one of the voices clearly hers. One of the other women told us her husband hit her with a stick. Didn't see her again until the next day. She had a smile on her face, was laughing that laugh of hers. I marveled how she found reasons to rejoice, despite a life full of drudgery and cruelty. She didn't choose her world, had no control over it, but still seemed at peace."

Ray noticed Morger's upper lip quivering, tears pooling in his eyes. Everyone noticed.

"Can't remember for sure what month it was, but there was enough of a chill in the air that Colette and I slept inside. The moon was full, made it seem like the village had streetlights. People were moving about well after dark, kids were playing. I was used to all the noise during a full moon, fell right to sleep. Must've been after midnight when Colette woke me. Could hear these panicked screams. I rush out to see what was the matter. There was a crowd around this hole in the ground—an open well—along the path running between our compound and a neighboring one. At the edge of the well, there's a woman, on her hands and knees, screaming frantically. Some women drag her away from the hole. Could tell right away it was Djeneba."

Morger steeled himself.

"She tries fighting her way back through the crowd, had to be physically restrained by several men. A man runs up to me shouting *juru juru*! The word for rope. I run back to our compound to get the rope we used to pull water from the well, give it to him, the men lower someone down into the hole. Not five minutes later, they pull the man back up, he has a child in his arms. Crawls out of the hole, lays this limp body on the ground. Djeneba lets out this blood-curdling scream, starts sobbing uncontrollably. Her youngest son. Dead."

Colette wiped tears from her eyes.

"He was six years old, a bit off mentally. During the day, he led his blind grandfather around the village, was so proud to do it, could see it on his face. This particular night, he went with his brother to a neighbor's to watch the television they ran off a car battery. Only TV in Gninela, attracted quite a crowd, especially for soccer matches or old American shows dubbed in French. Walking home, probably half asleep, he stumbled right into the well. Most likely hit his head on the way down, probably was out cold before reaching the water. By the time help came, he was gone."

Morger spoke so softly he could barely be heard from five feet away.

"The whole rest of that night Colette and I laid in bed, hearing Djeneba sobbing and wailing, rambling incoherently. Thought she was going mad. Only once could I make anything of her ravings. Could tell she was praying, asking God to take pity on her son, watch over him. After her prayers there'd be these tortured screams. Prett-near all the women in the village congregated in Djeneba's compound. Didn't say anything, just sat with her."

If Morger was aware that Chris and Colette were sitting next to Ray listening, he didn't show it until now.

"I'm sorry, Chris. This is no story to have to hear on your first day with us."

"No, no, keep going," Chris protested.

"The shrieking carried on all night long, 'til nearly daybreak. You know what really got me? Her cries ended with that same whoop you always heard when she laughed. Shows how fine the line is in a place like that between joy and sorrow, life and death. The funeral was the very next day. Generally speaking, funerals in Mali are drawn-out affairs, often lasting several days for an influential elder. Seem almost festive. This one wasn't anything like that. The death of a newborn or an infant is so common it's not considered tragic, it's regarded as natural. A six-year-old is another matter. This child had 'taken' or 'arrived,' as they say. He was supposed to be in the clear."

Morger looked up at his audience.

"You still want me to finish the story?"

Three heads nodded.

"Colette was expected to be with the women who gathered near Djeneba's hut. The men were on the other side of the compound near her husband's. For better than an hour, we sat there together in the courtyard, probably 50 men. Hardly a word was said. Then the imam arrives with his entourage, the men pray. The boy's body is wrapped in white cloth, taken to the burial ground near the sacred forest on the edge of the village, lowered into a freshly dug grave. That was that. A few days later, Djeneba pays us a visit. For some reason she felt the need to apologize for not coming to greet us in the days before. She brings up the circumstances of her son's death, is matter-of-fact about it, almost serene. I wanted to say something—anything—to let her know she owed no apology, how deeply sad we were for her, but the words weren't there. All I could do was repeat a few death blessings I had memorized. In a few more days, that laugh returned. I'd heard it so many times before, but it wasn't until then that I realized it was a scream turned inside out."

The old man patted both arms of his chair with his hands, his eyes misty, focusing on Ray.

"Now you know why I didn't find missionary work to be worthwhile. Why would I try to give my God to someone who already has a God, is more spiritually grounded than I will ever be? What could possibly be accomplished by converting her to Christianity? Couldn't make her a better person. She made me better. She didn't need Jesus, she needed for there to be some damned justice in the world. She needed more to eat, never to be beaten again. My religion couldn't do that for her. But I'll tell you this, knowing Djeneba taught me there's a big difference between religion and morality, between church and faith. I got way more than I gave over there. Learned far more than I taught."

No one moved a muscle or spoke a word. Morger sighed.

"I miss Mali. I'm reminded of her often. Little things. I think of Mali every time I pass a stranger without so much as making eye contact. Being alone in the house, Mali always comes to mind when I'm by myself. They're living pretty much the way they did a thousand years ago, will probably be living that way a thousand years from now. People in this country look down on them, think they're backward. You know what? They may be poor in the ways we're rich, but they're rich in ways we're poor."

Colette was the first to rise, figuring this was as good a place as any to end the story, seeing how it was about time to start making supper. Ray started to follow her but stopped when Chris cleared her throat. "If school was about this kind of stuff, I'd consider going back."

Without missing a beat, Morger replied, "if school was about this kind of stuff, I never would have left."

The cryptic remark piqued Ray's interest.

"Why *did* you leave teaching?"

"I didn't leave of my own accord, I was shown the door," Morger answered.

"Wait, you were a teacher?" asked Chris.

"And you were fired?" Ray chimed in.

"Yes," Morger replied, first addressing Chris, then turning to Ray. "And yes."

"It's a *long* story," Colette warned loudly from the kitchen but Ray and Chris acted like they didn't hear her.

"I taught for better than 25 years, 'til '78. The beginning of the end was when I taught about sundown towns in my history class. Folks around here didn't take kindly to that. Got a lot of complaints. People went to the principal and the school board."

"What are sundown towns?" Ray inquired, feeling ignorant.

"All-white communities with either written decrees or unwritten rules keeping blacks out. If you weren't white, you couldn't be there after dark. Faith was a sundown town. Most of the little towns around here were. Colby. Loyal. Abbotsford. Owen. Greenwood. Thorp. Stanley. Medford. Neillsville. All were thought to be sundown towns. It's an untold part of our local history. Thought it was important to know. Seems I was about the only one who thought so."

"They're sure not teaching that in school now … when did this sunset crap stop?" wondered Chris.

"Hard to say. Some believe there are still sundown towns around these parts, just not as open about it as before. Obviously quite a few Mexican and Central American immigrants are moving into Faith. Some of the locals here accept it, others not so much. Ray, there was a time not that long ago when your mother wouldn't have been allowed to bring you here, not that it's easy even today. But times are changing, thank goodness."

Ray remained quiet, but Chris urged Morger on.

"They didn't fire you for that, though."

"Not for that. But it put me on thin ice. The thing that sealed my fate was teaching about a group called the Posse Comitatus. First started gaining a foothold around these parts in '74 or '75. A Korean War vet by the name of Thomas Stockheimer got it going in Wisconsin, organizing the capture of an IRS agent they lured to a farm. Held him for several hours. Assaulted him."

Anger swelled in Morger, after all these years.

"It was one James Wickstrom who took the Posse to a whole 'nother level in this area. Tool salesman from Michigan, became a preacher. Preached pure hate. Did radio shows, speaking tours. Followers of his worked to start a church affiliated with the Posse right here in Faith. To me, they were Nazis; it was Hitler all over again. Here, let me show you something."

Morger rose from his chair, excused himself and headed down the hallway leading to the bedrooms. Moments later he returned with a typewritten flyer on a yellowed, dog-eared sheet of paper with an old mimeograph machine's faded blue lettering. Handed it to Ray, whose eyes intermittently squinted and bulged while reading.

Jew run banks and federal loan agencies are working hand in hand foreclosing on thousands of farms right now in America. They are in essence, nationalizing farms for the jews, as the farmer becomes a tenant slave on the land he once owned. The farmers must prepare to defend their families and land with their lives, or surrender it all.

The farmer's debts and taxes are illegitimate under the Constitution, and the Federal Government's fiat money is not valid because it is not backed by gold. The economic hardship these devices create is part of a plan to destroy the White, Western Race by means of the Federal Reserve and Internal

Revenue Service. God's true chosen people must unite against the Jews and mongrel races seeking to help Satan destroy civilization.

We all must prepare for a war of attrition that can bring people together and continue on to terrorism and-or guerrilla war against who is in power. These Jews all need to be brought to the VA and tied in chairs. Bring veterans down who have been physically mutilated, their lives ruined without the opportunity of a family or children, and give them baseball bats and let them beat these Jews to death! Every one of them! Even the women and children. Take these Jews after they're beaten to death, throw 'em in the wood chipper! Let the remains go into a big incinerary truck, give them the holocaust they rightly deserve!

There is no legitimate form of government above that of the county and no higher law authority than the county sheriff. If the sheriff refuses to carry out the will of the county's citizens, he shall be removed by the Posse to the most populated intersection of streets in the township and at high noon be hung by the neck, the body remaining until sundown as an example to those who would subvert the law.

The Holy Bible calls us to action. The Anglo-Saxon race descends directly from Adam and Eve, whereas Jews are the descendants of Cain, who was begotten through Eve's intercourse with the Serpent of Eden through which Satan's seed passed. These products of sin, blacks and jews, are the direct biological offspring of the Devil and must be crushed by any available means.

-MOD

"Sheesh, what was up with these people?" Ray muttered. "Is incinerary even a word?"

"A made-up one," Morger replied. "Yeah, ugly stuff. Got my hands on this in about '76."

"What's MOD?" Ray asked, pointing to the bottom of the page.

"Guessing it's somebody's initials. Never was able to figure out whose," Morger answered. "They never put names or phone numbers or addresses on any of their leaflets. They were paranoid as hell. When the Posse's organizers found people who were interested, they were careful to tell them face-to-face where to go for meetings or training."

"Who would possibly fall for this garbage?" Ray wondered, handing the leaflet to Chris.

"Farmers were easy pickings. They were losing their shirts. The Posse preyed on their anger to get them to join, told them they were victims, gave 'em someone to blame. I showed this to my students. Showed them Hitler's *Mein Kampf* so they could see the parallels. Didn't go over too well with a lot of parents."

Morger paused, drew a deep breath, and Chris jumped in.

"That's when you were fired?"

Morger nodded.

"What happened to the Posse?" asked Ray.

"Eventually more or less disappeared, most likely just went into hiding. That church of theirs never got started here. I hope maybe I had something to do with that. Wickstrom concentrated his efforts to the east of here. Set up a cluster of mobile homes, declared it a township, refused to pay taxes to the actual local government, drew up all kinds of documents declaring their trailer park outside the jurisdiction of all government authorities. Ended up being convicted of impersonating an elected official, went to jail for a short time. He's still out there, still alive, back living in Michigan. One of his converts introduced Timothy McVeigh to fertilizer bombs. He's the one who blew up the federal building in Oklahoma City in '95."

"It sucks that you lost your job for teaching about Nazis," Ray asserted emphatically.

"Actually, the stated reason for letting me go was failure to follow the history curriculum. It called for teaching a unit about World War II and I did that. Thought it would feel more real to students if they saw how Nazism was rearing its head in their own home town. Needless to say, the principal and school board and a whole lot of parents didn't see it that way."

"That blows," Chris said.

"Never lived that down, never was able to get back in the good graces of the community."

"I bet that's why people tell their kids your house is haunted, why the Moose always warned me to stay away from here," Ray speculated.

"Probably a safe bet," Morger replied with a wry smile. "Don't go feeling sorry for me; the only regret I have is how all of this has unfairly affected Colette. She doesn't deserve that. As for me, I loved teaching, but if I had it to do over, wouldn't change a thing."

Morger excused himself to go for a walk before supper. Chris and Ray went to help Colette in the kitchen. Twenty minutes or so later, the table was set and Colette served roast beef with all the fixings. Chris ate like she hadn't in a while, something not lost on the other three.

The school year was winding down fast, graduation approached. Ray was going through the motions, mind wandering, paying enough attention in class to earn passing marks but not enough to learn much of anything. Nearly every hour outside of school was spent making Ebiyan House come to life.

There had been a time when Ray and Ev Meaney felt more than a little overwhelmed by the project, but now they had more help than they knew what to do with. Ray brought Gin into the loop. Like the others, she was discreet, doing her part to keep Moose in the dark. Morger enlisted the help of a retired industrial arts teacher to assist with drawing up blueprints, furnishing tools, helping Gin secure donated building materials. He also talked a recently retired county public health nurse into being a volunteer advisor once the shelter started operating.

Gin used family clout to grease the skids with local officials, leaning on the county zoning department to cough up a building permit, exploring the process for getting the shelter licensed as a care facility. Her sister Grace made a surprisingly large financial contribution, as did the Meaney family. Lisa Lewandowski threw her support behind the endeavor, donating both money and labor. When Chris wasn't helping Colette with chores, she lent a hand to the building crew and persuaded her brother Mickey to help too. Ev got his sister Linh involved. All Ray needed to do was ask, and Frankie López, Willie García and Rosa Vazquez pitched in as well.

The school year came to a close, nearly two weeks earlier for the seniors than for underclassmen. Without classes to attend, work on the shelter intensified. The bigger the circle of helpers, the harder it was to keep the whole business under wraps. Word was leaking out; besides, work was plainly visible at the construction site. When several people asked Gin about it at the graduation ceremony, she knew it was only a matter of time until Moose would know what was up. Ray was not enthused about her proposal to talk to him soon.

"He'll just throw cold water on it, try to derail the whole thing. I know he will."

"Leave dealing with him to me. There are cards I can play. Trust me."

Ray relented and Gin mulled over when to fill Moose in. She pondered asking him if he wanted company that night and making Ray's project the subject of pillow talk afterwards. The prospect of manipulating him didn't concern her half as much as the idea of sharing a bed with her husband again. She decided to wait until morning, retreating to the room Mark and Steve shared as children, where she'd been sleeping for years. Over coffee the next day, Gin delivered the news. Moose responded the way she knew he would.

"What a bunch of damn foolishness."

"Way to keep an open mind, big guy."

"Oh, come on Gin, this makes no sense and you know it. With this kind of operation, you need permits and licenses. To get those, you need professional credentials. You have to have financing. To get that, you need a business plan. You're doing him no favors by going along with this fairytale. He's not six. He's a high school graduate now, for crying out loud, with no fucking clue what it means to enter the real world."

Those last words stuck in her craw, but she knew there was some truth to what Moose said. She had enough experience with business dealings and navigating bureaucracies to know there were hoops to jump through. Countless other potential pitfalls raced through her mind. Still, she pushed back.

"You really have no idea who Ray is."

"What's that supposed to mean? You're talking nonsense."

"It doesn't make any sense to you because you have no idea who Ray is. To you, people are whatever you think they should be."

Moose let out an exasperated sigh.

"It's not complicated, darling," she said in a tone dripping with sarcasm and resentment. "Ray is doing this, I am helping, and so will you."

"The hell I will! This is a fool's mission, and if you think I'm taking this trip to fantasyland with you all, you got another think comin'."

"You listen here, you f ..." Gin spurted before biting her tongue. "I know all the hurdles that have to be cleared. Some might trip us up. If that happens, we'll go around them. Don't worry about asking permission, go ahead and do it, ask forgiveness later, that's my attitude. This is a small town, a lot's done outside the rules. You can make things a hell of a lot easier for us. You own half of this town ... and I own half of you."

The amused look on Moose's face washed away, replaced by an incoming tide of confusion and anger.

"We live in a community property state, what we have isn't yours, it's ours. We get divorced, everything gets split fifty-fifty. Say the word, I'll have the divorce papers drawn up ... go ahead, test me."

Gin could sense violence welling up in Moose.

"You so much as lay a hand on me, I'll make the rest of your days a living hell."

Moose stood there, rigid, eyes vacant, face blank.

"Get this through your thick skull, here's how it's gonna be. You're going to use your connections to make any barriers to Ray's shelter go away. Anyone balks, well, you own the only newspaper in town, you'll make them see the light. You'll make a generous donation to the cause. A very generous donation. And get others to do the same."

"How'd you become such a conniving bitch?"

"Observed the master."

Moose did everything Gin demanded and then some. He donated, threw his weight around, twisted arms, called in favors. Gin's research into licensing options unearthed only a series of dead ends. Each option was a round hole, Ebiyan House was a square peg. Somehow Moose finagled approval, getting the county and state to recognize it as a shelter care facility. Gin wondered if the arrangement was truly on the up and up, but knew what not to do with gift horses.

CHAPTER 19

THE SECOND TUESDAY IN SEPTEMBER was the kind of day to bottle and store. The sun shone brightly, the temperature in Faith reached 80 degrees, a refreshing breeze kissed cheeks and tousled hair.

After a five-day stay in Faith—her second of the summer—Annie had left to start her freshman year at Macalester College, intending to major in anthropology and study abroad at the first opportunity. Everyone working on Ebiyan House's construction missed her; she'd proven herself handy with a hammer or saw.

A work crew consisting of Ev, Ray, the retired shop teacher Mr. Jeske and Willie García got an early start that day, at it by sunrise. Across town, Moose grabbed a quick bite before heading out to check that all was right with his world. Gin lingered over her morning coffee, tuned to a talk show on public radio, only half listening. The host was interviewing a guest from New York City by phone. Some kind of expert discussing something or other.

The interview took an abrupt turn when the man on the phone gasped, horrified, describing what he saw out his office window, grabbing Gin's attention. A jet airliner, crashing into one of the twin towers of the World Trade Center. An explosion, a huge ball of fire, smoke billowing out of a massive gash torn in one side of the skyscraper. For several minutes Gin listened intently as the man spoke, the emotion in his voice palpable, his mind reeling, scarcely able to believe what he was seeing with his own eyes, this terrible accident, this inexplicable mistake.

It occurred to Gin to turn on the television. Every news station was showing images of the stricken building, a giant plume of smoke the sole cloud in a clear-blue sky. Gin stared at the screen, utterly transfixed. Not even 20 minutes after the man on the radio started recounting what he was seeing, the idea that this was some freak mishap born of human error or mechanical malfunction was blown to smithereens.

A second passenger jet appeared in the sky, banked sharply, slicing into the southernmost tower, slightly below where the first tower was hit but still close to two-thirds of the way to the top, causing another massive explosion, showering flaming debris over nearby buildings and onto the streets below. What moments earlier was so confusing, so surreal, came into sharp focus. The country was under attack.

Gin sat on the floor, eyes glued to the TV, more numb than frightened, as reports of a third plane crashing into the Pentagon came barely 30 minutes after the second tower was struck. Twenty minutes later, news bulletins reported a fourth plane crashing in a field in rural Pennsylvania. Not long after, Gin watched live footage of the World Trade Center collapsing, first one tower, then the other.

She had always felt perfectly safe in Faith, never minding being home alone. It was a strange sensation, sitting in her house, not vulnerable in the least but feeling like it. She thought about trying to reach Moose, but phoned Colette instead.

"Have you heard?" Gin asked without even identifying herself.

"It's horrible. Just terrible," Colette replied.

"Is Ray over there working on the shelter?"

"I think so. They're inside doing interior finishing. Can hear them working, though."

"I'll be right over."

Gin hopped in the car, minutes later pulling into the Morgers' driveway. She felt obliged to stop in and say hello. The door was open wide, so she let herself in, called out a greeting. Seeing no one in the kitchen or dining room, Gin proceeded to the sitting room. Colette and Morger stood in front of the television, mouths gaping.

"The world's going mad," Colette muttered before greeting her guest with a kiss to both cheeks.

"Crazy, isn't it?" Gin mumbled.

"This is only the beginning," said Morger ominously.

They stared at the TV, Gin finally breaking the silence.

"I think I'm gonna go over and see if I can find Ray."

Having neglected to offer a slice of pie or a cup of coffee to their guest, Morger and Colette tried herding Gin toward the dining room table, imploring her to sit for a spell. Wanting to be on her way, Gin begged off. Morger and Colette insisted on accompanying her on the short walk to the construction site.

The nearly finished structure now wore a hand-carved sign, maybe three feet high and seven feet long, with dark lettering burned into the blond woodgrain. Engraved to the left of the letters were a pair of pine trees, to the right was foliage in the shape of an archway. The building itself was an elongated log cabin, the wood stained a rich golden color, with a roof covered in bright green shingles.

When no one answered several knocks on the front door, Gin poked her head inside. She could hear voices and the whirring of power tools several rooms away, followed the sounds, Colette and Morger behind her. Willie García didn't stop what he was doing but waved, pointing to the next room. There they found Ray, Ev Meaney and Mr. Jeske on their knees installing flooring in the makings of a kitchen.

"Your security is awfully lax," Morger teased. "You let any old Tom, Dick or Harry just wander in off the street."

"That's the whole point of this place," Ray shot right back. "Open to anyone. Even old grumps."

"Quite the sign you've got over the front door. Where'd that come from?" Gin interjected, as much to abbreviate the juvenile ribbing as out of genuine curiosity.

"Ev made it. By hand," Ray replied.

"Beautiful work. Getting noticed, can tell you that. Already had two different people ask me what Ebiyan House is going to be." Gin pronounced the name with a short e, an error promptly flagged.

"It's abe-ee-yon," Ev corrected.

"I understand it means heaven in your tribal language."

Ray could tell Ev regretted correcting her and tried lightening the mood.

"You guys checking up on us, making sure we're keeping our noses to the grindstone? Truth is we were loafing around, saw you coming, quick made it look like we're actually working."

"Must have the Seven Dwarfs working for you. Place looks almost finished," said Morger.

"Only got six. Grumpy stays holed up in that old house across the field, refuses to help," Ray answered with a wink.

Everyone laughed but Gin, who looked tense, Ray noticed.

"What's up, Mom?"

"S'pose you heard what happened."

Three blank faces.

"Two passenger jets flew into both towers of the World Trade Center this morning. Another hit the Pentagon, and one headed to Washington crashed somewhere in Pennsylvania," she reported grimly. "They're saying on the news it looks like it was a coordinated attack by Islamic terrorists."

Ev and Ray gasped, Mr. Jeske's jaw dropped.

Morger bristled. "Whoever did this are no Muslims. They may quote the Koran and claim to be following Allah's orders, but they're just murderers. Every religion's been embraced by criminals looking to sanctify their crimes; Islam's no exception."

Judging from the lunch crowd bellying up to the bar at Moose's tavern, no one else in Faith saw things as Morger did, but reactions to the day's events were all over the map.

"I'm tellin' ya these goddamn Moslems are out to destroy America," one loudmouth declared. "Best thing we could do is nuke every last one of them Arab countries, wipe 'em clean off the map."

"Got that right," said another. "Them towelheads want to start some kind of holy war, bring it on! Let's get the party started."

"Come over here, attack our country ... We got no choice," chimed in a third.

Up and down the bar, heads nodded. At least one shook.

"Who exactly we going to war with? How we supposed to know which country's responsible? You're a bunch of damned fools if you believe what the media's putting out there. Could just as well be those self-flying planes going haywire."

Several at the bar hooted and jeered, but the dissenter was undeterred.

"Don't you dipshits know nothin'? Jets fly themselves now. Takeoffs and landings are controlled by computers, pilots are just along for the ride.

What happened today could've been one big computer system failure."

That was met by more hoots and jeers, but a customer at the far end of the bar piped up in the man's defense.

"Someone coulda hacked into the airline's computer system and redirected those planes," he said in a loud enough voice to be heard throughout the establishment.

A paunchy, graying man sitting two stools away looked like he had a bad case of indigestion.

"You got shit for brains if you think computers done this. Ain't no accident New York and Washington got hit. All that's there is a bunch of fruitcakes and street hustlers. Crooked politicians, Wall Street hucksters. God done sent a message. They got what's coming to them."

This clearly resonated with one of the younger patrons, who turned to the three men whose appetite for bloodshed matched their thirst for beer.

"It don't exactly break my heart that a building full of bankers and stockbrokers got blown up. What've they ever done for us? They milk us dry, fill their pockets. Why in the hell should we go to war for them? No Arab's ever done me any harm."

When Ray, Ev, Willie and Mr. Jeske knocked off for the day, Ray paid the Morgers a visit an hour or so before suppertime, hoping they might know Chris's whereabouts.

"Stay for a bite?" asked Colette.

"Nah, just wanted to see if there's any more news."

Morger drifted in from the sitting room to join Colette and Ray in the dining room.

"It's going to take a long, long time to sort out what happened. Doubt people are willing to wait for the evidence to be gathered. When it's not clear who to blame, scapegoats get created."

"So, you're not thinking it was Muslims?" Ray asked.

"They may call themselves Muslims, but they're murderous fanatics. That's not any Islam I'm familiar with. We spent a full year in a Muslim country, never saw so much as a fistfight or even a good shoving match."

Ray stayed quiet, which Morger took as an invitation to say more.

"Look, many a war has been fought in the name of Jesus. I don't doubt for a second that killing in the Prophet Muhammad's name is just as irresistible to those who lust for war in places where Islam is practiced.

Doesn't matter where you are. People make their God like them rather than making themselves like their God."

Ray glanced over at Colette, then back at Morger.

"Any idea where Chris is? Haven't seen her today."

"She helped me with housecleaning jobs on the Hill for much of the day, then with chores around here," Colette said.

"Might want to check the cathedral. Saw her headed in that direction," Morger advised.

Ray swung open the screen door, descended the steps in a single stride, dashed up the driveway and along the road past the cemetery, taking the fenced dirt path into the woods, through the thicket, across the stream, up the ridge, over the crest, down the swale, to the archway. Chris was lying on the bed of pine needles that covered the forest floor.

"Another message from the cookie jar," she said, extending her arm to Ray, a thrice-folded sheet of ruled notebook paper in her hand. Ray unfolded it. This time the message was but 10 words, again handwritten in blue ink, the same flourished pen stroke.

Miracles are not a matter of chance but of design.

"Whadya make of this one?" Chris asked.

"How long you been here?"

"Dunno. Lost track of time. So, what's this mean?"

"You doin' okay?"

"Yeah, I'm fine. I come here whenever ... I mean, um, you know ..."

"Know what?"

"Whenever you're on my mind. This is, like, your place."

Chris turned toward Ray, resting on one elbow. "I love you. Just want you to know that."

Ray's head swam.

"I feel close to you when I come here."

"Um, you see me every day. You can be with me whenever you want."

"I was hoping you'd come looking for me. I wanted to be alone with you, away from the others, so I could tell you how I feel."

Now Ray felt faint. Chris could tell and sat up, nervous laughter escaping like a belch.

"It's taken me a long time to work up the courage to say that."

She patted the ground next to her. "Sit. I won't bite."

Ray's legs felt on the verge of buckling. The act of sitting required extra concentration.

"You saved my life."

"Not sure what you mean."

"Why'd you do it?"

"Do what? You've lost me."

"Care about where I was living, what I was doing, get that dear old couple to take me in. I haven't had one of those awful headaches in weeks. My stomach stopped hurting. I'm not on anything anymore, even stopped smoking. Then I find that," she said, pointing to the note Ray held.

Silence stretched, a few seconds seeming much longer.

"You didn't want all the gory details." Chris continued, taking the hand holding the note in both of hers. "You accepted me when I didn't deserve it, made me feel like I was worth something when I didn't feel that way myself."

Ray felt a familiar surge of energy, followed promptly by pangs of guilt for getting aroused as she poured her heart out.

"I know what the message means," she said, her eyes piercing, drilling down to Ray's core.

Ray mimed uncertainty.

"What happened to me wasn't an accident. You made it happen."

"Miracles might not be accidents, but it's not like you can whip one up like baking a cake. What you're feeling is nothing magical, it's the difference between being used and being loved."

Chris beamed. "Sure feels like magic to me."

Ray looked at the message on the note one more time, thinking about what Morger always said, wishing for some explanation to reveal itself.

"You coming to work on the shelter tomorrow? Would love to see you there. It's nearly done."

"Tomorrow and the next day and the day after that."

Ray stood up, extended a hand to Chris, helping her to her feet. She stumbled slightly as she rose, careening into Ray. When she righted herself, they were face-to-face and their lips met. They both jerked back ever so slightly before Chris pulled Ray to her.

Long bewitched by her looks, Ray was now mesmerized by her feel, how velvety and delicate her skin was to the touch. Her hips, rounded, soft. Her lips, supple, agile, deliciously so. For who knows how long their kiss continued, as if by some immutable law of physics. Then it ended, just like that.

"We better go," Ray whispered. "Before they send out a search party."

CHAPTER 20

THE NEXT DAY WAS AWKWARD. Work on the shelter was wrapping up, the light at the end of the tunnel so close it seemed possible to reach out and touch it. Willie, Frankie and Rosa all showed up to work. Mr. Jeske and Ev were there, as usual. Ev brought along his sister Linh.

Morger came by to lend a hand. Colette and Lisa Lewandowski stopped in to offer encouragement. So did Moose, oddly enough. Jim and Maggie Slater too. Also checking in on the project's progress every few days, including this one, was Corrine Thorson—Cori to everyone who knew her— who worked for the county health department, the sole nurse shared by nearly a dozen schools in the area. She was prim and proper with a rather brusque manner, although Ray suspected kindness lurked underneath.

When Chris arrived, she made a beeline for Ray, who barely said hello and was noticeably standoffish. The division of labor was done in such a way that Chris and Linh were assigned a cleanup task at the front entry while Ray was working with Ev and Rosa out back under Mr. Jeske's supervision.

During breaks, Ray hung with the group, thwarting Chris's hopes for a moment alone. She noticed that when she made eye contact, Ray looked away. By mid-afternoon, hardly a word had passed between them. Chris decided to clear the air, quite forcefully pulling Ray aside.

"What's up?" Anger was written plainly on her face.

Ray looked dumbfounded and ambushed.

"You haven't spoken to me all day. It's like you're avoiding me, acting like I'm invisible."

Surprise, then a sort of defensive resolve and, finally, dismay flashed across Ray's face.

"Do you regret what happened last night?"

"No ... it was amazing."

"What then? What gives?"

"It's just ... I don't know, it's just a lot to ... um, I don't really know how to ... you know ..."

Chris rolled her eyes, then her expression softened.

"I'm sorry if I made you uncomfortable. Maybe I shouldn't have said what I said or done what I did, although I have to say, you seemed to be enjoying yourself."

"I *was* ... I mean, I did ... Aaaaaah!" Ray exclaimed, venting frustration loudly enough to be within the entire crew's earshot, then motioning in the direction of the front door.

"How 'bout we go outside, take a walk or something."

Ray alerted Mr. Jeske they were stepping out but would be right back, ushered Chris out the door, not speaking until they reached the edge of the highway, only then turning to face her.

"I wanted to do that for a long time. Kiss you, I mean."

"Why didn't you?"

"Too 'fraid, I guess."

"Are you glad we did?"

"I am, I really am. But I'm still 'fraid."

"Afraid of what?"

"Maybe afraid's not the right word. I know I love you, but what I don't know is if I love you as a friend, or like a sister, or if it's more than that. I don't want to lead you on ... I'm not sure I can be the person you need me to be."

"You don't have to be anything different for me. I love you just the way you are."

"That's the thing ... the way I am in your eyes is not what I really am."

"What's that s'posta mean? You got some deep, dark secret?"

"There's something about me you don't know, and I'm not sure I'm ready to tell you about it yet. If we're going to be more than friends, you deserve to know. I just can't explain right now."

"Does this have to do with all these strange things you make happen? If that's it, I gotta tell ya right now, I can handle being with someone with superpowers." She had that mischievous twinkle in her eyes.

"That's not it. It's not about what I can or can't do, it's about who I am. I wish I could tell you ... I want to be with you. Can't stop thinking about you. I'm just not sure I can handle everybody knowing this about me."

"Everybody doesn't need to know. You can just tell me. I can keep a secret."

"I shouldn't have said it that way. I don't care about everybody else. I'm afraid this will change the way you feel about me. I want us to at least be friends. I couldn't bear it if we couldn't at least have that."

"What could possibly be so bad that you can't tell me about it? My God, Ray, think about what you know about me. If you can look past all that, what makes you think I couldn't look past whatever you're so scared to tell me?"

"It's nothing I've done. It's something you don't know about me as a person, and I can't help thinking it will change how you feel about me."

"Let me be the judge of that. I might surprise you."

"You're right. And I will, I promise. Just not right now."

"When?"

"I don't know. As soon as I can work up to it. I wish I knew how long that'll be, but I don't."

"So where does that leave us?"

"Friends, I hope. Look, I know this is weird. You must think I'm some kind of head case, playing mind games. But I really, really want to stay friends. I hope and pray that can be enough for you ... for now, anyhow."

"You're a mysterious one, Ray Glennon. You're lucky I'm a sucker for complicated types." Chris stopped, turned to face Ray, smiled impishly, came to attention with rather dramatic flourish, chest out, shoulders back, feet together, ceremoniously extending a hand.

"Friends."

Ray laughed a grateful yet sheepish sort of laugh, shaking her hand for an instant before drawing her into a careful embrace.

On the walk back, Ray felt a weight had been lifted. Though another remained, it felt half as heavy as it had moments earlier. At one point along the way, Chris took Ray's hand in hers, intertwining their fingers. She let go once they were within 50 yards or so of the construction site for the sake of appearances, not that anyone was watching.

Soon enough they were at the front door, went in, got back to work. But now they made a point of working on the same tasks, in close proximity, talking, teasing each other, taking breaks together, sharing ideas on how Ebiyan House should operate once it opened. They hashed over who could live there and for how long, how to raise funds to pay the bills, how to furnish the place, how to make sure there was not only a roof over the residents' heads but also food on the table. Close to an acre was fenced off behind the building for a garden to be planted the following spring. A corner of the Morgers' barn was fashioned into a coop for keeping chickens.

Better partners would be hard to conjure up. Ev was a fixture at Ebiyan. Having Cori Thorson on call with decades of experience as a health professional gave the whole operation an air of legitimacy. But Ray and Chris were the center's backbone.

Opening day came before anyone felt ready. Chris and Ray cooked, cleaned, swept, mopped, troubleshot, problem-solved, improvised. They recruited volunteers, solicited donations, scoured the landscape to identify children and adults in danger or otherwise in need of assistance.

When someone spray-painted a swastika on the front of the building, they scrubbed the log wall with solvent, removing all but the slightest shadow of the graffiti. Chris spent her spare hours working toward her GED and helping the Morgers. She toyed with the idea of continuing on with school after earning the equivalent of a high school diploma.

Ebiyan's very first guests included a penniless woman Chris had gotten to know while living at what used to be the Hideaway. A 16-year-old truant who found life at home so intolerable he was sleeping outside, one night under the rickety bridge, the next behind the hedges lining the battlefield or in a discarded industrial canister behind the shuttered paper mill. Two battered wives. A migrant couple with two children, all undocumented, who came to the area looking for a better life in a place remote enough they could stay off the authorities' radar. The father discreetly looked for farm work but found none. The mother was sick and too weak for the family to move on, the boys too young to help out much.

Ebiyan House also offered refuge to a 13-year-old girl whose circumstances reminded Ray of Chris's, along with two teenage runaways—Native girls who were being trafficked at a truck stop along Highway 29, whose disappearance came to Ev's attention through tribal contacts.

The rustic warmth of Ebiyan's exterior stopped at the front entrance. On the inside, the shelter was plain and rather antiseptic, more doctor's office than chalet. The walls were bare, with an orange-peel texture, all painted the same off-white. The front entrance opened to a cramped lobby with nothing but a desk, a coat rack and a few chairs. Straight back from the lobby was the dining room, to the left a spacious but sparsely appointed kitchen, to the right a recreation room just large enough for several card tables and a ping-pong table.

Hallways ran both ways from the common area to the guest bedrooms and shared bathrooms. Accommodations were spartan; each resident had a bed and either a bureau or a trunk for belongings. Closets were roughly the size of phone booths. The flooring was either linoleum or tile throughout, a throw rug in the lobby being the closest thing to carpeting anywhere in the building.

Eventually all beds in Ebiyan were spoken for. When still more sought shelter, first Ray and then Chris surrendered their beds. Ray took to sleeping on a fold-up cot in the front lobby. Most nights Chris opted for the soft mattress in the Morgers' spare bedroom but occasionally would curl up in a sleeping bag next to Ray's cot. Those nights they invariably discussed expanding the center before drifting off to sleep.

At a quarter past two on one of those nights, Ray and Chris were awakened by shouting and pounding on the door. Alarmed, Chris sprang to her feet, peering out a front-facing window. Outside, a hulking man, staggering, obviously impaired, loudly demanded to see his wife. Ray headed for the door.

"You're not going out there, are you?" Chris demanded incredulously.

"Lock the door behind me!" Ray ordered, slipping quickly outside, securing the door before turning to face the man, who was not eight feet away, swaying slightly.

"You have no business here; you need to go home."

The man advanced, gesturing menacingly. "My wife's in there ... I ain't leavin' without her."

"Police have been called, will be here any minute," Ray called out loudly, as if addressing a crowd.

At first the man looked around, puzzled, then his bewildered expression quickly turned to amusement.

"And I suppose a shrimp like you is gonna stop me from goin' in there, gettin' what's mine."

"Don't want any trouble ... you're not allowed in, there's nothing here that belongs to you." Ray spoke sternly but felt defenseless. Claiming that police were on their way was a bluff.

The man took two steps forward, threw a punch that came out of nowhere, his right fist landing flush on Ray's lower left jaw. Ray took the punch without so much as dropping to a knee or being thrown back a step. Watching from the window, Chris let out a scream, waking everyone inside. Ray prayed she'd stay put.

The adrenaline rush of what had just transpired appeared to have a sobering effect on the man, who suddenly seemed steadier on his feet, his eyes no longer quite so bleary. As he grew more clear-headed, he became more unnerved, unsure of what to do next. Ray stood there before him, showing no inclination to either retaliate or capitulate. The stranger got the same kind of look on his face Paul Driscoll and Nick Szymanski had— Ray recognized it at once—surprised, confused, scared. The man looked around, nervous like. Noticing headlights coming down the road from the northeast, he ran off without another word.

Once the threat was out of sight, Ray heaved a sigh of relief and hastened to get back inside, rapping on the locked door. It burst open. The entire Ebiyan community was there, still in their nightclothes, all but two of them barefoot. Chris threw her arms around Ray, but their hug was brief in the interest of avoiding questions. Soon the commotion died down and everyone returned to the comfort and security of their beds.

Dawn's maiden rays created a spectacular effect the next morning as they tickled the thick frost coating the fields and yards and rooftops. Temperatures these days were above freezing in daylight before falling enough to deposit a shimmering glaze on the landscape. The air's chill numbed fingertips, set noses to running, turned each breath into thought clouds. Made warm beds hard to leave, blankets difficult to surrender.

It was nearly nine by the time everyone was up and about. Chatter around the breakfast table focused on what had transpired in the middle of the night. Residents knew there was a confrontation, that Ray was punched at some point. Chris supplied details, giving a thorough recounting of the drama.

"Didn't you hear me say the police are coming?" Ray asked everyone in a scolding manner. "That means everyone was to go below." Only Chris actually heard Ray mention the police, the agreed-upon signal to head down to the cellar by way of one of the trapdoors under false flooring built into the shelter's design at Ev's insistence. Ray had thought this feature unnecessary, but Ev's escape hatches proved their value again less than two weeks later when two unsavory-looking characters showed up in broad daylight, demanding that their property be returned to them. Meaning the two Native girls rescued from the truck stop and brought to Ebiyan. That time too, Ray stepped into the fray, loudly warning police had been summoned, keeping the two men at bay long enough for the girls to disappear into the hidden cellar.

"We know they're here. You have what's ours and if we don't get 'em back, we'll torch this place," one of them threatened. As he sought to push past Ray, the sneer on his face evaporated upon encountering the business end of a 12 gauge.

"You set foot on my property ever again, you'll be leaving in a body bag. When I came home from the war, I promised myself I'd never kill again. You don't want to go causing me to make an exception now, do you?"

That ended that. The two men fled, never returning. Morger's heroics had Ebiyan's residents buzzing, but not without some ribbing courtesy of Ray. "I thought you didn't have any guns, gave 'em up after the war."

"All I recall telling you is I'm not a hunter 'cause I know what it's like to be hunted. Have had this old thing for years. Trouble is, don't have any ammo. It wasn't loaded."

That revelation was met with amazement, admiration for the old man's sheer nerve. Gratitude too. Morger and Colette offering land for this refuge, then Morger scaring off intruders, earned him license to come tell stories whenever the spirit moved him. Unafraid of wearing out his welcome, Morger dropped in virtually every day, sometimes before supper, most times after.

His audience fluctuated; rarely did everyone gather around, but every so often the whole household did. Morger told of farming in the old days, what Faith was like in his childhood. He'd share gossip from the here and now, never failing to embellish the mundane. Colette accompanied him from time to time, sharing memories of Africa or life in France as best she could remember. Morger couldn't resist the occasional history lesson from his days as a schoolteacher, telling of the Posse Comitatus, how Faith was once a sundown town, how teaching that history cost him his job.

History was an abstraction to Ebiyan's residents, pushed to the margins of consciousness by recent traumas and current struggles. But Morger's gentle demeanor, kindness and brave interventions were no abstractions. They were keenly appreciated by all who called the place home even for the briefest stays. Indulging Morger and celebrating his eccentricities was rent they cheerfully paid.

Ray, on the other hand, quiet and inconspicuous, went unnoticed most days.

"I wish I could tell stories like you do," Ray told Morger one day while chaperoning a contingent of Ebiyan's youngest guests on a visit to Colette's kitchen, introducing them to the delights found within a certain ceramic jar. Morger replied in an indecipherable tongue.

"Fo ko nyuman nee tyen tay kelen yay."

Ray figured it was an African proverb but mimed surrender.

"It means eloquence and truth are not the same."

Ray stared blankly, pondering Morger's explanation. "Are you saying your stories aren't true?"

"No, I'm saying just because words are used cleverly doesn't mean they are any more relevant or truthful than words spoken clumsily. Besides, there's more truth in doing than in saying."

Ray's attention shifted to the cookie jar full of fresh snickerdoodles. Everyone at Ebiyan was welcome in the Morger home and visited regularly. Though Colette was now baking cookies for a dozen or more people, she showed no sign of being inconvenienced or unable to keep pace. The jar always was full or nearly so, regardless of the number of visitors on any given day, a fact that never ceased to amaze Ray. Even more curious—to Chris and Ray at any rate—was that no Ebiyan guest ever found a note in the jar.

Weeks later, winter rudely announced its arrival, sending mild autumn temperatures fleeing with bitter northerly winds. A light dusting of snow threw a veil over frost-stricken blades of grass. More than half of Ebiyan's residents were at the Morgers along with Ev, Chris and Ray. Cori Thorson was there as well. Gin too. Most of the group crowded the kitchen, many hovering near the counter where the cookie jar sat.

The jar's lid was lifted, hands plunged in, the lid was replaced, only to be lifted again moments later. Ray drifted over near Gin, who was deep in conversation with Colette, before being brushed from behind. There was Chris holding the lid aloft, beckoning Ray. Ray reached in, struck by how empty the jar was, then surprised to find the first thing encountered wasn't a cookie at all but a folded piece of paper.

Ray casually slipped out of the kitchen, down the hallway, unfolding the page in the privacy of the bathroom. Same ruled white paper as before, 10 words, same hand, same color ink.

Feeling what others feel is the surest way to heal.

This one gave Ray chills. Emerging from the toilet, inching back up the hallway, peering around the corner at the spacious kitchen melting into the dining area, Ray spotted Chris and tried getting her attention by whispering her name once, a second time a little louder, a third time with greater urgency still. When she finally looked over, Ray motioned to her to come. She hesitated, looking wary, then made her way over to where Ray awaited her.

"Why are you hiding over here?"

Ray did not answer but took her by the arm, leading her down to the end of the hall.

"There was another note in the jar, how'd you not see it?"

"There was no note in the jar."

"It was in there when you opened the lid for me," Ray insisted, revealing the sheet of paper as proof.

"No way. That is so weird. What's it say?"

Ray handed Chris the note. She looked it over, seeming agitated.

"How are you s'posta make any sense of that? What's this even about? Jeezus, this is so fucking weird."

"I need to tell you something," Ray said.

Chris looked worried yet intrigued.

"I keep noticing this strange thing happens to me when someone's hurting. I start hurting in the same way they're hurting. Like when Rich Boniewicz was given the treatment freshman year. My crotch started burning. Honest to God. Does that ever happen to you?"

"I think I'll keep how my crotch feels to myself."

"Come off it, I mean, when someone's in pain, do you ever start feeling the same kind of pain? Been reading up on it, seen it called sympathy pain. The medical establishment ain't convinced it's a real thing; they think it's just in people's heads. What I don't get is if something's in people's heads, why don't doctors consider that real? Just because they can't explain it doesn't mean it's not happening."

Chris arched her eyebrows. "Good point."

"Also saw it called mirror touch something or other, the last word is like anesthesia 'cept starting with an S. And there's Couvade syndrome with pregnancy. When women are expecting, sometimes their partners will start having nausea, bloating, stuff that mimics pregnancy. Bizarre, huh?"

Chris's silence made Ray think she suspected madness.

"You prolly think I'm crazy."

Chris still said nothing.

"What's really nuts, when I start hurting the same way someone else is, they stop hurting. Lisa Lewandowski, saw her at a Christmas party. Could tell her chest hurt."

"Lisa Lewandowski, isn't she like 20 years older than you? And whadya mean you could tell?"

"Not 20. She was still in high school when I was born. Stayed at our house when my mom and I were in the Cities."

"Whatever … how'd you know her chest hurt?"

"I told you; I could feel it." Ray placed a hand over Chris's heart, causing her to smirk.

"I started having chest pains and hers went away, right then and there. Same thing happened with you, 'cept it wasn't quite so immediate."

"Come again."

"When you were … you know, when, uh … when you were having those horrible headaches and your stomach was bothering you … I started having bad headaches and stomach cramps. Yours went away."

"You never said anything … did they go away?"

"Yeah, eventually."

Ray paused, started to speak again, hesitated once more, then continued. "There's more."

"Why am I not surprised?"

"You know how sick Bella has been," Ray began, referencing Isabella, the migrant mother staying at Ebiyan. "She's getting so thin, can't be a hundred pounds anymore. I know Rami is worried she's not going to make it but is afraid to take her to the hospital, their status and all."

Chris's eyes got big. "You haven't …"

She ruminated on a thought, then let it go.

CHAPTER 21

A MILKY FILM FROSTED OVER ALL THE WINDOWS at Ebiyan, nature's artwork that to one eye resembled feathers, to another delicate leaves. Scraping off the frost did little to help visibility, as snowdrifts resembling sand dunes outside blocked any line of sight.

Ray was first to rouse this particular morning. Bella and Rami stirred not 20 minutes later. She looked peaked, her frame gaunt, her eyes sunken yet unusually bright. There was a bounce to her step not seen in many a day. Upon seeing Ray her face lit up, she started babbling excitedly, a steady stream of words Ray could not understand.

"¡Mi ángel! ¡Tú me sanaste! ¡Tú me sanaste! ¡Me curé completamente! La enfermedad se ha ido."

Rami took a stab at translating with his few words of English.

"Sick. No más. Gone. ¡Gracias a Dios!"

The ruckus awakened several others, including Chris, who rushed to Ray's side.

"I think she's better," Ray told her.

Chris surprised Ray when she addressed Bella in Spanish. "¿Cómo estás?"

"Muy bien gracias," Bella replied. "Mucho mejor."

"What did you say to her?" Ray asked Chris. "And what'd she say back?"

"I asked how she's doing; she says much better. You have anything to do with this, anything you're not telling me?"

"No ... whadya mean? No."

Chris fixed Ray with one of her piercing gazes, one demanding disclosure. Ray promptly relented.

"Look, you know what's been going on. Diarrhea so bad it's gotten to the point where she's dehydrated. D'you know she fainted in the bathroom the other night?"

Chris shook no.

"Middle of the night, everyone was sleeping. Heard a loud thud on the floor. Found her passed out. She came to but looked so weak, didn't have the strength to get up. Rested her head on my lap; must've sat there with her for a half hour. I think this is what the latest note is about."

"How d'ya mean?"

"It's about Bella. You. Lisa Lewandowski. Feeling what others feel brings about healing."

"Jeezus, Ray. I mean, strange things have a way of happening whenever you're around, but this ... I dunno, your imagination's running a bit wild, don't you think?"

"I had diarrhea the next morning."

"You're shittin!" Chris blurted out incredulously before dissolving into laughter once her choice of word came in for a landing.

"Literally." Ray turned serious.

"It's hard to know what Bella's thinking cuz it ain't easy understanding her, but it's like she thinks I took whatever she had, so now she ain't got it no more."

Chris looked shaken. "Come on, you gotta admit, this is freaky."

"Listen, all I did was sit there with her for a little while, until she had the strength to stand. Helped her back to her room. Next thing I know I've got the runs and she doesn't. That's the whole story. I wish I could make sense of it all, but I can't."

Bella gained strength by the hour. Ray's illness passed too. Cori Thorson could detect no fever, no stomach discomfort, nothing, in either of them. When Chris and Ray filled Morger in, his response was as predictable as sunrise and sunset.

"What can't be explained is magic."

Willie García was far more helpful. He wasn't around Ebiyan every day once construction was completed, but often was summoned when Ray, Chris or Cori was in need of a translator. Willie talked with both Bella and Rami, passing along more to Chris than he shared with Ray.

"Bella's convinced Ray healed her. Hard to say with Rami. Tells me it's beyond any of our understanding, says God cured her. Bella about bites off his head, insists it was Ray who made her better. Then he says it's clear God worked through Ray."

Ray heard enough murmured remarks, saw enough furtive glances, to get the gist of what was circulating around Ebiyan and filtering out into the broader community. It was all so familiar, the way it always was in high school whenever something odd happened in Ray's presence.

After dinner one rudely cold night, Ray assembled everyone in the rec room. All 12 guests along with Willie and Cori. Ev happened to be around as well because he'd supplied the fish that had been that evening's main course. Colette had done the cooking and was cleaning up with Chris's help. Morger was pretending to help too, slipping into the rec room more or less unnoticed as the meeting was about to start.

"Well, uh, just wanted to say something. Okay, um, yeah, regardless of what you've heard … or think you've seen," Ray began haltingly. "I'm no doctor. I don't know what makes people sick or how to make them better."

"Oh yes you do," Chris interrupted as she stood at the edge of the dining area looking into the rec room. "No idea how you did it, but you made me better when I was sick, and I know Bella believes the same as I do."

Bella perked up when she heard her name, but didn't follow what Chris said. Willie leaned over, whispering in Bella's ear. Her eyes widened, Willie whispered something more, she nodded vigorously.

"It's not like I can stop infections or make diseases go away. There are doctors and medicine for that," Ray protested. "Dogs sense when you're hurting, have this natural ability to make you feel better, seem to understand healing better than us humans. I don't know, maybe I have some kind of dog sense. You might too and don't even know it."

Willie was in Bella's ear again, pulling away only long enough to whisper translations to Rami as well. Both laughed at the part about dog sense.

"Me curó," Bella said to the group, a look of stubborn determination etched on her still-haggard features. "El es mi ángel de la guarda."

Rami looked crossways at her; Willie emitted a muffled gasp. No one else knew what she said, no translation was provided. Ray didn't want to know, afraid it might open a can of worms, preferring to leave well enough alone.

"Anything I can do, you can do, I'm sure of it. The power to hurt comes naturally. Everyone knows how. Why is it so hard to believe that all of us might also have the power to heal?"

No one in the room disputed what Ray said, but no one looked satisfied or persuaded either. Noticing this, Ev did what he almost never did. He spoke.

"You are right that animals can sense things humans cannot. They know when storms are coming, long before we do. They can sense injury, soothe suffering, in ways we can't. My people revere animals, see them as brothers and sisters. I am connected to them, get guidance from them, but I am limited in my understanding of what they feel, what they know, what they can do. I am just as limited in my understanding of what you can do, Ray. You can do things I cannot, things that no one else here can do."

Chris stared at Ray until their eyes met, at which point she telegraphed a facial expression and hand gesture across the room that Ray took to mean told you so and get this through your thick skull. Ray felt ordinary, hating how others interpreted what they saw as exceptional.

"Would anyone mind me sharing a few thoughts?" Morger said from the back of the room.

No eye-rolls, no wincing.

"I don't mean to pile on, Ray, and hope you won't hold it against me if I tell the others what I've told you. You do have a power that few others possess. It only seems magical to those who can't understand it. You know how to use it, maybe not in your head, but your heart knows. I don't know how you came by it, but there's more than one person in this room who's convinced you saved them. I'm inclined to believe them because you also saved me, just in a different way."

Ray regarded the old man, at a loss for words, partly irritated, partly confounded, curious about what that difference might be.

"When you're as old as I am, you can hardly help having learned a thing or two along the way. Thing is, knowledge and experience bring you to a fork in the road. One way leads to arrogance. The other way takes you to humility. With the wisdom gained through humility comes the realization you're no better than anyone else. Different, but no better. Makes you kinder, more willing to cut others some slack. When I reached the fork in the road in the past, I turned toward arrogance, thinking I had everything figured out. I'm afraid I'd still be headed in that direction if not for you. You saved me, Ray, by showing me it's possible to turn around, retrace steps, go the other way at the fork. For that I thank you."

Any fleeting gratitude Ray felt gave way to embarrassment leavened with the simmering frustration that comes with feeling misunderstood. Trying to explain away or downplay the strange circumstances surrounding Bella's mystifying recovery, and Chris's before that, was pointless. The sensible path forward was to spend less time trying to explain the unusual, more time attending to the ordinary.

CHAPTER 22

A SEASON PASSED, THE SNOW MELTED, the ice broke. On cue, buds that appeared for all intents and purposes dead turned from gray to green, bulging expectantly. Ray stayed busy, ignoring gossip and speculation, finding peace of mind in an occasional walk in the woods that invariably led to the cathedral.

There was the garden to plant out back of the center, three kinds of squash, two kinds of melons, four kinds of beans, sweet peas, green and red peppers, yellow and green onions, garlic, potatoes, yams, pumpkins, cucumbers, lettuce, spinach, cabbage, broccoli, and five rows of sweet corn. Close to two dozen tomato seedlings nursed indoors at the tail end of winter were transplanted.

The plot was huge as gardens go, nearly an acre, promising a bounty to eat and plenty to sell, with everyone staying at Ebiyan pitching in. Residents all shared the load indoors as well, cleaning, taking turns cooking meals. When not on kitchen duty, several would go fishing with Ev or foraging the landscape for berries, nuts, mushrooms, wild greens and other edibles. Others collected eggs from the henhouse.

Seven more seasons came and went. Bella, Rami and their children had moved on once Bella regained her strength, looking for a place offering more opportunity and hoping to stay one step ahead of immigration authorities. Their place at Ebiyan was taken by several newly arrived migrants. Soon thereafter others arrived at the doorstep, two runaways, a domestic abuse victim, a trafficked teen, a homeless parolee. So did Sara, a stout farm girl and recent college graduate from the area who secured a license to practice social work but not a position in her field anywhere close to home. The aim of her narrow job search wasn't to ward off homesickness, it was to have the support of family after she learned she was pregnant.

Living with her parents outside of Unity, she heard about Ebiyan through the grapevine and was eager to volunteer as a way to gain experience. Her help was warmly welcomed, but her addition made close quarters feel crowded. They didn't trip over each other for long before deciding to build a new wing, adding an office for Cori and Sara along with more guest rooms, showers and toilets.

A second wing was added before the new year. The shelter now resembled a squared U, donated aluminum siding on the wings giving it a patchwork look. Gifts from near and far—money and materials—made it all possible, heartening signs of support that belied the misgivings and persistent grumbling of some townsfolk.

Faith was changing and changing fast, to the point where the locals took pains to distinguish between Old Faith and New Faith. When the paper mill still operated in the '70s and early '80s, jobs were easy to come by. Many a family and local merchant were sustained. When the plant shut down and the mill money dried up, about the only thing left was farming.

Families working the land and tending herds sent their kids to school in town, spent at the grocery store, dime store, feed mill and implement dealer, occasionally splurging to take in a movie or grab a bite at a local eatery, keeping those establishments going. Some family farmers waved the white flag in the early '80s, done in by collapsing commodity prices and unsympathetic bankers. Others weathered those storms, only to be slowly squeezed and eventually financially strangled by competition from the massive industrial feedlots and assembly-line-style milking operations that were beginning to dot the landscape.

Forced to choose between getting big or getting out, dozens if not hundreds in the area got out. As one after another left the business, their kids left them. This grim, involuntary exodus to faraway places in search of employment doomed Faith to a death spiral, making the community a shell of its former self. With the elementary school closed for lack of enrollment, sitting empty and decaying, young families had little incentive to move to

Faith.

Owners of the handful of gigantic agricultural factories couldn't come close to replacing hundreds of farm families when it came to filling classrooms and buying groceries or appliances or cars or clothes or the cafe's meatloaf special. Lights were turned out, windows were boarded, further pulverizing the ill-fated burg. One of the few growing enterprises was Ebiyan House, as the ranks of the afflicted and dispossessed relentlessly mushroomed.

Faith hung by a thread. Surviving businesses—like Moose Glennon's— provided employment for a few. Factory farms proved to be powerful magnets for migrant workers willing to perform the backbreaking tasks done there. These newcomers earned modest but regular paychecks that made them welcomed patrons of local stores. Their ways of doing things were greeted less warmly.

With time it became evident that the old-timers in town could tolerate— if only barely—a little cultural diversity if it meant an influx of consumers to buck up the local economy. Doing work whites in Faith considered beneath them paved the way for the migrants' acceptance as pivotal, if not permanent, fixtures in New Faith.

Other occupants of New Faith were not so readily embraced by the old guard, their presence producing ongoing friction. They were migrants of sorts as well, having traded the frenetic pace of city life for the tranquility of country living. That they took advantage of losses so many suffered with the collapse of local property values to scoop up land at bargain prices was a sore point for Old Faith, so sore that letting bygones be bygones was close to unimaginable.

One of the most striking qualities of these pilgrims was how oblivious they were to the grudges their neighbors bore against them. They threw their economic weight around, establishing upstart businesses instead of patronizing the old ones, each new enterprise rubbing more salt in Old Faith's wounds.

Nick and Dana Wilder started a small cheese and gift shop on the edge of town, opting against locating on Main Street alongside shuttered storefronts. Nick had been an advertising executive in the Cities, while Dana was a supply chain manager at a national electronic components conglomerate. The couple fled urban life to raise their two children in a small-town setting.

Nick jumped off the corporate treadmill to take up beekeeping, selling the honey he harvested at the gift shop. Dana learned the art of cheesemaking and had 10 Jersey cows, whose milk she turned into specialty cheeses sold in the shop. She told anyone who cared to listen—and few outside New Faith cared—that hers was a vertically integrated value-added operation, jargon from her industry days, meaning she raised the cows, milked them, made the cheese, packaged and sold it, no middlemen. Old Faith wondered why she didn't just say that.

In time, the Wilders branched out, making their artisan cheeses and honey available for purchase at Dicks Natural Food Cooperative. The pint-sized grocery was opened by Josh Dicks, a psychotherapist from Madison who'd grown disillusioned with the health care bureaucracy's meddling in his practice. Everything in his store was locally sourced, fresh produce from Ebiyan House and other area growers, grass-fed beef produced by two more urban transplants, Dan and Greta Schmitz.

That Josh entered into direct competition with Glennon's grocery was one strike against him with the locals. That he once called Madison home was another.

About the only place new and old mixed in Faith was Moose's tavern. It was the only watering hole in town, an oddity of the highest magnitude in a part of the country with more bars per capita than just about anywhere. From time to time the grocery wars would come up in conversation.

"I prefer Dicks," one fairly recent arrival asserted, paying no mind to double entendre.

"I bet you do," a lifer fired back with a smirk, prompting snickers up and down the line of barstools.

Quarrels originating at Moose's had a way of circulating through town, although blow-by-blow accounts varied from the old side of town to the new. That fact alone became a subject of discussion at a gathering of Ebiyan guests at the old Morger place.

"People here carry on about the free market, how good competition is, how evil socialism is, but how dare anyone come in and open a new grocery store," Willie observed.

"You ask me, it's not a new grocery store they have a problem with," Morger responded. "It's that the owner's not from around here."

"Why do people here hate Madison so much?" Ray asked Morger.

A wry smile grew on the old man's face as he pondered the question. Age was taking its toll, his appearance was more unkempt, his clothes hanging more loosely over his withering frame. His voice, however, was as commanding as ever. He spoke with meticulous clarity and methodical cadence, often starting out calmly before quickening the pace, turning up the volume, then downshifting to a gentle, kindly tone. This time, he struck a monotonous, almost weary note.

"Madison's a real nice town. I don't hate it the way others do," he began. "Part of it is probably jealousy. There's a lot of money in Madison, a lot of power. Comes across as overbearing, rubs folks the wrong way. Madison's a privileged place, quite impressed with itself, always careful to be politically fashionable, embracing all the right social causes, but numb to poverty. Tough place to be poor. At least that's what it feels like to outsiders like me."

"Sounds like you know it pretty well," said Ray.

"I've never advertised it around town, but Colette and I lived there for nearly a year after returning from our mission. Lots to do, always something happening. But for some reason, never felt at home, never fit in. Guess you can take the boy off the farm but can't take the farm out of the boy."

"What were you doing while you lived there?"

"I was substitute teaching. Colette worked at the Ovens of Brittany. Fancy joint compared to anything around here. Had two or three locations, best I can remember. Heard the last one closed a few years ago."

"If you'd stayed, you could've kept teaching."

"True enough, although at that time it wasn't easy getting a foot in the door. Full-time positions were hard to come by; no guarantee I ever would've been able to do more than sub. But even if I could have, not sure I would've wanted to. Couldn't see living there over the long haul."

Chris cut to the chase. "People here disowned you, forced you out of teaching. Spread horrible rumors about you, told their kids your house is haunted so they'd keep their distance, afraid you might rub off on them. If I were you, I'd want to be just about anywhere but here."

"You may be right, I may be overly stubborn, but this place is as much mine as it is theirs. I love this land, these woods, this old house. This is home. No one can tell me I don't belong. No one has the right to say Josh and Cindy Dicks don't belong. Or the Wilders. Or the Schmitzes. Or you Willie. Or you Ev. Or you Ray."

All but Chris nodded in agreement. She couldn't hide feeling sorry for Morger, something not lost on him.

"I can't make people agree with the way I've lived my life. I made my choices, got no regrets. Nothing's gained by sitting around stewing about how you've been treated. Spending your time being mad is a waste. Like the old saying goes, anger is like drinking poison and expecting somebody else to die."

Four faces exhibited not even a hint of recognition, proof enough that the saying was familiar only to Morger.

"Having something you value taken away can be a blessing in disguise. Creates an opportunity to discover something even more valuable. If my teaching career hadn't ended, most likely never would've gone to Africa. Highly doubt all of you would've come into my life. In a way, the people here did me a great favor."

All four in his audience knew to one degree or another how it felt to be ostracized, but could scarcely imagine how Morger managed to be so stoic and forgiving about it. Little did they know that their own responses to such treatment would be harshly tested in the days to come.

Ebiyan House was not exactly welcomed in Faith to begin with, and the Morgers allowing it to be built on their property, helping to make it happen, didn't sit well with a number of locals. Doc Szymanski and his family weren't fans. Nor was Pastor Cash. Butch and Claire Barber rarely passed up an opportunity to badmouth it.

What started as good-natured mocking turned into caustic grumbling, done in hushed tones out of respect for Moose's outward support of the project and the backing of other Good Samaritans like the Meaney family and the Slaters. But Ebiyan supplying produce to Madison transplant Josh Dicks loosened tongues and had even Moose openly complaining.

Someone went so far as to lodge an anonymous complaint about goings-on at Ebiyan, first with the county, then with state authorities. The deed was done on the sly, making it impossible to know which detractor was the culprit. With Cori Thorson running interference for the center, no county health department inquiry materialized. Luck ran out once grievances reached the state capital. Even though Ebiyan took no government funding, a state human services department auditor by the name of Cook was dispatched, tasked with looking into whether the center should continue to be allowed to operate as a shelter care facility.

Cook was a letter-of-the-law type, and the measures he took upon arriving in town felt more like an inquisition than an audit. He made little effort to conceal his preconceived judgments, clearly taking a dim view of an operation with no paid professional staff, apparently under the direction of a high school graduate and a dropout, only ostensibly guided by a trained health care provider. The state inspector was barely more discreet about what he thought of Faith, a forsaken backwater he could not put in his rear-view mirror quickly enough.

The handwriting was on the wall.

COUNTY
Q

CHAPTER 23

WITH NO HOTEL OPERATING IN FAITH ANY LONGER, Cook took up residence in the Abby Inn in nearby Abbotsford for the duration of his planned three-day stay. By the second day, boredom after work hours led him to make the 15-minute drive down Highway 29 to Meadowview Golf Course in Owen. After a late-afternoon round, he grabbed a bite in the clubhouse, then a seat at the bar, where he stayed until well into the evening.

Whether by serendipity or by design—to this day, no one knows for sure—Gin happened to be there. Only eight people sat around the circular bar, all except one in groups of two or three. Gin sidled up to the solitary stranger, between his barstool and the empty one next to him, perching an elbow on the bar.

"You look like you could use some company."

The bespectacled interloper shot a fleeting glance in Gin's direction, back to the glass in front of him, then returned to her. She didn't look like she was pushing 50, easily passing for 15 years younger, still trim, still stylish, still blonde without so much as a hint of gray, one more button on her blouse unfastened than modesty prescribed.

"Mind if I join you?"

Cook seemed incapable of speech, instead gesturing in a comically overzealous way, his hand hovering above the padded round seat, palm up, fingers outstretched beseechingly. Gin was amused but hid it well, planted herself on the stool, got the barkeep's attention, ordered her namesake with tonic. She downed one and started on a second before the conversation advanced beyond mindless discussion of the weather and area golf courses.

Gin got Cook talking about where he was from, where he attended college, his work, found it all mind-numbingly dull. She brought up Jim Slater, only to discover the angular, bookish bureaucrat knew nothing of baseball. When she tried a few tidbits of gossip to enliven their conversation, he scoffed at what passed for local drama, prompting her to segue to recollections of teen angst and high school hijinks.

By her third cocktail, Gin was telling of the time the local sheriff caught her in the car, half undressed, making out with the star of the football team. She spared no detail, embellishing here and there. She leaned in close, her voice barely above a whisper, disclosed that the sheriff was her father.

Telling this tale—aided by alcohol's effects—loosened things up considerably. After going Dutch the first few rounds, Cook saw fit to buy Gin's next drink. They toasted, laughed, swapped more stories. He coyly rested a hand on the small of her back, gravity guiding it downward at a glacial pace until it rested over the left rear pocket of her jeans.

"I'm married," she announced coolly.

Cook abruptly withdrew the offending hand, returning it to his lap.

"Didn't say that so you'd move your hand," Gin said nonchalantly. "Just wanted to be sure you're okay with it before we go back to my place."

Cook's posture stiffened. He appeared rattled, then awestruck.

"What about your husband?" he inquired nervously.

"He's an early riser. Fast asleep by now. Sound sleeper, that one … could sleep through a tornado. Can't imagine we'll make that much noise. Not that it matters. He and I don't … been three, going on four years since … you know, we live in the same house but don't sleep in the same bed."

"We could go back to my hotel … just to be safe."

"Don't be silly, you're not the first guy I've brought back to the house. I wasn't about to be abstinent for the rest of my life, and besides, he might not even be there … he's got two lady friends who look after him."

Cook tried unconvincingly to look sympathetic.

"Deb ..." Gin snarled, her voice dripping with contempt at the mere mention of the woman. "Agent with his real estate company, about our same age. Then there's Carrie ... pretty young thing ... tends bar at his tavern. Tends to him after closing time."

"Why do you stay married?"

"Our lives are so entangled. Everything's tied together, 'cept the sex."

"He knows about the other men?"

She smiled sheepishly, nodding.

"And he knows you know what he's up to?"

"Course he does. He plays them off against each other ... has them competing. Probably so they try outdoing each other in bed. Works out nicely for him, I'm sure."

Gin gathered her belongings from the bar, Cook rose from his stool, righting himself after staggering slightly, escorting her from the clubhouse, returning a hand to the base of her back, this time not so tentatively.

"You better drive," Gin said, not flinching as his hand migrated to her bottom. "I've probably had one too many."

Cook thought of the logistical inconveniences and ethical quicksand but wasn't about to lodge a protest as she looked at him impishly. Her eyelids drooped slightly under the weight of the cocktails but not enough to mask a suggestive leer, a devil-may-care invitation to indulge in carnal delights. On the drive out of town, Cook tried one last time to suggest it might be better to go back to his hotel room but a strategically placed hand on his upper thigh put an end to that.

He pulled in the driveway on the Hill, followed her to the front door. She let them in, turning on no lights, led him to her bedroom. There she flipped the switch to light the room and turned down the covers.

"I'll be right back," she said, unbuttoning her blouse.

When Gin returned several minutes later, Cook was lying on the bed wearing not a stitch of clothing, his swollen manhood pointing due north.

"Oh my, you look ready to go. We've got all night, cowboy."

She sat momentarily on the bed at his side, eyeing him as if admiring her catch. She rose, faced him, began wriggling out of her jeans, then paused.

"Forgot something. Be back in a second."

What seemed like several more minutes passed before she reentered, holding a half-full tube that she set on the nightstand. Cook had gone soft.

"A little something to make things go more smoothly," she said, gesturing to the tube. "Why don't you flip over. I give killer back rubs."

He did as commanded, turning onto his stomach, his head cocked so he could see as she joined him on the bed and swung a leg over him as though mounting a stallion. "Mind if I leave the lights on for now?" she asked as she began massaging his shoulders and arms. No answer came, and she didn't wait for one, kneading his back muscles, first near the shoulder blades, next along the rib cage, inching lower and lower, lingering just above the buttocks.

"You're so tense," she cooed. "This feel good?"

Cook groaned contentedly.

Gin shifted position so she could proceed lower still, rhythmically pressing first her thumbs then the rest of her fingers into his rump before moving to his hamstrings. When she reached the back of the knees and ran her hands slowly up the inside of his legs and down again, she could feel him tremble. As she retraced her path, she detected a pulse where none could be felt before. Her own quickened.

"You tense anywhere else?" she asked in a teasing tone.

He craned his neck and shoulders to look up at her, a wry smile on his long, lean face. She lifted her weight from his legs just enough to enable him to flip over.

"Oooh, found where you hold your stress," she said playfully, her hands hovering over his nether regions, which had snapped back to attention. "Let me see what I can do."

She lightly ran her fingertips up his arms to his shoulders and down across his chest, her feathery touch barely grazing the surface of his skin, migrating to his navel, where she lingered, circling with an index finger. This had him throbbing, oozing a clear secretion. Gin felt lightheaded, warmth spreading through her body.

"I'll get the light," she said, her voice wavering ever so slightly as she dismounted, scooted herself over to the edge of the bed, made her way unsteadily to the switch. The room went so dark Gin could no longer see the bed or what was waiting for her there. Cook could hear the faintest rustling from what seemed like five or six feet away, but could see nothing. He was tempted to call out, but held off, then whispered her name. As she brushed against him, he could tell she'd shed her undergarments. She rested her head on his shoulder, a hand on his chest, a leg draped over his.

"Did you think I lost my nerve and wasn't coming back?" she teased. She began passing her lips ever so tenderly over one nipple, then the other, to his stomach, lingering again at the belly button. Each time her lips moved on her hair swept softly over the vacated area until the muscles there quivered. She looked up but could not see his face. He could not tell she was smiling.

"Gonna get a little better acquainted," she said almost inaudibly, inch-worming toward the end of the bed, lowering herself until he felt a pendulous breast come in contact with his scrotum. He stared up, unable to discern anything in the pitch blackness. She remained still, as though holding her breath. Just when he could stand the suspense no longer and words queued at his lips, she began, undulating over his midsection, deliberately to begin with, the pace accelerating, then slowing again.

He writhed beneath her, grimacing, overpowered by a pain so exquisite, a pleasure so agonizing. Twice he raised an arm, holding it over her, ready to tap out. Each time she sensed he was nearing the point of no return and paused, bided her time, resumed, drew back.

"Want me to keep going?"

Cook issued something of a grunt that didn't quite pass for an answer one way or the other. His eyes longed to communicate what his voice could not, searching for even a silhouette in the dark. Seeing none, he scanned the room, hoping to locate even the scantest glimmer. His heart still racing, his breathing still labored, every muscle seized up, for any practical purpose incapable of movement. Cook was helpless as she resumed and utterly unprepared for a clicking sound that punctured the silence accompanied by a blinding flash of bluish white.

A half-beat later night was blasted into premature dawn as the whole room flooded with a softer but equally piercing light, stabbing his eyes, jolting him from his altered state. Startled, Gin abruptly released him, cupping the back of her hand at her brow as she wheeled around. Cook lurched out from under her, blurting an expletive, instinctively throwing one hand over his eyes, the other down between his legs to provide at least partial cover.

Snap.

Through squinted eyes Cook could make out an imposing figure standing just inside the doorway, a massive man even taller than him and nearly twice as broad, gripping with both meaty hands a small rectangular black object with a snout of some sort pointed in his direction. He groped the nightstand in search of his glasses, inadvertently knocking them to the floor.

Snap.

Cook slumped over the crumpled sheets.

Snap. Snap.

"Look who's caught with his hand in the old cookie jar," came the voice from the indistinct form in the doorway.

Snap.

"Richie, put that down!" Gin sprang from the bed, marched over to her husband, snatched the camera from him, began gathering up the clothes strewn across the room.

Cook located his glasses. As his eyes adjusted to the sudden and unexpected illumination, the room came back into focus. He could see Moose clearly now. Taking a cue from Gin, Cook retrieved his clothing and began dressing, panicked, speechless. Gin stood between him and her husband, camera in one hand, her clothes in the other.

"Get dressed," Moose directed his wife. "Not gonna harm him, gonna interview him."

He rounded on Cook. "I'm the publisher of the local paper … Since I've got you here, how 'bout you tell me how this investigation of yours is gonna turn out."

"I'm not at liberty to discuss that with you," Cook replied.

"Of course, you're under no obligation to talk," Moose replied calmly. "But since you're in a rather compromised position here, so to speak, I thought maybe you'd be in the mood to cooperate. Otherwise, you being in my house, doing what you were doing with my wife, well …"

Cook appeared ready to be sick. Considering the hour, Gin decided against putting her clothes back on, instead rifling through a dresser drawer for her favorite summer nightshirt.

"Now then, let's talk next steps," Moose continued. "I know you were just following orders coming here. There were complaints from an ignorant few, you've got to do your due diligence, I get that. I'm sure your bosses expect you to be all hard-ass about your rules. But when those rules cause a small town like ours to lose a resource like Ebiyan, people who really need help have nowhere to go. You want that on your conscience? Then there's the little matter of you and my wife."

Moose let his words sink in as he could tell wheels were rapidly turning in Cook's mind. Gin, for her part, stopped rummaging around in the dresser, not sure whether to be mad about privacy invaded or thankful for her husband's intervention on Ray's behalf. She stood there, still naked, not self-conscious in the least, gaping at Moose, showing neither anger nor gratitude.

"There won't be ... well, I can say ... for certain ... make no mistake," Cook stammered. "There won't be any next steps. No action needed. I consider this case closed."

His eyes dropped from Moose to the floor and he made for the door as though hoping no one would notice him leaving. He passed Moose, disappeared into the darkness of the narrow hallway. Gin remained frozen in place for several awkward moments. As she watched her one-night stand flee, she suddenly felt conspicuously bare.

"Better make sure he finds his way out," she muttered as she hurried past Moose, out the door, down the hall. Halfway down the stairs, she watched Cook step out into the night and close the door behind him, never to be seen in this neck of the woods again.

Gin dropped to the floor, her back up against one of the foyer walls, her knees drawn up tightly to her chest. She sat there a good long while before pulling herself to her feet and returning to her room.

Moose was no longer there, so she walked the short distance down the hall to his room. The door was closed, the lights off. Gin figured he couldn't possibly be asleep. She turned the knob, opened the door a crack, reached in with her hand, feeling for the switch, flipping it on. He swore as the light assaulted his eyes. He was not in bed but in a chair next to the bureau, sitting hunched over, head down.

"Jeezus, do you mind?" he bellowed.

"Exactly what I was thinking a moment ago," Gin shot back. "I respect your privacy; you should respect mine."

"I did you a favor. You should be thanking me."

Gin knew exactly what he was saying but pretended otherwise.

"And how's that?" she inquired in a sarcastic tone.

"You know how. He was most likely going to shut down Ebiyan. Now he's not. You're welcome."

"Why'd you do it?"

"You heard what I said to him."

"You were lying through your teeth. A few complaints, my ass. There's not 20 in the whole town who'd shed a tear if someone put a match to the place, and you know it."

"Ray and the others have worked hard, done good things, even if hardly anyone appreciates it."

Gin's expression softened, her posture relaxed. "Your timing could've been better."

"Wasn't trying to save you from yourself, only wanted to catch him in the act. Everyone at Ebiyan deserves better than being a notch on some ladder climber's belt. Smartass from Madison comes here, tries throwing his weight around, he got what he had coming. And, hey, if he didn't satisfy you, I'm happy to be a stud for hire."

"I'll pass."

"I know all the secrets. He couldn't have possibly solved the riddle in one night."

"Not that desperate."

"Suit yourself."

Gin turned to leave but the sound of Moose's husky voice caused her to linger in the doorway.

"Not buying that you brought that scrawny little prick home cuz you couldn't resist his bony ass. You did it for Ray, I know you."

Gin didn't turn around to face him, instead making her parting comment loudly enough so he'd hear it even as she walked back down the hall.

"Thank you."

CHAPTER 24

GIN DROPPED IN AT EBIYAN THE NEXT DAY. Everyone was relieved, pleasantly surprised that Cook cut his investigation short and was not sentencing the shelter to death or even mandating notable changes. To a person, it felt like a bullet dodged.

"The way he was talking, I was sure we were goners," said Chris.

Huddled in a cluster spilling from the dining area into the game room, staff and residents alike took turns telling of their encounters with Cook and feelings of impending doom. Even Morger revealed he had been bracing for the worst.

"Was thinking you'd have to do a Hail Mary ... as a last resort declare this place a church, to get the bureaucracies off your backs while keeping tax-exempt status."

"Hold on to that idea, still might need it someday," said someone from the back. Everyone turned around at the sound of a voice not often heard at Ebiyan. No one was more surprised than Ray, though Gin and Morger came in a close second and third. The voice belonged to Moose.

The room fell silent.

"I, uh, just wanted to say congratulations, I'm happy for you," Moose began haltingly, all eyes on him. "You've got a good thing going here. I don't mind admitting I was skeptical at the beginning; didn't think you were going to make this work. You proved me wrong. What you've done is a credit to our community, a tremendously valuable asset. Keep up the good work."

"Miracles never cease," Morger said under his breath. Gin's mouth hung open; Colette's eyes were swimming. Chris looked over at Ray, hoping their eyes would meet, but Ray was studying Moose. As the meeting broke up, Moose headed for the door, not wanting to overstay his welcome. Ray intercepted him just before he reached the exit.

"Good of you to come, Dad."

Ray never said much but had a knack for using precious few words to great effect. That last word hit with the force of a bomb. It left Moose speechless, scrambling to herd stray emotions back into their pen. Gin had never seen him lose his composure like this, rarely saw him look less than confident. He looked uncomfortable, awkward, afraid Ray might hug him or something. He was spared.

Once Moose left, Gin threw her arms around Ray.

"You never stop surprising me," she muttered upon releasing her grip.

"He's not my father, but he's been a dad. Not always a good one, but he's done a lot."

Gin shook her head, held a hand to her mouth for a few moments before reaching out to run her fingers over Ray's hair pulled back into a bushy tail.

"Your hair looks nice like this."

"Been needing a haircut, don't like it this long. Been thinking of getting a buzz cut, just haven't gotten around to it."

Gin wanted to protest but bit her tongue.

"I know what happened wasn't an accident," said Ray matter-of-factly.

Gin looked stumped.

"The man had his mind made up. Next thing we know, he drops the whole thing, high-tails it out of town," Ray continued. "There's a reason, you and the Moo ... you and Dad ..."

"Honey, I ..." Gin interrupted.

"I love you, Mom," Ray said, not letting her finish her thought. "It's not like this place is mine. Belongs to everyone; what happens here is done standing on the shoulders of others. I'm glad so many look out for us."

"How much do you know about what ..."

"Doesn't matter. I'm thankful you care."

"You don't ... you're not ..."

"I love you, Mom. Nothing you do will ever change that."

A flood of emotions inundated Gin, tying her tongue: embarrassment, shame, gratitude, motherly devotion.

"Can you do me a favor?" Ray asked, breaking the silence.

"Anything."

"Can you give me a ride over to the church later?"

"Sure. What for?"

"Tom Tetzlaff's dad's funeral. You heard he took his life. I was in Tom's class."

"Wasn't he the one who ..."

"Yeah."

Gin looked past Ray to Chris, who was listening from behind Ray, her face a blend of anger and admiration.

"He humiliated my brother in front of basically the whole school," she told Gin, her eyes steely. Then she turned to Ray. "Can't imagine he's going to be happy to see you. You made him piss his pants."

Ray cringed, remembering. "Their farm is being taken away. The way I hear it, Tom and his mom can stay in the house but are losing everything else."

Chris said nothing further. She knew of the Tetzlaff family's plight, everyone in town did. Charlie Tetzlaff learned the ways of farming in his youth when neighbors banded together in threshing gangs to harvest their grain and came to each other's aid when calamity struck, pooling their resources and labor to sandbag homes against floodwaters, raising new barns to replace ones demolished by a tornado or destroyed by fire.

That was then. No neighbors came to the rescue when the bank sent notice of impending foreclosure as Charlie's family reached the brink of financial ruin. When they could no longer keep up with loan payments due to rising expenses and falling milk prices, there was no government bailout, no union marched in solidarity with them. Charlie Tetzlaff looped a length of rope over a rafter in the shed where the tractors and other farm equipment were stored and hung himself.

He left behind his wife Phyllis and two sons. The younger, Tom, worked at his dad's side on the farm; the older, Gary, was doing jail time for a series of thefts. Charlie's suicide and loss of the farm staggered the family emotionally and financially. Tom only knew farming; other gainful employment proved elusive. Gary briefly got out of jail, only to violate the terms of parole.

A full two years after losing Charlie, with Gary back behind bars and Tom not bringing in any money, Phyllis stubbornly refused to apply for public assistance. Instead, she let the insurance on the house lapse. The electricity was cut off and the telephone disconnected, and she relied on church pantries for what food they couldn't grow or scavenge. Well into her 70s and in faltering health, now lacking electricity, Phyllis lit her home with candles and a kerosene lantern, heating it in the winter months with an old wood-burning stove claimed from the town junkyard. Though no authorities ever determined the cause with certainty, it was widely suspected one of the candles caught some drapes on fire, engulfing the old farmhouse in flames.

The local volunteer fire department wasn't summoned until Tom ran almost half a mile to the nearest neighbor to put in the call. There was no saving it—the house was a total loss. The family's few possessions were gone. Without insurance, there was no way to rebuild.

Tom Tetzlaff's surprise at Ray's presence at the funeral was nothing compared to his bewilderment when Ray suggested Tom and his mother move into Ebiyan House temporarily. He was downright shocked when Ray organized friends, neighbors as well as local Amish families to build the Tetzlaffs a new home. The retired shop teacher Mr. Jeske procured building materials and oversaw construction. All the people who built Ebiyan pitched in once more, plus many others from the area.

Moose jumped in with both feet, providing both funds and sweat equity. With many hands making light work, the house was finished in less than two months. The entire time, Tom only spoke to Ray twice. When construction commenced, he thanked Ray in one clipped sentence for paying respects after his father's passing and extending hospitality to him and his mother when they had no place to go. About a week before Tom and Phyllis left Ebiyan to move into their newly built home, Tom found himself alone with Ray in the lobby after others retired to their rooms.

"You and your mom have been through a lot," said Ray. "It won't be long now, things will be better."

Tom didn't want to sound ungrateful but had a hard time imagining life getting better.

"Bankers, ag extension agents, they all tell you, gotta get big or get out.

Like it's a choice. T'aint no choice. Dare ain't no way to get as big as the outfits movin' in from Texas, Oklahoma, Florida. You don't get to choose when to get out. Gets decided for you. They just take your land, take your herd, take everything you worked for."

He remembered vividly how he treated Ray in school, how most everyone treated Ray. How he did nothing to prevent the abuse or soften the blows, how he did the deeds himself or at least cheered on the bullies. At the same time, even after all these years, he bore something of a grudge against Ray for intervening to such humiliating effect when he was hazing Chico Driscoll. Yet he couldn't help but feel guilty about that grudge given the present circumstances. He couldn't fathom the kindness now being shown but was in no position to turn down the help.

Chris remembered too, bore her own grudge against Tom, likewise struggling to comprehend Ray's willingness to give someone a helping hand who'd done nothing to deserve it. She kept her thoughts to herself for the longest time, until after the construction was completed, when Tom and Phyllis Tetzlaff left the shelter to move into their new accommodations.

"I wish I could be like you. It's like you have amnesia," she said to Ray as the two scrubbed pots and pans after dinner one night. "You forget and move on. I remember and am stuck."

"I remember," Ray replied softly.

"You remember what that greasy little fuckwad did to Mickey? You remember what he did ... what all those asswipes did to you, day after day?"

Ray nodded.

"How do you just put all of that out of your mind?"

"I don't."

"But you offer him and his mom beds here."

"They lost theirs."

"You don't have one yourself! You sleep on a damned cot!"

Ray shrugged.

"Then you build them a new house! Who does that? For someone who shit all over you?"

Ray dried both hands with a towel, pulled a folded-up dog-eared piece of ruled white paper out of a pocket, handing it to Chris. She knew instantly what to expect, unfolding it hastily, needing only seconds to read what was handwritten on the page.

Roses and thistles each are prickly and both bloom.

"You found this in the jar. When?"

"A while ago. I was starting to think maybe the messages had stopped."

"Why didn't you show me?"

"Wasn't sure we'd agree on the meaning."

"You took it to mean you're obliged to help the Tetzlaffs?"

"Took it to mean there's good and bad in all of us, nobody's always right, nobody's always wrong. Took it as a reminder that our best hope is forgiveness. Forgiving doesn't mean forgetting. I remember all of it. I can't un-remember it, but can try to rise above it."

Chris took the towel from Ray, wiped her hands, tears streaming down her cheeks even as indignation smoldered in her eyes.

"You know, sometimes I feel like I know you, am madly in love, other times I feel like I don't know you at all, hate you for hiding what's inside you. I once was willing to wait for you to open up, was sure it'd be worth the wait. I gave up expecting it to ever happen. Getting through each day is easier when I'm not playing some endless waiting game."

She buried her face in the towel. A wave of emotion crashed over her, then receded. She withdrew the towel. "I hate you. I really do. And I hate myself for that, because you're the most amazing person I've ever met. I love you so much I hate you."

She brought the towel to her face once more, sobbing. When Ray embraced her, she initially pulled away before accepting the gesture. Her agonized cries drew the attention of several residents, who followed the sound to the common area, keeping their distance but obviously concerned. Once Chris became aware her outburst was attracting a crowd, she calmed herself, trying her best to downplay the theatrics.

"Just been a hard day ... I'm okay," she assured six or seven onlookers before vacating the premises.

What came to be antiseptically referenced as the Tetzlaff matter was a tender subject around Ebiyan. Some who knew the high school history or who'd fallen victim themselves to Tom's bullying ways—like Ev and sister

Linh—were confounded by the generosity Ray extended to the Tetzlaffs. Others sensed it was a source of tension between Ray and Chris and skated around the topic.

A few marveled at what confused so many. A middle-aged migrant woman named Elena heard about what happened with Bella, knew of many other similar occurrences, then saw with her own eyes what Ray pulled off on the Tetzlaff family's behalf. More than once she nodded toward or pointed to Ray, making declarations—exuberantly, almost worshipfully—that nobody understood. No one was at the ready to translate. Willie, Frankie and Rosa had succumbed to Ray's arm twisting to help build the house, but made themselves scarce after the work was done.

For weeks that soon stretched into months, Ray gave Chris a wide berth, treading softly when task or circumstance did thrust them together. Finally, whether worn down or fed up, something snapped.

"You don't have to wait," Ray blurted out in a rare private moment.

"Say what?" replied Chris in a tone of voice every bit as puzzled as the look on her face.

"You shouldn't wait for me to open up. You deserve to be able to move on, find someone else."

Chris breathed a heavy sigh, mouth shut, lips pursed, puffing out her cheeks. She looked weary, older than her years. "I don't want to move on, not interested in looking for someone else. Never had any luck with men, can't imagine my luck changing. 'Member that time we were out back of my old man's garage, what I told you?"

Ray nodded.

"You were the first, the only."

Ray got the feeling Chris was moving in for a kiss.

"Well, that's ... that, uh, you know, is the thing ..."

Chris laughed heartily at the sight of her friend stammering, recoiling, shrinking before her. "Oh my God you're hopeless, you know that, don't you? Don't worry, I stopped waiting. Now that I think about it, I guess I have moved on."

Ray looked stricken, absolutely crestfallen, not needing to say so much as a word for Chris to get the picture. Her smile vanished, her shoulders slouched, her demeanor softened.

"Ray," she said gently, trying to make eye contact. "Ray, look at me … Listen, I don't expect anything to change between us. I did stop waiting for that to happen. But I didn't stop loving you. Ray, look at me … I still love you. I love you even though you're pathetic."

Both of them laughed through tears at that.

"Even if I can only have part of you, I'll take it."

COUNTY
Q

CHAPTER 25

"YOU GOT A MINUTE?" Ray saw the figure standing in the lobby, heard the voice in the same instant. Both seemed out of place. Of all the people showing up on Ebiyan's doorstep, sometimes out of curiosity, usually out of desperation, that it was Lisa Lewandowski took Ray by surprise. Still, Ray recognized her at once.

"Lisa! Oh my God, it's great seeing you."

Appearing relieved not to be mistaken for a stranger, Lisa took several steps forward, surveying the place.

"It's been a while," said Ray. "Come and sit."

Lisa always had been on the heavy side, but curvy in her youth. Now she was wider and rounder. Years had turned pert dimples into drooping jowls. Hair once shoulder length was now cut much shorter and flecked with gray.

"What can I do for you?" Ray asked.

"I'm getting married next month, would like you to be at my wedding."

"That's wonderful, congratulations! Course I'll come, just let me know the date. Who's the lucky guy?"

"I'm marrying my partner Jan."

Ray felt about a foot tall. The embarrassment showed.

"No, Ray, don't worry about it. We've always kept our relationship on the down-low. Now that the Supreme Court has made it legal, we decided to make it official. Been a long time coming."

"It was stupid of me to assume. I'm really happy for you."

"No need to beat yourself up. You being willing to come is enough. My folks won't. Neither will Jan's. We're not even sure where we can have the ceremony. No church in town will do our kind of wedding. Maybe we'll just do it in the backyard."

"You can always do it here. Or, if you want an outdoor ceremony, there's the cathedral."

"The what?"

"That's what Morger calls it. Out in the woods, underneath the twin steeples. You know them, right?"

"Those I know."

"If you walk out towards the twin steeples, you come to this cluster of trees and bushes that looks like a big meeting room. Darnedest thing, like someone sculpted it. Morger swears it's natural. If you're interested, I can take you and Jan out there and show you."

"We'd love to see it, even if we don't choose to do the ceremony there."

With Ray not saying anything in return, Lisa fidgeted in her seat for a spell, gathering her thoughts.

"I should've told you when I moved in with your family. Didn't feel safe saying it back then. What I told you about wanting to get out of my parents' house, that's true. Wasn't trying to get in between your mom and Moose, also true. Never been attracted to men, that I left out."

She drew a breath.

"Jan and I are both 49 now, we're not keeping this in the shadows anymore. Getting on with the rest of our lives, regardless how others feel. Thanks for being okay with it; most people around here aren't. Nice of you to offer to host our celebration. Means a lot."

Lisa did return with Jan days later following up on the offer to use the Ebiyan grounds or the woods for their ceremony. Despite the challenging trek down a rutted dirt path, through thick tag alders, fording a narrow stream, traversing uneven ground, the couple was enchanted by the preternatural setting, especially the ready-made tent the forest provided. They fell in love with the idea of exchanging their vows there, both surprising and delighting Ray.

Wedding day was one of summer's dog days as July gave way to August.

Barely a dozen guests, counting Ray, gathered next to Ebiyan's garden before seeking shade under one of the big trees in front of the Morger house. A few close friends of Lisa's and several of Jan's were there, no parents, no aunts or uncles, no cousins, no former classmates. Maggie and Jim Slater were the only neighbors from the Hill in attendance.

Colette served the group lemonade while waiting on the justice of the peace to arrive. No ministers within 50 miles of Faith would preside over a same-sex wedding. No local judges were comfortable officiating either. Just as the search began to feel futile, a state appeals court judge from Madison whose district included Clark County agreed to make the trip, even waiving any fee. She was nearly a half-hour late arriving, quite taken aback when informed where the ceremony would take place and what was involved in getting there, but was a good sport about it.

There was a minimum of grumbling about bushwhacking through tangled underbrush, only slightly more when a few dress shoes sunk in the muck along the shallow stream. Misgivings dissolved and eyes widened as the wedding party and judge passed one by one under the archway that seemed too perfectly formed, too symmetrical, to be a natural coincidence.

Lisa, Jan and the judge took their places at one end of the more or less oval-shaped chamber, a ceiling of tightly clustered leaves and branches rising to a peak above them. Everyone else gathered around. The judge wasted no time starting the ceremony.

"It is an honor to be here with you in this beautiful spot to celebrate the marriage of Lisa and Janice. Considering that less than two months ago such a marriage was not legally recognized in our state or in most parts of our nation, I thought it would be appropriate and inspirational to read from the majority opinion of the United States Supreme Court written by Justice Anthony Kennedy."

She recited how marriage transforms strangers into relatives, binds families and societies together. "It is written that marriage responds to the universal fear that a lonely person might call out only to find no one there. It offers the hope of companionship and understanding and assurance that while both still live there will be someone to care for the other."

She looked up from the text, smiling warmly at Lisa and Jan, both towering over her. Lisa was at least five-foot-nine, Jan stood even taller, all of six feet with more of a lean athletic build. Neither wore a dress, opting instead for pantsuits.

The judge continued reading about how homosexuality was classified as a mental disorder in 1952, remaining so until 1973. How the court eventually invalidated laws making same-sex intimacy a criminal act. How freedom does not stop there. "Outlaw to outcast may be a step forward, but it does not achieve the full promise of liberty. It would misunderstand these women to say they disrespect the idea of marriage. They respect it so deeply that they seek to find its fulfillment for themselves. Their hope is not to be condemned to live in loneliness, excluded from one of civilization's oldest institutions. They ask for equal dignity in the eyes of the law. The Constitution grants them that right."

Tears welled up in Lisa's eyes, not escaping Jan's notice, causing her to lose her composure as well. Once more the judge paused, drawing a breath, thanking everyone for bearing with her, assuring them they were being spared, for she was not reading the court's ruling in its entirety.

"This landmark decision makes it possible for Lisa and Janice to exchange vows and enter into matrimony and allows me to stand before you today and confer upon their relationship the official status of marriage," the judge said. "Without further ado, Lisa will you repeat after me: I, Lisa, take you, Janice, to be my lawfully wedded spouse, to have and to hold, from this day forward, for better, for worse, for richer, for poorer, in sickness and in health, until death do us part."

Lisa recited the words with some coaching from the judge, who then turned to Jan, prompting her to repeat the same vow, which she did well enough, if not exactly word for word. The judge called on the two of them to exchange rings, done in turns with each making a memorized declaration. "I give you this ring as a symbol of my love, my faith in our strength together, my promise to learn and grow with you."

"By the power vested in me by the State of Wisconsin, I pronounce you a married couple," the judge announced, her voice filled with emotion. "You may kiss."

And they did. Everybody burst into raucous applause. The rest of Faith didn't see Lisa and Jan kiss, the sound of their friends cheering couldn't permeate the forest's walls, not the way gunfire at the shooting range does.

In the days to come, Lisa and Jan as well as Ray and the others at Ebiyan fell back into routine. The day-to-day grind was mercifully interrupted when Annie came to town for a visit. She'd been a stranger for quite some time, immersing herself in her studies in St. Paul, spending a semester in Norway, returning to finish up school. She went back to Norway for more than a year after graduating, lived in the Denver area for a spell before landing a job in a museum in Phoenix. She got back to the Cities maybe twice a year to visit her mom, her stays brief, rarely allowing enough time to squeeze in a trip to Faith.

Annie's manner was as remembered, engaging, blunt, ever the wiseacre. She colorfully described her vagabond existence, comparing and contrasting the places she'd been, unblushingly recounting trysts she'd had, profiling men she'd bedded. Then she began pumping Ray for information, not getting nearly the level of disclosure she desired.

"Why'd you stay here?" she asked abruptly and rather crassly. "Why not go back to the Cities? You liked it there."

"I like it here too."

"The world's a big place. There's so much to see, so much to experience. You could make a far greater impression, get more attention, help so many more people."

"I'm not looking for attention or trying to make an impression. There are people everywhere needing help. Don't have to go anywhere to find people hurting. There's plenty of hurt right here."

Annie started to argue, but Ray cut her off.

"Finding meaning in life isn't hinged to a place, it's found in here," Ray said, bringing hand to heart.

"It's that jar, isn't it?"

Ray didn't see that coming. A comeback didn't immediately come to mind. Annie pressed her case. "That's why you won't leave ... it has a hold on you."

"My mom's here, a lot of people I care about are here. The Morgers are family to me."

"Don't you wish you could call your own shots? Won't you ever stop waiting for directions from that old coot or his wife or whoever he has writing you those notes?"

"The messages don't come from Mr. and Mrs. Morger."

"I know you say that b ..." Annie started to say before again being cut off.

"The messages aren't theirs."

"Whose are they?"

"Wish I knew. I have a hunch, can't be sure."

"Do tell."

Ray decided against answering. The whole conversation got Annie to thinking she and Ray should pay the Morgers a visit. That would have to wait. They'd already told Ray they were getting a lift to Marshfield; seems they needed to see a lawyer to put their affairs in order.

Later that day, Ray and Annie stopped by to see if they were back. No one answered the knock on the door, unlocked as usual, the two let themselves in. Ray called out upon entering; that too went unanswered. By force of habit, Ray drifted into the kitchen, over to the counter, lifting the lid to the cookie jar. In it, barely an inch below the lip of the opening, another folded sheet of white paper, the ruled kind, resting on top of a mound of chocolate chip cookies.

Ray removed it along with two of the treats, taking a bite of one, offering the other to Annie. With Annie looking on curiously, Ray unfurled the find, being careful not to tear it. On one side, middle of the page, eight words handwritten in blue ink, the familiar stately cursive.

It is time to show your true self.

Ray showed the note to Annie, who regarded it skeptically at first, her expression changing as she absorbed the message.

"I could have told you this, it's not wrong. You should've unburdened yourself of that years ago."

"Are you saying what I think you're saying?" Ray inquired uneasily.

"Yeah, pretty sure I am," Annie answered without a beat being missed. "Known for a while now, don't know, a few years maybe. I think Mom's known all along."

That was something of a shock to Ray. "I thought only my mom and the Morgers knew about that."

"Haven't told another soul," Annie reassured Ray. "It's for you to decide when to tell others. Far as I'm concerned, I don't know what you've been waiting for."

"You make it sound like it should be easy."

"Not easy. It's just if I'm in your shoes, I'd want people to know. I wouldn't want to keep that kind of thing to myself forever."

As Ray was measuring words, the front door could be heard opening. Colette's voice called out from the entryway. "Chris, is that you?"

Before Ray could answer, Colette and Morger emerged from the front hallway into the dining room.

"Ray! Soyez la bienvenue!" Colette exclaimed. "Oh, Ann! What a pleasure seeing you. It's been such a long time. Such a treat to have you come visit."

Annie beamed, pleased to have been recognized after a years-long absence. She noticed at once that Colette and Morger had aged plenty since she'd last seen them. Morger was thinner, more bedraggled, moving stiffly with a shuffling gait. Colette looked haggard, unsteady on her feet. That didn't stop her from making her way to the kitchen to retrieve the cookie jar.

"Please, sit. Can I get you something? Lemonade, juice, milk. Could make some coffee."

Annie declined the offer, leaving Ray feeling obliged to properly acknowledge the hospitality.

"Just some water, please."

Colette obliged. The four sat at the dining room table.

"What brings you to our neck of the woods?" Morger asked, but before Annie could answer Colette redirected the inquiry.

"Where are you living now?"

"Phoenix. Came up to visit my mom, thought I'd swing over here to see Ray and you folks."

"So glad you did. Kind of you," Colette replied.

"It's impressive seeing how much Ebiyan has grown," Annie said. "A lot of other places could use this kind of thing. Far bigger places. The impact would be so much greater."

Morger bristled at the remark, though his response was characteristically measured.

"Now don't you go trying to steal Ray from us," he said with a wink. Oblivious to her perceived slight, Annie forged ahead.

"All I'm saying is Ray could stand to be more ambitious, dare I say evangelical. At the very least, create social media accounts, share Ebiyan's story that way. Might just go viral."

Ray looked intrigued, Morger's countenance made it plain he took a dimmer view.

"Far as I'm concerned these social media sites are among the worst inventions in human history. Making our country into one giant middle school."

Annie was like a dog with a bone.

"It's the way of the world, today's marketplace of ideas, what a free press looks like in the 21st century."

Morger sighed, shaking his head.

"Freedom's a wonderful thing, but when it's exercised childishly, it's lethal. America's in that lethal phase. Do as I damn well please, I know my rights, don't talk to me about my responsibilities. Don't you dare put any limits on my freedom, but go ahead, take away someone else's. All this is a big old barrel full of gasoline and social media's the match."

Morger's lecture gave Annie pause, but it was a much pithier comment that stopped her in her tracks.

"*Lord of the Flies*," Ray said wryly.

"Touché," she replied with a hint of a smile.

As usual, Colette smoothed things over, redirecting attention to the cookie jar, deftly steering the conversation to less rugged terrain. Plans to make roasted chicken and baked potatoes, would Annie and Ray care to stay for supper. How people came together at Ray's behest to build the Tetzlaffs a new house after theirs burned down. The town's latest marriage, first of the same-sex variety.

"Times are changing, we'll be better for it in the end," she said cheerfully.

"Over a few dead bodies I'm afraid," Morger chimed in, dousing the mood, earning a stern visual reprimand from Colette.

"You might not like it, but it's true. Some folks ain't gonna take what's happening lying down. There'll be blowback, mark my words."

Ray found it hard to disagree with either Colette or Morger. Which made tomorrow feel both too long in coming and speeding too fast for conditions.

CHAPTER 26

MORNING'S FIRST RAYS BRIGHTENED THE SILL above Ray's head but left Ebiyan's interior dark. Those that followed pelted the windows with increasing intensity, some sneaking through cracks in the blinds, landing on closed eyelids, beckoning them to open.

Chris was first to rouse this morning, emerging from one of two rooms unoccupied by guests. The sound of someone stirring woke Ray, who'd spent the night on a folding cot in the lobby. Annie remained sound asleep in the other guest room not currently spoken for. No residents were up and about yet, leaving Ray and Chris alone to begin making preparations for breakfast.

Chris started brewing coffee while Ray cut up some fruit and put out assorted boxes of cereal. Having just rolled out of bed, they looked it, equally disheveled, both unshowered and uncombed. Each still wore nightclothes, Ray a ratty old T-shirt and gym shorts, Chris a stretched and graying tank top so oversized it could pass for a mid-thigh dress. She stood bleary-eyed, slightly bent at the waist, her arms spread-eagled, hands gripping the kitchen countertop, not realizing Ray had crept up behind her.

"I'm ready," Ray announced, startling Chris a bit.

"Ready for what?"

"To tell."

"Tell what?" Chris retorted, sounding unenthusiastic about any further suspense.

"What I've been holding back ... about me."

Chris wheeled around, looking surprised, then happy, then skeptical, then relieved. Suddenly self-conscious about being underdressed for the occasion, she tugged at her tank top in hopes of greater coverage.

"I'm, well ... not strictly speaking ... you know ... oh man, this is hard. I've been thinking about what to say, should've practiced how to say it."

"Spit it out."

Ray was trembling now, wracked with nerves nearly to the point of fainting.

"I'm not ... well, anatomically at least ... you know, a man."

Chris's eyes grew large. Her mouth hung open. Questions bombarded her mind; just as she was about to ask one, three more threw themselves on the pile.

"I feel like a man, 'cept ... that's the way I think of myself, but ..."

"You don't have a ..."

"I've got one ... it's an innie, not an outie."

Chris tried but failed to suppress laughter. "Sorry."

"No, I mean, I know this is a lot to process."

"So, you have ..." Chris started to say, miming the rest of the question by bringing a hand to her chest.

"Always been flat-chested, they've been easy to hide. Nobody's ever noticed."

"Who else have you told?"

"No one. You're the first. My cousin Ann and her mom already knew. So did the Morgers. Mom must've told them, or they figured it out for themselves. The Moose doesn't know."

"You're kidding!"

"No, he has no idea. Mom kept it from him. Even when I started having my period, we were able to keep him in the dark."

Ray could tell Chris was searching her mind for signs or hints or clues she'd overlooked all these years.

"I've gotten good at making sure no one knows it's that time of the month."

"Still, you think of yourself as a man."

"I do. Always thought of myself as a boy when I was in school. Always wanted to hang out with other boys, got crushes on girls. Had a major crush on you, biggest one I ever had. Me being a couple of years younger, I figgered you didn't know I existed."

"I didn't, until what you did for Mickey."

"Yeah, that. The cat was almost out of the bag right then and there, in front of the whole school."

"I've thought a lot about this thing you've been keeping from me. This was never one of the possibilities I considered."

"Worse than you imagined, or not as bad?"

Chris pondered the question for a good long while, started speaking, then stopped.

"Nah, not bad. Just wasn't thinking along those lines at all. Thought it must have something to do with these things you keep making happen, didn't want anyone else knowing how you do it. Or maybe it had to do with where you came from. That whole story, your mom losing a baby, leaving, returning years later with you, you being adopted, always seemed off somehow."

"With good reason."

Chris's eyes got big again.

"I'm not adopted, Mom had me. Says she doesn't know by who."

"Oh my God ... How can she not know who the father is?"

"Dunno."

"That doesn't bother you? Don't you want ..."

Ray talked over her. "The Moose sent her away ... to the Cities 'til I was like eight. Took us back, on the condition that everyone be told I'm adopted."

"Wait, so how does the Moose not know you're a ... you know, were born female?"

"As soon as he saw my skin color, he freaked out. Left the hospital, didn't wait to see whether I was a girl or boy, didn't want anything to do with naming me."

Chris clearly was struggling to process all this. Ray gave her time to let it sink in.

"Obviously knowing you were a girl, why'd your mom name you Ray? That's what, short for Raymond?"

"It's short for Raejean. R-a-e-j-e-a-n. And I'm not a girl. At least I don't think of myself as one."

"Sorry, it's gonna take me some time to talk about this without sticking my foot in my mouth."

"No sweat. I was a baby girl to my mom, until I got closer to school age. She could see I was acting like a boy, making friends with boys in the neighborhood, didn't want to dress like a girl, didn't want to do girl things. It's why we came back to Faith."

"Wait, what?"

"I don't think she wanted to ever come back. I don't think she was interested in patching things up with the Moose, she was fine being single again. She loved living in the Cities, liked her job. Especially liked being close to Aunt Grace. She did it for me ... came back here to make things easier for me."

Ray's lips quivered, tears leaking.

"How does being here make anything easier? This place isn't exactly overflowing with tolerance."

"She didn't bring me here cuz she thought I'd be accepted. She thought it'd be easier here to keep my sex a secret. Told everyone I was a boy; everybody took her word for it. The few who knew kept it to themselves. Enrolled me in school, filled out all the forms saying I was a boy, nobody questioned it. Doctored a copy of my birth certificate to make it look like I was born a boy; don't know if she ever had to show it."

Chris marveled at Ray, like she was looking at an entirely different person.

"Holy smokes, it's hard to believe this has gone on so long."

"There were close calls. It's why I stopped playing sports, dropped gym class as soon as I could. Too risky to keep going in the boys' locker room. When I got pantsed in the hallway, was sure the underwear would be next to go. Dodged that bullet. There was that one time here, you walked in on me as I got out of the shower. Thought you got a clear look—guess not."

"Only saw you for a split second, could tell you were naked, wasn't about to stare. Now I wish I did."

"It's not a pretty sight; prolly would've turned your stomach."

A frown forming on Chris's face turned up into a smile. "Let me know the next time an exhibition is scheduled."

Ray wasn't sure how to take that, but sorely wanted it to be a sign of acceptance.

"So do you think you can ... we could ... I mean, even though I don't ... I'm not ... I can't, you know ..."

"You want to try saying that again?"

"Do you think ... oh hell ... should I still be afraid of what I was afraid of before?"

"Sorry, not sure what you're trying to get at."

"I told you before, I was afraid that if you knew this about me, you'd be grossed out or feel misled or something, wouldn't want to be friends anymore. Now that you know, I'm wondering ..."

Ray's voice trailed off. Chris didn't let the unfinished thought hang there for long.

"We can still be friends. Or more than that ... if you want ..."

Chris paused, battling cotton mouth. "I want that. I do."

Now Ray's eyes got big. Breathing suddenly got substantially more challenging.

"Oh my God, are you serious? Even though I'm not ... I don't ..."

"For chrissakes, shut up already. It's adorable when you get tongue-tied and all, but yes, even though you don't have a dick. You're man enough for me."

Ray lurched into her arms. They reprised the kiss shared so many years earlier in the cathedral. Coming up for air, Chris ran her fingers across Ray's velvety smooth cheeks.

"I always noticed you didn't shave, assumed you were a late bloomer when you were still in school. Later on, thought maybe it had something to do with your skin condition. Somehow, it never occurred to me ... Looking back on it, I feel really stupid now."

"Don't. I was always afraid my ... you know ... the way I look ... I mean ..."

"I love your skin, it's part of who you are. I love what's underneath even more."

From that point forward, the two spent not only their days together but also nights whenever a bed was available at the shelter, not escaping notice by staff and guests alike. When the shelter was full up, they shared the Morgers' spare bedroom, signaling unmistakably to Colette and Morger that at least one of Ray's secrets had been revealed to Chris, much to the hosts' delight. Soon enough, they became aware that Chris was now privy to two of the confidences they'd been guarding for so long.

The rest of Faith was none the wiser. Aside from the widely shared view that the couple was living in sin, everything else about them appeared unchanged. Ray was the adopted son of an upstanding and tragedy-tested family. A mongrel to be sure, no small thing, but trivial compared to the strange occurrences and associations making him a man to be wary of. Chris was widely regarded as trailer trash, daughter of two lowlifes, an apple who fell not far from the tree. Graced with good looks but imbued with loose morals, possessing no qualities she could possibly leverage to improve her lot in life. Useful enough flat on her back, the locals supposed, but not good for much else.

Chris and Ray were hardly oblivious to their standing in the community or the many whispers circulating around town. They went about their business. In the rare instances when enough hands were on deck at Ebiyan to allow them to get away, they went to visit Grace in the Cities and—one time—Annie in Phoenix. But for the most part, they were planted in Faith, toiling away.

The better part of a year after their trip to Arizona, Annie came back to Faith, just after the holidays. She lodged with Gin and Moose for the duration of her stay, but spent most of her time either at Ebiyan or the Morgers. She looked forward to Colette's cooking, but that wasn't to be. Chris or Ray came over to make meals most days, or brought food cooked at Ebiyan. Colette had fallen several times recently, one of those times breaking a wrist.

Morger was more or less confined to his easy chair, rarely venturing outside anymore, moving only to use the toilet or fetch something from the fridge. The one thing he could still do like a much younger man was talk. His voice was raspier, and stringing together more than a few sentences unbroken by pauses left him out of breath, but his memory remained remarkably reliable.

"It's about time to toss me in the dump with the other trash," Morger muttered with a hint of a smile. Others in the room groaned in protest, failing to knock the old man off topic. "A Malian friend of ours got to come over here, some exchange program, visited a nursing home. Will never forget what he told me: You Americans treat your most valuable asset like garbage."

He wheezed as the last word left his lips, coughing to clear the phlegm from his throat.

"People in places like Mali, there's prosperity in their poverty. Here, it's the other way around," he said, looking at Ray.

Everyone else looked at each other, not knowing quite what to say, hoping someone would think of something kindly, or distracting. Morger didn't see well anymore, but well enough to notice their discomfort.

"Oh, come now, you can tell the old geezer he's full of crap. You needn't worry, I'll be gone soon enough."

"Don't talk like that," said Chris.

He waved dismissively, then winced. "Not to worry. Comes a time when pain is a favor. Makes moving on appealing. Death's nothing to fear. Dying is like the sun setting. When the sun drops below the horizon, it's not gone. It shines elsewhere."

A faint smile formed on Morger's lips and no one else's.

"There's a hell of a lot more behind me than up ahead. After all this living, there's so much I don't know, so much that's unknowable. Where knowledge ends, belief begins, faith takes over. I suppose that's what led me to church."

His voice weakening, he finished his thought barely above a whisper. Then he rallied.

"For all the worshipping going on, there's very little faith, certainly not in each other, not even in a power higher than ourselves. I swear, if a second coming actually happened, the messiah wouldn't be persecuted, wouldn't be crucified. Would be overlooked entirely, I'm sure of it."

Morger said no more. He looked like he wanted to, but lacked the stamina to do so.

Some weeks after Annie's visit, Morger roused well after sunrise, shuffled to the kitchen, opened the fridge, stared absent-mindedly at the sparse contents, closed it again without taking anything out. He proceeded to the dining room table, pulled out a chair but did not sit. Just then, Chris and Ray came by with a hearty farm breakfast—scrambled eggs, toast, bacon, fried potatoes.

"Good morning!" Chris called out, seeing Morger but not spotting Colette. "Where's your better half?"

"In bed."

"Still in bed? Not like her to sleep in this late. She feeling all right?" Chris set a platter on the dining room table, headed for the hallway leading to the bedrooms.

"She won't stir."

"Whadya mean?" Ray asked imploringly.

"She won't wake," Morger repeated, staring out a window.

Chris reappeared from the back rooms, a hand cupped over her mouth, her arms noticeably trembling, her chest convulsing. Ray immediately broke down. Morger turned and faced them.

"She's not gone. She's shining elsewhere."

CHAPTER 27

RAY AND CHRIS HAD NO CLUE HOW TO PROCEED, no experience dealing with death. Ray summoned Gin, who was a godsend. She alerted the proper authorities, lined up an undertaker, gently coaxed answers from Morger about his preferences for funeral arrangements. Wrote an obituary, got it in Moose's hands for publication in the local paper. Figured out how to notify Colette's remaining kin in France. Cooked, cleaned, ran errands as needed, welcomed all who came calling.

Morger was stoic, emotionally paralyzed, saying little, doing less. He was in his 90s and had looked it for some time, but nonetheless appeared to age years in a matter of days. At the dining room table over a cup of coffee he was letting turn cold, with Gin standing behind him, Ray and Chris seated on either side, he pointed to a manila envelope at the far end of the table.

"I need you to know about this before ... well ..." he said somberly.

Ray slid the envelope to Chris. She opened it, removed its contents, lingering over the first page, then rifling through the remaining pages fairly quickly. She passed the document to Ray, who likewise studied the first page intently before flipping through the rest. It was the last will and testament Colette and Morger had the lawyer in Abbotsford draw up, bequeathing not only the land where Ebiyan House stood to Ray and Chris in equal shares, but also the farmhouse, outbuildings and their entire 120 acres.

Ray looked up at the old man. "You sure you want to do this?"

Morger nodded solemnly. "More than anything I've wanted my whole life. It's Colette's wish as well."

Ray looked over at Chris, then back to Morger, nodding consent. "I love you, Grampa."

"Love you too. All three of you."

The mood around the house lightened somewhat in the next few days. A date for the burial and memorial service was set, Gin managed every detail while darting out from time to time to attend to personal business. Ray and Chris had to take time away as well to defuse a dispute at Ebiyan that produced a minor skirmish the day before. When they returned to the house, they found it empty.

Assuming that Gin had taken Morger somewhere, they waited for them to return. When Gin called close to an hour later from the grocery store and Ray learned Morger wasn't with her, panic set in.

"He's not with Mom! Where the hell could he be?" Ray shrieked to Chris, heart racing, mind reeling. It was the dead of winter; he couldn't have gone far. His winter coat was hanging on a hook in the entryway. They searched the grounds, the barn, the shed. Gin arrived on the scene moments later and called her father, who notified the new sheriff. A search party was formed, fanned out across town. Morger was nowhere to be found.

"You don't suppose," Ray mumbled, just loudly enough for Chris to hear.

"What're you thinking?"

"He once told me his father always said that when it was his time to go, he wanted to do as dogs do, just go off on his own, where nobody's around. Told me his dad waited until everyone left his bedside, was all alone when he passed. Morger might be doing the same."

Ray knew. "The cathedral."

"He couldn't possibly make it there. Not in his condition. No way."

"You wouldn't think. But we should check."

It seemed the longest of longshots, but Chris followed Ray out past the cemetery, into the woods. The bushes and brambles were easier to plow through in the winter with leaves dropped, the slopes and gullies more arduous on account of a deep snow cover. The stream was ice covered but for a few patches where water still flowed, the bogs were frozen solid. No visible tracks, no sign anyone had come this way.

Snow and ice coating the tangled branches made the enclosure look vaguely like an igloo. Its rounded opening was unobstructed by winter's deposits, allowing Ray and Chris to enter. When they did, they discovered to their utter amazement they were not alone. A wave of relief washed over the shock Ray initially felt. There was Morger, sitting upright, his back to them, wearing no coat, at the far end of the cavern where past visitors had built fires. Chris called out to him in a low voice. No answer came.

"Mr. Morger," Ray repeated softly. Again, no answer. Chris approached Morger, slowly, as if sneaking up on him. Upon reaching his side, she could see that his eyes were closed, lending the impression he was lost in prayer. She spoke his name once more, barely above a whisper, then turned to Ray.

"I don't think he's breathing."

Chris reached for his wrist to check for a pulse, recoiling instantly as he was cold to the touch. She dropped to her knees on the carpet of pine needles and started to weep, gently at first, more forcefully once she felt Ray's hand on her shoulder. She looked up, her face mangled by grief, trails of frozen tears etching her cheeks.

"How in the world did he get all the way back here?" she asked, not expecting any answer, knowing there was none.

"Where there's a will, there's a way," Ray replied. "He must've had a mighty powerful desire to be here at the end."

Chris resumed bawling, sending tears cascading down Ray's cheeks as well. One week, to the day, that's what separated one terrible loss from the next.

Arrangements were made with Gin's guidance to retrieve the body from the forest. That grim business was taken care of before night fell. The local undertaker who'd been handling preparations for Colette's burial took on the added task of readying Morger for the grave, recommending plans be rearranged so the couple could be interred together, with the military honors due Morger. The couple had not been of one mind when it came to funeral arrangements, Colette preferring a church ceremony, Morger wanting anything but.

Pastor Cash was quick to make his church available, provided a proper donation was forthcoming from the estate. Ray, Chris and Gin decided to forgo a church service, instead planning an evening visitation at the funeral home in three days' time and a memorial gathering at Ebiyan the following morning. Veterans affiliated with three different local VFW chapters agreed to come to the cemetery for the burial and do a 21-gun salute.

The visitation was sparsely attended, the mood understandably somber, dampened all the more by what happened the night before. While everyone at Ebiyan slept, a message was spray-painted in large red letters on the outside of the Morger house facing the road, misspelled but unambiguous.

TRAITERS

Ray and Chris spent much of the day of the visitation trying their best to remove the graffiti, scrubbing the wall in the bitter cold, immeasurably compounding the pain accompanying the moment. That night, they returned from the funeral home to the house that now was theirs. They sat at the dining room table, each remembering the many meals shared at that table, neither saying a word.

Ray pushed away from the table, wandered into the kitchen, opened and promptly closed the refrigerator door, turned on the faucet at the sink, let the water run for a moment for no reason before turning it off, lifted the cookie jar's lid to find only crumbs.

Chris stood in the sitting room, surveying its spartan furnishings. Then she made her way down the hallway to the master bedroom. On the dresser sat the Morgers' sole photo album. She opened it, soon noticing Ray looking over her shoulder. Near the back were pictures of Africa they'd seen before. Before those were ones they'd never been shown, childhood photographs of Colette in France and Morger on the farm. Pictures from basic training at Camp Claiborne, including a group photo of his entire tank destroyer battalion. Some with college friends, two from his graduation ceremony. Quite a few taken in school settings, some of Colette in school cafeterias, others showing what must have been Morger's classrooms.

What appeared to be vacation photos, mostly trips to France, were sprinkled throughout. Dozens from Mali, some showing the landscape, most showing friends made in various villages. As Chris went to close the bulging album, she noticed two envelopes tucked inside the front cover. One was folded in half; neither was sealed. Chris unfolded the one, its contents spilled out. Two medals, a Purple Heart and a Bronze Star.

"He never mentioned receiving these," she said to Ray. "I think this one's for those injured or killed in combat. This one's for bravery. Did he ever say anything to you about being wounded?"

Ray shook no.

Chris lifted the flap of the other envelope to find two pictures, both taken with an old Polaroid instant camera, the kind that spits out a photograph that develops on the spot. One taken in their bedroom, Colette standing, abundant curls freshly permed in her hair, wearing only black nylon stockings and matching high heels. The other showed her lying on the couch, right arm tucked under her head, propped up by a pillow, wearing bright red pumps, nothing else.

"She's so young in these," Chris marveled.

"Maybe we should get rid of these," Ray said. "They were private."

"She never struck me as the type who'd be bothered by someone seeing them," Chris countered. "Didn't seem ashamed to show what God gave her."

"To Morger," Ray protested.

"And the camera," she shot right back. "I'm sure he saw her in her birthday suit plenty, didn't need pictures. She must not've minded being photographed, can't blame her, she had a pinup's body. I'm not gonna pass them around town, but we don't need to destroy them either."

Ray still saw the matter differently, but protested no further. Chris returned the medals and pictures to their envelopes, closing the album. They left the bedroom, Ray shut the door behind them. Shortly, they left the house, spent the night at Ebiyan, even though all beds were spoken for. This time, Ray insisted Chris take the cot, curling up at her side in a sleeping bag.

The next morning after breakfast, folks started arriving at Ebiyan for the memorial service. Residents usually scattered once a meal was finished, but they stayed assembled in the dining area. Two who'd long since left Ebiyan came back, blending right in as though at a family reunion. Chris greeted them all, thanked them for coming.

"When I was young, I was told to stay away from the Morgers. I know Ray was too," she began. "You can see from the turnout today, most people in town stayed away. They don't know what they missed. I'm glad Ray and I didn't do as we were told. They were real special people. Giving people.

Kind people, the both of them. They will be missed. They're missed already."

She hesitated, turned to Ray, then faced her audience again.

"One more thing. They weren't traitors. Ray and I just found out last night that Mr. Morger was awarded the Purple Heart and the Bronze Star. He never told us he was a war hero; never told us he was wounded in battle. He did his duty, came home, brought Colette back with him, they got on with their lives. Many of you know, some of you might not, that Mr. Morger was a teacher, was fired for teaching things that some around here wanted to keep hushed up. Being fired for telling the truth doesn't make him a traitor. He was a patriot and a hero. And Colette was the kindest, most decent soul I've ever met."

Abruptly, she stopped, sat down. Ray's turn.

"Um ... well, you know Grampa Morger was good with words, loved telling a good story. I wish I could tell one like he could. I don't know many who can; I sure can't. He always said he thought about what to say but Gramma Colette thought about what to do. It was her idea to give us the land Ebiyan House is built on. Everyone who knew her also knew her cookie jar. Was never empty. Seems every time you reached in you found something different. But in a way, it was always the same thing. Kindness. She didn't need to say a thing, she lived it. When I was little, I remember Grampa Morger telling me that a full life is better than a long one. Turns out he and Gramma Morger were lucky, they got both. Now they live on in all of us. Makes us lucky too."

A few others gave brief testimonials. Gin told of canning vegetables with Colette. Mr. Jeske spoke of Morger's devotion to teaching and his sadness when his colleague was let go. Then everyone bundled up, proceeding on to the cemetery. Military rituals were performed, the two caskets were lowered into their graves at the foot of Morger's parents, to the right of his grandparents.

Days passed before Ray and Chris returned to the Morger house. Weeks passed before they spent the night there, even though every bed at Ebiyan was taken that whole time. Winter was giving way to spring before they decided to make the old house their home. They packed away some of the Morgers' personal belongings, gave others to Ebiyan residents. The photo album got a new home on a sitting room shelf. The cookie jar was kept too, of course, not without discussion of whether it should be stored for safekeeping or put to ongoing use. Fear won out, the risk of it breaking deemed too great.

Chris removed the portly woman's upper torso that served as the jar's lid, meticulously enveloping it in several layers of wrappings before placing it in the box. Ray went to do the same with the jar's lower half, balling up several pages of newspaper to stuff inside, fixing to shake out any crumbs before being stopped cold. At the bottom of the jar was a folded slip of paper.

"Oh my God!"

"What?" exclaimed Chris. "Did you break it?"

"No! Look!"

Chris gasped. In Ray's hand was a now-unfolded sheet of ruled white paper with a single sentence handwritten on it in blue ink.

The next time will not be the second.

Previous messages always struck a chord with either Ray or Chris, made some kind of sense to one of them. This time, neither could even hazard a guess. But at least one thing was now clear.

"They always insisted these messages weren't theirs, I guess I never really believed them," Chris said. "Now ..."

As her voice trailed off, Ray filled in the blank. "Now we're in the twilight zone, through the looking glass, however you want to put it."

"So freaky," Chris readily agreed. "Makes you wonder ... maybe this place really is haunted."

CHAPTER 28

GIN POPPED IN TO EBIYAN AT LEAST ONCE A WEEK to help out, stopping by the house much more frequently, every other night or so. More than once she brought some small housewarming gift, a throw rug one time, a wall hanging another. A new frying pan, bed sheets, towels, toiletries. Often her stays were quite lengthy, sometimes stretching from before supper until 11 o'clock or even later. On a few occasions, Chris excused herself, retiring to bed when the hour grew late, leaving Ray and his mother to finish the visit alone.

"You thinking of painting the place?" Gin inquired one such night. "Sure could use it, inside and out. I'd be happy to spring for the paint. I'm no professional but not bad with a brush."

"For now, we're leaving it like it is," Ray answered. "I'll let you know if we change our minds."

Gin was dubious but took the look on Ray's face to heart, changing subjects.

"You heard some reporter's been sniffing around? From Milwaukee, I hear. Been here for a few days talking to folks."

"About what?"

"Ebiyan ... You ... Mostly you."

"Me? What for?"

"Only know what I've heard secondhand. Get the impression somebody's planted a seed in the guy's mind that there's something suspicious about Ebiyan ... like it's some kind of cult."

"People been telling him Ebiyan is a cult?"

"He's gonna want to talk to you."

"I'll be sure there's no Kool-Aid in the fridge when he comes around."

"Rage, I don't think you can just blow this off. This could be bad, could cause big headaches."

"Better stock up on aspirin then."

The very next day, the reporter did indeed come calling. Ray was pointed out to him.

"Ben Abrams," he said by way of introduction. "I'm a freelance journalist, worked out of Chicago for many years, based in Milwaukee now."

"Pleased to meet you."

"Just wanted to follow up with you about some conversations I've been having."

"Who've you been talking to?"

"I'd rather not say at this point if that's all right. It's Ray Glennon, right? Let me make sure I have the correct spelling of your name."

"G-l-e-n-n-o-n. What're you talking to them about?"

"You've lived here your whole life?"

"I lived in the Twin Cities until I was almost nine."

"Minneapolis or St. Paul?"

"St. Paul."

"I understand you're adopted."

"Is that what you've been told?"

"Is that not true?"

"What's this about? Who asked you to come here?"

"You started this Ebiyan House?" the reporter asked, mispronouncing the name with a short e.

"Abe-ee-yon."

"Oh, right, thanks. You started it?"

"Not alone. Had a lot of help."

"How old were you?"

"Eighteen."

"You started a care facility at 18. That's pretty remarkable. Not the kind of thing you hear every day."

"Got a lot of help."

"What do you do here?"

"It's for people who can't afford to stay where they are but have nowhere else to go."

"Are you providing treatment or any kind of care? What qualifies you to be a provider?"

"We provide shelter to people who need it. A safe place to stay, a warm bed, home-cooked meals. We do have a trained nurse helping us."

"Is that Corrine Thorson?"

Ray nodded.

"How much is she paid?"

"Nothing. We all work as volunteers."

"I'll want to circle back to that, but tell me about this cathedral out in the woods. What's that? Did you build that too?"

"Nobody made it. It's not a building, it's a cluster of trees and bushes."

"It's not an actual cathedral."

"That's just what people have always called it."

"What's it used for?"

"It's just part of the forest."

"Was there a wedding performed there, or did I hear wrong?"

"No, yeah, there was, one time. The couple wanted to be married outdoors, liked the natural setting."

"Did you perform the wedding?"

"What do you mean, did I perform it?"

"Did you preside over the wedding? Did you officiate?"

"Lord no, was just there as a guest. A judge came from Madison."

"Let me ask you this, have you ever told anyone you can heal people?"

"*What?*"

"Do you believe you can heal the sick and do you tell others you have this ability?

"No."

"More than one person has told me you can. Why would they say that?"

"Who told you that?"

"I'm not in a position to say. Have you done things to make them think that?"

"I don't tell people I can do that. I say the exact opposite."

"One person I interviewed told me you were la segunda venida. Do you know what that means?"

Ray shook no.

"It means the second coming. Do you believe you are?"

"Are what?"

"The second coming."

"Who'd you talk to? Bella?"

"Again, I'm not at liberty to reveal my sources. But I can tell you this much, this particular person's name is not Bella ... You know what, let's stop there for now. If I have more questions, do you mind if I follow up with you?"

"Not at all."

That was a lie. Ray would've rather been boiled with the potatoes that were for supper that evening than talk to this man ever again. The exchange did cause Ray to recall what Morger said about a second coming. Also brought the message sitting on the bedroom dresser to mind.

Abrams did come back. The second conversation was even more awkward and painful than the first.

"How do you support yourself?"

"What do you mean?"

"I mean you're working as an unpaid volunteer, do you have any income, how do you eat, where do you live?"

"I eat here with everyone else. A lot of the food is our own harvest, we collect enough donations to buy what we can't grow or gather for ourselves. Sometimes I grab a bed here if one's free, sometimes I sleep in the house next door."

"Do you own all this? This building, the house, the land."

"It was given to us."

"I understand the land for your facility was gifted to you at the time it was built. I'm told you were bequeathed the rest when the estate was settled, is that correct?"

Ray nodded.

"I'm told an elderly couple lived in the house until very recently."

"Yes."

"And I understand you were there when the woman was found dead, and you were the one who found the old man dead in what you call the cathedral, is that correct?"

"Me and someone else brought them breakfast. Mr. Morger told us his wife had died in her sleep."

"Who was the other person?"

"Chris."

"Is that Chris Driscoll?"

Ray nodded. "Mr. Morger went missing a week later, we notified the sheriff's office, they searched, couldn't find him anywhere. Chris and I found him in the woods."

"In the cathedral, right? Dead, correct?"

"Yes."

"When they died, you already knew about their will, that you and Chris Driscoll stood to inherit the whole farm, all the buildings, the land, everything, is that correct?"

"Yes ... What're you trying to say?"

"I'm just trying to make sure I have the story straight, make sure what others have told me is correct."

Abrams leafed through his notepad, underlining something on one page, scribbling a few words on another.

"You went to Colby High School, right?"

"Yes."

"Ken Kaczmarczyk was a classmate of yours, is that correct?"

Ray nodded.

"I understand there was an incident involving the two of you, some kind of medical emergency. What happened?"

"I don't know what was wrong with him. He started having trouble breathing, broke out in hives."

"I'm told you had something to do with this, some say you caused it."

"No one knows what caused it. We had a disagreement, we tussled. He was on top of me, had me pinned to the ground, when it happened."

"When what happened exactly?"

"Like I said, he started having trouble breathing."

"I've been told you did something and his symptoms disappeared. Is that true? What'd you do?"

"I didn't *do* anything. One second, he was having a hard time catching his breath, the next thing we knew he wasn't. He was convinced he had some kind of allergic reaction."

"But other students didn't believe that, did they?"

"There were a lot of theories, but nobody actually knew."

"There also was an incident in school with a Tom Tetzlaff, another classmate of yours. Do I have that name right?"

Ray nodded.

"What happened with him?

"He peed his pants."

"Did you do anything to cause him to do that? I heard you did."

"Didn't touch him."

Abrams rifled through his notepad again, staring off into space, a mixture of disappointment and frustration plainly displayed on his face.

"Anything else I should ask? Anything else you care to say?"

Caught somewhat off guard by the abrupt end of the questioning, Ray thought for a moment.

"Prophets and saints do live among us. The next one won't be the second."

"Not sure I'm following you," Abrams said pensively.

Ray studied the floor below.

"Your questions, they give me the feeling you're convinced I'm something I'm not."

Abrams closed his notebook. "Who are you?"

"Just someone who sees people hurting, thinks I should at least try to help, give them a place to come where they can put the hurt behind them."

"I talked to the publisher of the newspaper here in town, Richard Glennon, your adoptive father I'm told."

"I'm not adopted."

"I was led to believe you are."

"You were led wrong. My birth mother is Virginia Glennon."

That additional twist in a hopelessly tangled state of affairs stopped Abrams in his tracks, giving him yet another reason to believe he had no story, at least not one he could tell with any degree of confidence.

"Well ... uh ... I'll be damned. Went to talk to him after we last spoke. About all these things I've been hearing about you, how the only way it adds up is if you were filling their heads with this stuff, had some kind of hold on them. He warned me not to trust what I hear, there's a lot that people around here don't know about you."

Ray wasn't sure what to say so said nothing.

"You definitely have a hold on him. Told me he lost everything on account of you. Asked what he means, seeing as everyone else I talked to told me he owns half the town. Says he lost the only thing that really matters to him ... your mother. Wishes he'd handled things differently as far as you're concerned."

Ray remained silent.

"To be honest, I don't have a clue what's going on here and highly doubt I have enough days left on earth to ever find out. I'm going to be moving on. I won't be bothering you further."

He was true to his word. Told his editor the leads he was pursuing didn't pan out, was time to cut their losses. Was never seen or heard from again in or around Faith.

CHAPTER 29

RAY BROKE THE NEWS TO GIN THAT THERE WAS NO NEWS.
None that would see the light of day, at any rate.

"How on earth did you chase him off? What'd he ask? What'd you tell him?" Gin probed, rapid-fire.

"He asked about Ken Kaczmarczyk, Tom Tetzlaff, you know, the stuff from school. Things at Ebiyan."

"What kind of things?"

"The whole business with Bella. The Morgers and their will, it was weird, almost like he thought Chris and I did them in so we could get our hands on their farm. Another weird thing, he talked to me like he thought I was a minister or something."

Gin looked both angry and validated.

"I told him I'm not adopted," Ray continued. "Not to worry, he ain't doing anything with that. Seemed surprised, though, said he talked to Dad. Know what he told him?"

She shook her head and beckoned the answer in one.

"Lost the only thing that really matters. You."

"That's rich."

"Wishes he'd handled the whole situation with me differently. Told the guy not to trust what he was hearing about me."

"Got that much right."

"You don't have to stay with him anymore for my sake. Or give him another chance if you want. From the sounds of it, he'd like one. Do whatever makes you happy; whichever way you go, I'll be fine with it."

"Appreciate that, Rage. Trouble is, I honestly don't know what would make me happy. We've lived separate lives under one roof for so long, changing it, I don't know. I've thought about starting over, something stops me, force of habit maybe. In the morning I don't want to give up on my marriage, by afternoon I can't see how it can possibly be patched up. At night, I'm amazed I let my life get like this."

She wiped tears from her eyes.

"I wish I could do it all over, but I know thinking like that does no good. What's done is done, the only question is what to do next."

Ray wanted to say something consoling, but words wouldn't come. They rarely did when needed most.

"About the only thing I don't regret is you. Makes up for everything else," she said, leaning in to give Ray a peck on the cheek, only to be pulled into a tight embrace. Torment melted away.

Now words came, a bit tardy, better late than never.

"Regret's necessary, prevents you from forgetting. Mistakes and losses must be valuable if it's important not to forget."

"How'd you get so wise?"

"Learned it from you ... Love you, Mom."

"Love you too, Ragin."

The two hugged again.

"Hey, you know, your ... he's gonna be home any minute. Any chance you could stay for dinner?"

"Not tonight, sorry, got kitchen duty. Why don't you stop by later, the both of you? Chris would love to see you."

"I'll check with him, see if we can."

Moose and Gin did come by Ebiyan after dinner, looking more at ease in each other's company than they had in quite some time, or so Ray thought. Stood shoulder to shoulder for several minutes at one point talking with Chris and Ray as the last of the dishes were scrubbed clean. After the kitchen was tidied up, Chris whisked Gin away to show her something or other, leaving Ray and Moose momentarily alone.

"Thanks, Dad."

"For what?" Moose answered, clearly unnerved but not nearly as much as the first time Ray called him that.

"For coming over tonight. And for saying what you did to that reporter."

"He told you he talked to me, did he?"

Ray nodded, smiling.

"He must've told you what I said."

"He did. Thank you."

This sent Moose back to herding stray emotions into their pen, stiffening his lip. But he did not shut down, willed himself to soldier on, speaking in a softer voice than Ray had ever heard from him.

"Ray, I'm so ... so terribly, terribly sorry. I didn't treat you right, from the beginning. Turned my back, didn't even know your mother gave birth to a daughter. I'll never be able to forgive myself for that, so I can't expect you to forgive me either."

"You're forgiven."

Moose broke down. Ray knew how utterly out of character this was, how impossibly difficult it must be for him. This man's man—hulking and hard-shelled—dissolved into tears, years of buried feelings erupting from beneath the surface like lava. Ray embraced him, Moose's bulging arms at first hanging limply as though paralyzed. Eventually they sprang to life, encircling Ray's back, squeezing with all their might, so tightly Ray could barely breathe.

Gin and Chris returned in time to see Ray still swaddled in Moose's arms, face pressed tight to the old linebacker's chest. A Bunyanesque mitt punctuated the hug with several pats to Ray's back, delivered with enough force to be heard across the room. Chris and Gin looked at each other—one of those have-to-see-it-to-believe-it looks—both their mouths hanging open.

No one said anything. There was nothing more to say. Bygones were bygones.

COUNTY Q

CHAPTER 30

FAITH REMAINS A PARADOX. Should you ever find yourself on the old county trunk road between Unity and Loyal—once as smooth as it is narrow, now pocked with potholes—you'll come to a place that looks pretty much as it did a hundred years ago and more or less as it will a hundred years from now. A quiet, peaceful place. And a perilous one. You'll meet plain, ordinary people—not many, mind you—who are hardworking and discouraged, hospitable and suspicious, upright and proud yet tormented by nagging feelings of inferiority.

If you allow yourself to slow to the pace of life in Faith, you'll notice there's a rhythm to it, one in concert with the surroundings. You'll come to no traffic lights. Those remain quite unnecessary. On Main Street, you'll see that roughly every other storefront is boarded up. Not far from there, you can dip your bare feet in the mill pond. Just don't swim in it, that's still not advisable. The plant that housed the paper mill is still there, empty and unused since the early '80s, showing every sign of advancing decay. Once you reach the edge of town moments later, farm fields and forests will stretch as far as the eye can see in every direction. You will feel isolated, maybe even a little vulnerable, but you will be as safe as can be.

If you pass through in the winter, chances are the snow cover won't be as substantial as in the past, bad for snowmobiling, convenient for squirrels and deer and other creatures foraging for a meal. If it's not the time of year when all is frozen, you'll see vast waves of green dappled with smatterings of yellow and violet and about every color of the rainbow summoning enterprising bees to feast on nectar.

Regardless of season, you'll surely hear and feel the wind—there is so little getting in its way, so few competing sounds. Sometimes gaining such steam it howls like the coyotes that lurk about the area, most times soothingly melodious, gently tossing your hair, ruffling the leaves and blades of grass.

You can walk out past the old root beer stand. Hasn't been open for decades but never was demolished or repurposed. What paint remains on its walls peels a little more with each passing year, weeds have grown up where cars used to park. Not far beyond is Ebiyan House, where Faith perhaps shines brightest, where people take solace in fellowship, picking up the pieces of broken lives. Yes, Ray still works there with Chris. They still live in the old Morger house, which remains unpainted. And no, most of Faith still does not realize what is in their midst, still can't see what is hidden out in the open. What they see is Ana, a pint-sized brown-skinned girl Ray and Chris took in as a foster child and now have adopted as their own.

Ev Meaney has taken over Morger's role tending the town dump, which bursts at the seams, so much has been discarded. Ev looks after the old cemetery too, where there are still unoccupied plots—room to die or room to grow, depending on how you look at it. He helps out at Ebiyan whenever he can, which keeps him from dwelling on his sister Linh's decision to move to the Cities a few months ago. Beyond the cemetery, a fenced dirt path still leads to the edge of the woods. From there it's hard to miss the twin steeples, still standing, still looming over the rest of the forest yet showing signs of stress, many brown needles intermingled with green.

The steeples seem close, but you lose sight of them as soon as you enter the woods. The underbrush is as tangled now as ever, the brambles just as barbed. If you don't turn back, you'll be covered in burrs—heaven help you if you're wearing shorts or a skirt. There's a sense of relief when you reach the stream, still lazily flowing, no more than six feet from one side to the other. The same three rocks roughly as big as decent-size pumpkins protrude from the water where they always have, creating the illusion of a bridge. The final step to the far side still requires a small jump; the footing there remains treacherous.

If you don't mind muddy shoes and take the leap, you proceed to higher ground, make your way to the crest, then down the ridge until you are drawn to a most curious sight. Bushes hugging the ground and tree branches above intertwine to form an arched passageway. Narrower than it once was but still plenty wide to walk through without turning sideways. As you enter, more than likely you look back, wondering if you are indeed alone, half expecting an unnoticed door to close behind you. Beneath you is a soft carpet of pine needles, above a thick mesh of branches forming a peaked ceiling. It's hard not to feel like you are trespassing, entering the forest's inner sanctum unauthorized. There are no such rules out here. Regulations are of human construction.

One thing you wouldn't notice unless you'd been to Faith many years ago is that people are more outwardly pious these days, but Pastor Cash's congregation is considerably smaller than it was. He's slowing down, grooming a replacement, but continues to preach, assuring those filling a third of the pews, half on a good day, that everything is as it should be in Faith. Few beg to differ openly, but most know better.

The few roads off the main county trunk highway that were once paved have been covered over with gravel rather than patched or resurfaced on account of the cost savings. It's not often said but frequently thought around here that returning paved roads to dirt runs counter to expected progress—a glaringly, embarrassingly visible sign the area is going backwards. Also starkly noticeable: water that once ran clear out of faucets, now the color of weak tea, giving off a typically faint but occasionally pronounced smell of cow manure.

Like so many of their fellow Americans, a segment of Faith's population— one so sizeable it's the rule, not the exception—arms to the teeth against imagined threats yet willfully elects to remain unprotected against real ones. Posse Comitatus mastermind James Wickstrom died in March of 2018. A modern-day version of the Posse has formed. Those involved call it a militia, a peculiar label, for it serves no military purpose. Brian Mientkiewicz belongs; so do Royce Ackerman, Jeff Czerniak and Bruce Boyle, among others.

They tried recruiting Tom Tetzlaff, unsuccessfully. Tom is around, still hoping to get back into farming one day. His mother Phyllis passed away not long ago. Tom's brother Gary is out of jail, doing seasonal work when he can find it. Humphrey Slobodnik remains in the area, has a steady job in construction, plans to marry and start a family. Law enforcement authorities never did find grounds to believe he had anything to do with the cache of weapons and bomb-making materials removed from the abandoned movie house and hotel. In the end, no one else was implicated either. The case was closed without anyone being charged with a crime.

Chris's parents live in the house where she grew up. It looks much the same, maybe a bit worse. Mickey now lives in neighboring Taylor County, working in a window factory there. Nick Szymanski, Ken Kaczmarczyk, Tom Arciczewski, Doug Palzewicz, Rich Boniewicz, Eileen Schneider, Lisa Wagner and Katy Cash all moved on years ago, scattering across the country in search of something better or at least different. Their departures make their parents the final generation of those families to call Faith home, breaking lineages in the community that in some cases go back a century or more.

Faith has taken a beating, pummeled by relentless body blows. Yet, amazingly, hope remains that better days are coming. The fragile armistice between newcomers and the old guard has held. Nick Wilder still keeps bees, tends his gift shop, Dana milks her Jersey cows, turns it into cheese, marketing her product at locations near and far. Dan and Greta Schmitz continue to raise grass-fed beef, as well as their children, on the outskirts of Faith. Josh and Cindy Dicks run their natural food cooperative.

Willie García, Frankie López and Rosa Vazquez all stuck around and are doing well for themselves. The once-homeless and still-undocumented migrant woman, Elena, left Ebiyan but stayed in Faith, inheriting Colette's housekeeping customers to supplement what she earns working at the Mexican cantina, now far and away the most popular place in town to eat.

Jim and Maggie Slater have their house on the Hill. Profits from Jim's memorabilia shops and chain of sports equipment stores far from Faith afford them the luxury of a life of leisure in a small town's tranquility. Lisa Lewandowski and her spouse Jan are a few doors away. Butch Barber recently passed; Claire is still living. Grace is in the Cities, retired from teaching music, comes to Faith when she can. Annie now lives in Seattle, rarely able to visit.

Gin and Moose have reached retirement age. Moose sold the car dealership. The new owners couldn't make a go of it. He still oversees the newspaper, keeps tabs on the grocery, tavern and liquor store. Agreed to let his brothers' children take the reins of the auction house and real estate agency. No longer sees much less carries on with Deb or Carrie. Gin hasn't had an overnight guest in ages. Out of force of habit, they still keep separate rooms.

They have Ray, Chris and Ana over to the house every couple of weeks, never turning down an invitation when the favor is returned. They've grown to love that drab old haunt, where the Morgers' photo album resides on the bookshelf alongside Donn Clendenon's ball, Jim Slater's rookie card as well as Chris's general equivalency diploma and associate degree in social work.

The cookie jar sits in its familiar place on the kitchen counter. There's a small chip in the lid now, a conspicuous white dot on the red bonnet. Though dated and no longer in pristine condition, this is no mere keepsake; it remains in use, Chris and Ray generally striving to keep it at least half full. Like Faith itself, the jar can be replenished, still capable of surprising if one only bothers to look inside.

As a matter of fact, another note appeared just the other day. Ruled white notebook paper, folded three times, a single line handwritten in elegant cursive, in blue ink, in the middle of the page.

One not heard. One never seen. One yet to be fathomed.

Ray knew what that meant, knew just what to do next.

Chris looked at the jar's message, then at Ray.

"What the hell?"

"Secrets. The most dangerous aren't those we keep from others. It's the ones that keep you ... keep you caged," Ray said. "Took long enough, but I finally found the key to the cell."

Chris sought no further explanation. This is enough. This promises to be magical.

ABOUT THE AUTHOR

Mike McCabe has lived his life straddling America's rural-urban divide. Reared on his family's dairy farm, he's called both cities and small towns home, even lived abroad for a time. Mike has been a farmhand, journalist, educator, civic leader and nonprofit CEO. He's had two nonfiction books published. *Miracles Along County Q* is his debut novel.

Made in the USA
Columbia, SC
20 January 2025

52186303R00143